BETTER DEAD THAN WED

Murder Blog Mysteries #2

PAMELA FROST DENNIS

BETTER DEAD THAN WED
The Murder Blog Mysteries #2
Copyright© 2015 by Pamela Frost Dennis
All rights reserved
ISBN-13: 978-1517078430
ISBN-10: 1517078431

Printed in the United States of America
First Printing: 2015
pamelafrostdennis.com
Cover: Bookfly Design

For permission requests:
pamelafrostdennis@hotmail.com

~ *A Big Thank You to* ~

Mike Dennis
*Thank you for always telling me I can do it
when I think I can't.*

Dr. Holly Dennis
*For proofreading, answering medical questions,
and being my dear friend and daughter-in-law.*

Dr. Dorothy Dink
Always my muse.

My Readers
*Your kind comments on Amazon and Goodreads
make it all worthwhile.*

THIS BOOK IS DEDICATED TO:
My number one fan

WELCOME TO MY BLOG

My name is Katy McKenna. I'm pushing thirty-two, happily divorced, and self-employed as a graphic artist.

I call my blog *The Murder Blog Mysteries*—not because I'm a crime-solving supersleuth like Miss Marple, Stephanie Plum, or Kinsey Millhone. Not even close.

The truth is, I have a bad habit of sticking my nose into other people's business, and it tends to get me in a lot of trouble. The deadly kind of trouble.

Most days my life is pretty ho-hum. And that's the way I like it. Get up, do my thing, maybe blog about it in the evening. Then watch a little TV and crawl into bed. I wouldn't mind adding some romance into the mix, but otherwise, life is good.

And then there are those other days...

CHAPTER ONE

After nearly getting myself killed while solving a cold case a couple months ago, Police Chief Angela Yaeger asked me if I'd ever considered a career in law enforcement. Nope. I'm a graphic artist. Make that an out-of-work graphic artist, because my broken elbow was collateral damage in solving that cold case.

While my elbow has been healing, I've had time to weigh my career options. I love being a freelance graphic artist, but there are some drawbacks, like: If I'm sick—no paycheck. Injured—no paycheck. No client—no paycheck. Vacation—who can afford a vacation? Benefits—what are those? Retirement plan—nope.

Fortunately, I made a tidy profit selling the grandiose house that Chad, my "was-band," had to have, or I'd be back in my old bedroom at my folks' house watching cat videos and blogging about my boring life. Oh wait, I *am* blogging about my boring life, and I *love* watching cat videos. Who doesn't?

Back to the law enforcement idea. My stepdad is a retired cop with a good medical plan, a nice pension, and a monthly disability

1

check for taking a bullet in the knee. I don't want to be shot in the knee, but Pop told me that in over twenty-five years with the Santa Lucia Police Department, he didn't draw his gun until his last day on the job. So the odds would be in my favor. Of course, your first day on a cop job has the potential to be your last day. But a steady paycheck and a medical plan paid by someone other than yours truly sure would be nice.

Yesterday I called the chief and told her I was seriously thinking about what she'd said, and she suggested I go on a ride-along to get a realistic feel for the job; so today, I went to the station to sign up. I was sitting in the police department lobby with a clip-boarded waiver on my lap, pen in hand, ready to sign. Then I read it.

I acknowledge that the work and activities of the Santa Lucia Police Department are inherently dangerous and involve possible risks of injury, death, and damage or loss to person or property. I further understand such risks may arise from, but are not limited to, civil disturbances; explosions or shootings; assaults and/or battery; vehicular collisions; and the effects of wind, rain, fire, and gas. I freely and voluntarily assume all possible inherent risks, whether or not they are listed herein.

That gave me pause. I'd pictured something a little different. Like going for donuts, helping little old ladies cross the street, getting a cat out of a tree, lecturing a truant kid, throwing the town drunk in the hoosegow. In other words, a ride-along with Sheriff Andy in Mayberry.

I stepped to the counter and slid the clipboard under the office clerk's nose. "Exactly how often do people get killed in ride-alongs?" I tapped the waiver. "This says there could be explosions and riots, terrorist attacks, car crashes, and possible death."

"Well…" She glanced at the form through red, half-rimmed specs. "Ms. McKenna."

"Katy."

"Well, Katy. I don't see anything here about terrorist attacks—"

"These days you never know."

"True, but this form is merely a formality to protect the department from potential lawsuits. I can assure you we've never lost a ride-along passenger in all the time I've worked here."

That was reassuring. "How long is that?"

"Almost four months now."

Not so reassuring.

The waiver included an area where you checked off a box indicating which days and shifts you preferred. I preferred Monday, eight a.m. to noon. I figured more crimes were committed on the weekends and criminals liked to sleep in on Mondays. Better safe than sorry, I always say.

CHAPTER TWO

TUESDAY · JUNE 11
Posted by Katy McKenna

Yesterday I arrived at the police station at 7:45 a.m., latte in hand, and dressed according to the ride-along guidelines. Nice pants, cute pink top, a cardigan to ward off the chilly overcast day, and semi-practical shoes.

After checking in at the lobby counter, I took a seat on a bench. A few minutes later, Chief Yaeger greeted me. "Katy. So good to see you." We exchanged a hug, then sat.

"Wow. You look fabulous," I said. "I love your hair that way."

Angela had let her hair go totally gray since I last saw her, and her new close-cropped hairstyle looked stunning against her warm, ebony skin tone.

She patted her hair. "I got tired of fighting the inevitable. I'd let it start to go gray, then I'd hate it and color it again. I finally got it all cut off and I'm loving it. Should've done it a long time ago." She paused, giving me a concerned look. "You okay?" she asked. "You look a little tense."

"The waiver I signed the other day kind of unnerved me. You know, car crashes, shootings, explosions."

She chuckled. "You know, we wouldn't have the ride-along program if there were a big risk of endangering our civilians." The woman's motherly smile calmed me.

"Yeah, I know. Just too many cop shows, I guess."

She patted my knee and stood. "Come on. Let's go meet your partner."

I followed her down the hall and out a door to the squad-car parking area. Shifts were coming in and departing. A brawny Latino officer leaned against his car, gazing in my direction. The thought of spending the next four hours cruising the town with that police-calendar stud gave me goosies.

"Is that him?" I said, feeling a mixture of hopeful dread.

"No." She snickered. "Talk about danger. That bad boy would eat you alive, girl."

And that would be a bad thing? Since my divorce, Grandma Ruby has been pushing me to get a rebound man. In other words, my sweet old granny thinks I need to get laid.

"There's your ride." Angela ushered me toward the squad car parked at the end of the lot. "Just to warn you, Katy. Your partner may seem a little rough around the edges, but he's very good at his job and you'll learn a lot, so try not to prejudge him."

A ruddy-faced man who barely met the minimum height requirement and was pushing the maximum weight limit ambled toward us. He stopped a moment to hoist up his pants and cock his hat at a jaunty angle.

"Sergeant Crowley," said the chief. "This is Katy McKenna. Your ride-along partner."

"Howdy, ma'am." Crowley tipped his hat. "Bob Crowley at at your service. I hear tell you're thinkin' about a career in law enforcement." He rehoisted his pants.

Was this a joke? It had to be. It were as if he had stepped out of one of those old *Smokey and the Bandit* movies that my dad loves. I glanced longingly back at stud-cop, but he was too busy flexing his perfect triceps to notice.

"Sergeant Crowley does all our ride-alongs. He's our top field-training officer," Angela said. "Katy is the daughter of Kurt Melby."

"Ya don't say. Good man and a fine officer. Darn shame about his knee."

"Katy's responsible for closing the case on Belinda Moore's murder."

"Chip off the old block, huh? Your daddy must be mighty proud."

"I'll leave you two to get acquainted." Angela turned to me, giving me a look obviously meant to remind me not to prejudge the sergeant, and told me to come see her after my ride.

"Well, little lady," said Crowley, "before we roll, let me give you a quick tour of my office."

I followed him to his car. "This sweet ride is a Dodge Charger." We stood at the front grill, and he caressed the gleaming, black hood. "She's got a 5.7 liter hemi—"

I nodded, acting like I cared.

"—V8 and 370 horsepower." Crowley moved toward the back of the car, running his fingers along its side. "She'll do zero to sixty in 5.4 seconds." He popped the trunk. "We got your first aid kit, your portable defibrillator, your fire extinguisher, your shotgun, your tools." He lifted out a Kevlar vest and handed it to me. "Put this on."

I slipped it on, made a few admiring noises, and then began to shuck the ponderous thing.

"Nope. You need to wear that during our shift. Department policy. That's an old one." He smacked his vest. "Now we wear load-bearing vests so we're not carrying all our gear on our belts, which was killing my back."

"What all do you carry?"

"A sidearm, two loaded magazines," he said as he patted each item in his vest, "a radio, a body camera, couple of cuffs, flashlight, pepper spray, baton, a Taser, and what-have-you."

"Don't you get hot?"

"I prefer sweat to dead. Besides, if I get killed on duty and I don't have my vest on, the little woman won't get her full benefits." He laughed, shaking his head. "LuAnn would whoop my ass for sure."

Crowley slammed the trunk lid, then opened the front passenger door. "Plunk yourself down, and we'll get rollin'." He shuffled around the car and settled into the driver's seat with a grunt. "You look a tad jumpy, Katy. Don't be. Nothin' ever happens on this shift."

The muscle car rumbled out of the lot onto Chestnut Street. "Now if you really wanted to see some action, ya shoulda rode on a Friday night. It's a college town, so we get a lot of drunk-and-disorderlies. Sometimes a pot bust. If we're lucky, maybe a burglary."

We left downtown and cruised to a seedy neighborhood near the industrial area. Crowley told me that junk cars in the front yard were usually a good indication that there was a meth lab operating inside the house. There were a lot of rusty cars in the weedy yards.

Up ahead, a scraggly bearded man wearing gravity-defying pants held up with one hand, stood at the edge of a thirsty looking yard, waving at us to stop.

"Probably havin' a tiff with the wife. Stay in the car, Katy. That's an order. Domestic calls can get real ugly."

"Officer. You gotta help me." The scrawny man was hopping around like his feet were on fire. "That bitch's crazy!"

Crowley approached slowly. "Calm down, sir, and tell me what the problem is."

"I'll tell you what the problem is!" screamed a chunky dishwater blond on the porch, aiming a shotgun in our direction. "That piece of slime molested my little baby, that's what the problem is!"

The slimy guy hollered, "No way would I touch Jasmine. I love my little girl."

"She ain't your little girl, and you are one sick pervert. The world is gonna be a better place without you in it." She stepped off the porch, advancing toward the quivering man.

"Ma'am, please put down your weapon." Crowley used an amiable tone, sliding his hand toward his gun.

"No! I'm gonna kill that son of a bitch once and for all." She pumped the shotgun and swung it in Crowley's direction. "Please take your hand off your gun… and… and put 'em behind your head. I got no quarrel with you, but there is no way in hell I'm gonna let that piece of shit walk away from this."

Crowley did as told, and she turned the gun back on the man, aiming at his crotch. "I caught you in the act, Leon, so don't bother denying it." She hiccupped a sob. "This is all my fault. I should've listened to my mama and never married you. She said you was trash."

"Please, Tanya. I'm begging you. Don't kill me. It's not my fault. I got a sickness. I need help so I can get cured."

"That's a joke, Leon. The only cured pedophile is a dead pedophile." A mangy calico cat curled around her legs, and she gently nudged her away with her foot while keeping the shotgun dead aimed on Leon. "I want you to take the officer's gun and bring it to me."

Leon sidled up to the sergeant, and with the hand not holding his pants; he slid the gun from Crowley's holster.

"Hold it by the barrel," Tanya ordered. "And remember—the closer you get, the bigger the hole in your chest will be."

I rolled up the car window and slumped low in my seat, keeping an eye on Crowley. He wore a police radio on his shoulder but didn't dare move to activate it. His eyes locked with mine. He seemed to be telling me something. He tilted his chin, looked at his radio, and then back at me. Call the police!

I scrunched down so no one could see me, dug in my purse for my cell, and pressed the Home button, and whispered to Siri, "Call 9-1-1."

"I'm sorry. I did not understand that."

"Call 9-1-1."

"Calling 9-1-1."

A moment later a woman answered. "9-1-1. What is your emergency?"

I peeped out the window. Leon was inching his way toward the squad car, aiming Crowley's gun at Tanya.

"I don't want to hurt you, Tanya!" Leon shouted. "Just let me go, and I won't shoot you."

No! Go the other way! I silently screamed. *Oh shit! Can a shotgun blast go right through the door and kill me?*

Tanya laughed. "No way you'll hit me, you low-life meth-head."

"What is your emergency?" The dispatcher spoke in a placid tone that made me want to strangle her.

I whispered, "I'm in a police car and a crazy woman has a shotgun."

"What is your location, ma'am?"

"I'm in Santa Lucia."

"Where in Santa Lucia?"

"God, I don't know. Can't you trace this call or something? It's a crummy area near the freeway."

"Ma'am, try to stay calm. Can you see a street sign?"

I raised my head just enough to look out the window, hoping my head wouldn't be blown off. Tanya had raised the shotgun, aiming at the car.

"Oh shit! She's gonna shoot!" Ducking my head between my knees, I heard Leon fire off a shot at Tanya from behind the car. Then the shotgun exploded, and the car shivered as a billion bullets slammed into it. Something thumped hard on the hood, but I kept my head down.

Crowley ordered the woman to drop the weapon and lie down, but she kept screaming she was going to finish off the good-for-nuthin' dirtbag.

I stayed down, praying to anyone out there who might be listening. "Please don't let me die. Please don't let me die."

The dispatcher said, "Please remain calm and tell me where you are."

"Stop telling me to stay calm!"

The driver's door opened and Leon dropped into the seat, still clutching Crowley's gun. His entire body seemed to be oozing blood.

"Get out!" we screamed at each other.

The coppery smell of blood mixed with Leon's reeking BO made my stomach lurch as I fumbled to unfasten my seat belt. I heard the *chung-chung* of the shotgun racking and glanced out my window. Tanya was advancing, presumably to finish Leon off as promised, which did not bode well for me.

I rolled down my window. "Please, Tanya! Don't shoot me!"

"Then, girl, you best get outta the car pronto."

I wailed pathetically, "I'm trying, but I can't get the seat belt off."

Leon had the motor running. "Shit, I can't see a fucking thing outta the window!"

The thump I'd heard on the hood had been Leon, and the windshield was spray-painted red with his blood. He flipped on the windshield wipers, smearing the gore back and forth with an eerie screech.

Leon tried to shift the car into drive, but his bloody hand slipped on the gear, and when he stomped on the gas, we shot backward, plowing into the truck parked behind us. My seat belt pinned me back hard, but Leon's skinny body pitched forward, slamming his face into the windshield.

"Oh shit, that really hurtsssss…" His body shuddered and collapsed, draped over the steering wheel, blood gushing from his wrecked face.

"Momma?" called a little girl from the porch.

"Go back inside, Jasmine. Mama's busy cleaning house. This nasty piece of trash ain't gonna hurt you no more, baby."

The child, maybe five or six, dressed only in a stained yellow T-shirt, underpants, and sandals, ran down the steps to her gun-toting mama and flung her skinny arms around the woman's ample thighs. Crowley eased the gun out of the sobbing mother's hands, and she sank to her knees, clutching her daughter as sirens wailed in the distance.

The sergeant emptied the shotgun, then came round to Leon and opened the door. "You're one lucky hombre it was just bird-shot, or we'd be scraping you off the sidewalk."

Leon didn't budge. Crowley felt for a pulse and then glanced at me. "Well, if that don't beat all. Dumb son of a bitch is dead. He say anything to you?"

I will never, ever forget his last words. "He said, 'Oh shit, that really hurts.'"

I tried to unlatch my seat belt, but my brain had disconnected from my quivering body, and my fingers couldn't comprehend my extreme need to vacate the car of horrors. Crowley came around, reached in, and released me. "You look a little wobbly. Take my arm."

He practically had to lift me out and carry me to the porch steps. A little while later, an EMT checked my blood pressure and gave me water, which I dribbled all over my blood-spattered blouse.

Leon remained in the car for the next few hours as the crime scene investigators collected evidence. A motley crowd gathered on the street, and the local news crews descended.

Eventually child protective services pried little Jasmine from her mother's arms, and Tanya was cuffed and hauled away, crying for her baby. It broke my heart. If I had a kid and someone hurt her, I would want to kill them, too. No doubt about it.

———

When I was finally allowed to leave the crime scene, an officer returned me to my car at the police station. Once I was behind the wheel, I must have shifted into autopilot, because the next thing I knew I was parked in my driveway.

All I wanted to do was get inside, bolt the door, set the alarm, and take a long, hot shower. Daisy, my yellow Lab, greeted me, and when she got a snoot full of blood, sweat, and tears, she slid into Mommy mode, trying to comfort me. Tabitha, my gray tabby cat, had preferred to keep a safe distance, staring at me bug-eyed in that freaky way that cats do when they are about to lose it.

I sloshed a hefty helping of Pinot Grigio into a plastic tumbler, leaving a puddle on the counter. After a few shaky gulps, I stripped to my skivvies and tossed everything into the garbage can, then headed for the shower where I let the hot water sterilize my body.

Feeling a little more human, I climbed into my favorite cookie-print flannels, grabbed the comforter from my bed, refilled my cup, and then curled up on the couch with my two furballs.

I always keep old movies recorded for when I need comforting. *Now, Voyager* with Bette Davis was exactly what I needed. A plain-Jane spinster who blossoms and finds impossible romance. The next thing I knew, sun was shining in my eyes through the french doors.

CHAPTER THREE

WEDNESDAY · JUNE 12
Posted by Katy McKenna

"You could have been killed," said Mom. "What were you thinking?"

"I was thinking about a career in law enforcement, and ride-alongs aren't usually dangerous or they wouldn't do them. Ouch! Don't pull my hair so hard."

"Sorry." Mom owns the Cut 'n' Caboodles hair salon near the downtown area of Santa Lucia, and I was in for a trim. Probably not a good idea considering how upset she was with me.

She sliced through another section of my auburn, shoulder-length hair and snipped the ends. "I'm still so upset. You cannot begin to understand what it was like to hear on the eleven o'clock news that my daughter had been in the middle of a gun battle. And then I tried to call you and it went directly to voice mail. Why didn't you call us?"

"I'm sorry, Mom. I wasn't thinking straight. But I *did* call you first thing yesterday morning."

"Only because I left about a thousand messages on your phone."

"If it's any consolation, I never even saw the messages before I called you because I'd turned my phone off. So I had no idea that you already knew or were worried."

Mom brushed away a tear. "Someday when you have kids of your own you'll understand." She lifted a big hunk of my hair, scissors poised in the air.

"Hold on there! What're you doing?" I said.

"Taking some of the bulk out so it'll lay better." She slashed through the hair like a kamikaze pilot on a mission. "How's your elbow feeling?"

I flexed my healing left arm. "Better. I almost have full extension. It's time to post an ad on Craigslist and quit dipping into my nest egg. And please don't trim my bangs. I'm growing them out."

"I worry about you doing that."

"Growing out my bangs?"

"No. The Craigslist thing. No telling what kind of weirdo will answer it. And I think you look cute with bangs."

"You could say the same thing about the weirdo posting the ad, you know. And bangs bug me."

The woman sitting in the next chair said, "I might have an idea for you. I get lots of interesting work through a temp agency here in town."

"What kind of work?"

"It varies. I've demonstrated products at Costco, taken surveys, filed, ran errands for housebound people, receptionist…" She scrunched her lips, thinking. "Product tester. I loved that one. I taste-tested ice cream for a local dairy. Can you believe it?"

Whoa! Hold the phone. That sounded right up my alley. "You actually got paid to eat ice cream? Where do I sign up?"

"I have a business card in my bag."

While she rummaged through her purse, I asked, "How long does the average job last?"

"Oh, anywhere from a half a day to a few months. By the way —I like your bangs. I think you should keep them. Now where did I stick that darn card? Usually, I put cards in the side compartment so I don't lose them. Oh wait—here it is." She produced a tattered card.

Nothing Lasts Forever Temps

The temp agency is located downtown on Olivera Street about three blocks from the hair salon, so rather than hunt for the ever-elusive parking spot, I left my car in the lot behind Mom's shop and hoofed it. The temperature was pushing eighty-five and I appreciated the cooling canopy of the old ficus and camphor trees that shade Santa Lucia's downtown streets.

One hundred and four Olivera Street is an old, three-story building with boutiques on the street level and offices upstairs. I found a directory posted by a staircase. Suite 304.

The office door was half-open and the receptionist's desk was vacant, so I called, "Yoo-hoo, anyone here?"

"Yeah! Be right with you," answered a gruff male voice from another room. "Have a seat."

I perched on a couch that was older than me and counted cobwebs. A few minutes passed before a tall, baggy-suited, balding man came out and stuffed a McDonald's bag in the wastebasket.

"Sorry. Lunch. Don't tell my wife. She worries about my cholesterol." He stifled a burp. "You here about the job?"

"A woman told me about your agency and gave me your card."

He nodded, opened a drawer in the desk, and handed me a form attached to a clipboard. "Fill this out and we'll talk." He went back to his office.

It was a standard application. Name, birthdate, address, phone, social security number, education... Position desired: ice cream taster. And finally: May we contact your former employer?

I worked for a few years as a graphic artist at an ad agency, then freelanced, then ran The Bookstore Bistro with my ex (which he got in the divorce settlement), and since then, one freelance graphics job for an upholstery shop.

References: Police Chief Angela Yaeger. That should impress him.

I finished and called, "All done." No response. I waited a moment and called again. Nothing. Another minute passed, and then I peeked into his office. He was slumped in his chair, slack-jawed.

I cleared my throat. Still nothing. "Excuse me?" Still no response. I returned to the front office door, opened it and slammed it, then sat down.

He trundled out, scrubbing his face with his hands, glanced at the door, then me.

"Just me." I waved the application. "Here you go. All filled out."

"Okey-dokey. Let's have a look-see." He motioned me into his office, and I sat opposite him at his cluttered desk and waited while he scanned the application. "Everything looks good. When can you start?"

"Right away."

"Good enough. Follow me."

He led me out to the front office. I assumed he would give me the address where I would be tasting ice cream. Instead he opened the door and pointed down the hall. "Bathroom's at the end. There's also a kitchen we share with the other offices with a fridge and a coffeemaker. I like mine black."

I like mine with two or three sugars and half-and-half but to each his own. Back in the office, he opened a small storage closet. "Office supplies are in here. We open at nine and close at five. Be here by 8:45. Half an hour for lunch. Any questions, Miss…" He glanced at my application. "McKenna?"

"Yes, Mister…"

"Musser. Paul Musser."

"Well, Mr. Musser—"

"We're not formal here. Call me Paul."

"Paul, I think there's been a little miscommunication here. As you can see on my application, I'm here for the ice cream tasting job." Yes—I realize now how ridiculous that sounds.

He gave me an are-you-crazy look. "What're you talking about? There's no ice cream tasting job."

"Then how about product demos at Costco?" I think my blog followers would agree that the snacks at Costco are the number one reason to shop there.

"All those positions are filled. I thought you were applying for the receptionist job."

I don't have much in the way of office skills, but how hard can it be to answer the phone, greet people, and file your nails? If I had any nails, that is. I keep them short. Too hard to draw with long nails. Okay, full disclosure, I bite them. But in my defense, it really is too hard to draw with long nails.

"I guess I could do that. Where's the temp job?"

"Here. And it's permanent unless you drive me crazy like the last gal, I mean girl, uh, lady—woman—person. She kept telling me I'm not PC and she was right, I'm not. Can you live with that?"

"Yeah, no biggie, but I'm really an artist, and I'm just looking for temporary work to fill in between graphic gigs."

"It pays seventeen bucks an hour."

I charge seventy-five bucks an hour—when I actually have work. But seventeen bucks beats no bucks.

"Okay, but only temporarily. Until you get someone else hired."

"Fair enough."

"So when do you want me to start?"

"Now's good. How about a cup of coffee?"

"Sounds good."

"Remember, I like mine black. Each office has its own cupboard in the kitchen. I think we still got some Fig Newtons if you want some." He went into his office, leaving the opaque glass door cracked.

I glanced around the shabby room. My new desk was an ancient oak monster, probably once a schoolmarm's desk in a one-room schoolhouse out on the prairie. There was a coat rack, and a threadbare, mauve plaid love seat fronted by a water-ringed blond oak table. A Motel 6 oceanscape hung crooked and off-center over the couch.

I sat at the desk facing the "art" and wondered what had just happened. One minute I'm thinking I'm going to be an ice cream tester and the next thing I know, I'm a receptionist in this dreary agency.

Coffee! Evidently that is part of my job description. Making coffee. I can do that. And then I thought, *Is that demeaning?* I pondered this for a moment and decided it wasn't, especially since I have no real office skills. *It's just coffee. If I'm making some for me, it's only polite to make some for Paul.*

In the kitchen there was a cupboard labeled "NLF." Inside I found a humongous red plastic jug of Folgers with a "Good until December 2008" expiration date on it. I brewed a pot in the crusty old Mr. Coffee and poured a cup for Paul and doctored a cup for me with generic powdered creamer and clumpy sugar.

Back in the office, I interrupted my new boss's online poker game to hand him his coffee and a couple of petrified Fig Newtons, which he accepted with a grunt. I returned to my new domain and yanked up the dusty mauve mini-blinds to brighten the gloomy room. The sunny day filtering through the filmy window only made the space more dismal.

The phone rang and I waited for Paul to answer. When he didn't, I realized receptionists answer phones. "Nothing Lasts Forever," I said cheerily. "How can I help you?" In my head, I heard my seventh-grade English teacher, scary Mrs. Wade, correct my bad grammar.

"Hello, dear. My name is Beatrice Johnson, and I'm looking for a dog walker," said a thin, tremulous voice. "I recently broke my hip, and poor Fifi and Babette are going crazy stuck in this house. Do you have anyone nice who could walk my babies once a day until I've recovered?"

"Uh, um." *Now what? Hello! A little training would be nice here.* "Let me take your name and number, and my boss will get right back to you."

I took her info, said goodbye, and went to Paul's open door.

He was glued to the computer and didn't look up, so I stepped in front of his desk and stared at him.

"Darn!" he slapped the desk and glanced up. "Sorry. Just lost ten big ones. Do you need something?"

I repeated Beatrice's request. "I told her you'd get right back to her."

"That's your job." He scratched his shiny head. "I don't think we have any qualified dog walkers on file. That's more of a big city gig. Maybe you could take it. You like dogs?"

"I love dogs. I have the sweetest yellow Lab. Daisy. I got her at the pound and—"

"Sounds great. I'm more of a cat person, myself. Low maintenance."

"Oh, I have a cat too. Tabitha. I got her from—"

"Yeah, yeah." His eyes slid back to the computer monitor, clearly wanting to get back in the game. "So you want the job or not?"

Not really, but poor Beatrice's broken hip. "I guess. What about my job here?"

"This must be your lucky day. Now you got two jobs."

———

I drive a 1976 orange Volvo 265 DL wagon that I christened Veronica when I was eight years old. On my seventeenth birthday, Mom begrudgingly gifted her to me. Cup holders, GPS, a CD player, no—make that an MP3 player—would all be nice, but I love my car and would never think of parting with her. Besides, I can't afford a car payment.

Beatrice's address was in the senior living complex where Grandma Ruby lives. After getting grilled by skinny George at the Shady Acres security booth, I drove a sedate fifteen miles per hour, knowing he would turn his radar gun on me the moment I passed through the gate.

I parked Veronica next to an old Ford Fiesta and rang the cottage's doorbell, causing a thunderous chorus of barking. I'd assumed that Fifi and Babette would be tiny little things, like Yorkies or Teacup Poodles. But from the sound of those woofs, I'd assumed wrong.

The door opened a crack and a dead ringer for Mrs. Claus peeked out.

"Hi. I'm Katy. The dog walker."

"Hello, dear. I'm Bea. Hold on." She unchained the door and ordered the dogs to stay back. The door creaked opened and sitting obediently behind Bea were two enormous snowy-white Great Pyrenees.

I edged around her walker, and she introduced me to Fifi and Babette. Twins, three years old. Bea had to be ten years older than my seventy-four-year-old grandma. What was she thinking, living with these two polar bear wannabes?

I strolled the girls around the senior community with several stops along the way to sniff lampposts, mailboxes, and flowers. I had no intention of charging Bea, so at 5:15, I told the well-mannered dogs it was time to head home.

The word "home" triggered the dogs into a race to see who could get there first, dragging me full tilt through the neighborhood. At Bea's front door, it was a tie with me in second place. I sagged into a rocker on the porch, trying to catch my breath while the dogs pawed at the door.

"Katy! What are you doing sitting on Bea's porch?" hollered Grandma Ruby from her 1963 Triumph Spitfire convertible.

"Hey, Ruby." Everyone calls her Ruby. Even her grandkids, although I tend to flip-flop, between Granny, Grandma, and Ruby, depending on the occasion.

She climbed out of her little red roadster and joined me on the porch. "I didn't know you're friends with Bea."

"I'm her dog walker," I said between gasps for air. *Make that— was her dog walker.*

The cottage door opened and my petite, stiletto-queen granny said, "Beatrice! If you need your dogs walked, you could have called me, you know."

"Oh, I don't want to be a bother. I called a temp agency, and that's how I found Katy. I had no idea she was your granddaughter. You look far too young to have such an old grandchild, dear."

The compliment mollified Ruby and her tone softened. "You work for a temp agency, Katy? This is the first I've heard about this."

"Actually, I'm the office recep-uh-administrator. I took this dog-walking job because we have no qualified dog walkers available."

"How much is Bea paying you?" asked nosy Ruby. "And tell me more about this temp agency. You know I'm looking for a job. Maybe you can line me up something."

Gramps left Ruby a hefty insurance policy, plus his teacher's pension, and she collects social security. But she worries, so she supplements with multilevel marketing home businesses. Her latest had been EZ Lips. Stenciled-on, semipermanent lip color. What a fiasco that was. Even worse than Rubberwear—clothes and purses made out of old tires.

"You know what, Ruby? I think my administrative position would be a better fit for you than me. How about I pick you up on my way to work in the morning and I'll see if I can work something out for you." *This will be perfect. I'll give Ruby my lousy job, and then I'll have the inside track for any cool jobs that come up.*

CHAPTER FOUR

THURSDAY · JUNE 13
Posted by Katy McKenna

"What do you think of my outfit?" Ruby twirled at her cottage front door when I picked her up this morning. "It's business casual. But is it too casual?"

In my world, business casual is sweats, and her outfit would be White House attire.

"You look like a CEO, and remember, I get those shoes."

She was wearing her adorable brown-and-cream spectator pumps circa early 1960s.

"It's in the will. But you never wear heels, especially size six." Ruby eyed my eights.

"I still get them."

"Sweetheart, when I'm dead you can have anything you want. Although your sister may want a few things, too."

"I was here first, so I get first dibs." Yeah, I know. Petty.

My soon-to-be-former boss took one look at my gorgeous granny and said, "Okay. She can have the job. But you have to train her. I'm too busy."

Yeah, playing online poker. "You didn't train me."

"What are you talking about? You know where the coffee machine is, right? And the office supplies?" He shrugged his baggy shoulders. "I trained you." He turned his focus to his computer monitor, clicked his mouse, then slammed the mouse. "Come on! Jack of diamonds! Jack of diamonds!"

"Alrighty, then. We'll let you get back to your work, and…" I said as we backed out of his office.

"I could use a coffee," he hollered.

Ruby filled out an application and we commenced training. On our way down the hall to the kitchen, we bumped into my next door neighbor, Josh, AKA Josh-the-Viking, although he has no clue I've dubbed him that. I thought Ruby would have heart failure when she first saw him. Not just because of his movie-star Scandinavian looks, but because she thinks he's the perfect rebound man for me. We had a date a couple of months ago, at least I thought it was a date, but evidently he considers me a buddy. His words.

I jump-started the conversation before my drooling granny had a chance to open her big mouth. "Josh. What are you doing here?"

"Hey, Katy. Long time, no see. Did you make a decision about joining the police department yet?"

"Nope. Still considering all my career options." I grinned, rocking on my heels.

He shook his head with a chuckle and turned to unlock a door labeled Draper Investigations.

"This is your office?" Ruby tried to peek inside over his too-tall shoulder.

He turned, leaning his muscular body against the doorframe. "Yup."

Josh had been a narcotics undercover officer with the Santa

Lucia Police Department. According to him, his job had ruined his marriage. Now he's a private investigator.

"Ruby just got a job at Nothing Lasts Forever." I caught a whiff of his sexy cologne and felt light-headed. To be honest, he could have been wearing vinegar, and I would've thought it was sexy.

"I guess that means we'll be neighbors," said Ruby. "Katy was just about to show me where the coffee is."

"How would Katy know that?"

"I used to work there," I said. "But now it's time for me to move on, so Ruby's taking over."

"Strange, I never saw you around here." He twirled his key chain on his index finger, probably wondering how to politely ditch us.

"She worked there exactly one day," said Ruby, hands on hips. "Yesterday."

"Actually, it was more like half a day, Ruby, but who's counting? Would you like a cup of coffee, Josh? I'm about to brew a pot."

"No thanks. Got my own little setup in the office. Why don't you come in and I'll make you a cup."

Josh's office is furnished in midcentury modern. Bold fresh colors, cool art, squeaky-clean windows, and not a speck of dust anywhere. I watched Ruby's expression, knowing she was comparing it to her dismal digs.

"What's your pleasure, ladies?" Josh stood at a teak buffet.

I glanced at Ruby and could see we were simpatico on that question. Oh yeah.

Josh, oblivious to our lascivious musings, asked, "Latte? Cappuccino?"

He moved to reveal a Nespresso Delonghi Lattissima Pro sitting on the buffet. I have wanted one for ages, but it's out of my price range. Way out. The investigation field must be a lot more lucrative than freelance graphic arts.

"So this is what it looks like in real life." My voice husky with desire, I delicately traced its sleek lines with my fingertips. "May I have a latte macchiato?"

"Sounds good to me," said Ruby, with no clue how cool the machine was.

"I've got some fresh cheese danishes, if you like." In a matter of seconds, Josh handed me a steaming macchiato, and I snagged a pastry from the plate he held out. I was in office heaven.

"Do you need any help, Josh?" asked Ruby. "Like a gal Friday? I could run errands, answer phones, go on stakeouts."

"I barely have enough work to keep me busy."

"Then how can you afford all this?" I waved my full hands, rudely talking through my pastry.

"Inheritance. My grandmother on my father's side. Oil."

I glared at my inheritance on Ruby's feet and snatched another danish. "Must be nice."

"Be nicer having my grandma still around."

It would have been rude to eat three danishes, so we departed for the tour of the hall kitchen. After Ruby brewed a cup of sludge for Paul, we headed back to NLF.

"Here ya go, Paul." She plunked the coffee on his cluttered desk and glanced at his monitor. "The flop is ace, ace, ten? What's your opponent got?" She leaned in over Paul's shoulder. "Full house? You gonna raise?"

I tugged her arm. "Come on, Ruby. Paul's busy."

"No, wait," said Paul. "You play poker?"

"Oooh, ya know. Every now and then with the girls at the senior center," she said, keeping a poker face. "I'm not very good, though. I always lose all my toothpicks."

Paul's eyes lit up. "Maybe we can play sometime."

"Only if you promise to go easy on me." She winked over his head at me. Ruby is a killer card shark. She and her gal-pals would clean up in one of those Vegas tournaments. No kidding, those ladies are seriously good.

"Maybe I can even teach you a thing or two. You know, to help you hang on to your toothpicks."

"Paul," said Ruby, all sweet and sly. "This is going to be so much fun."

———

I was home scrounging in the fridge, trying to piece together a semi-healthy dinner when my phone vibrated on the counter.

"So help me, if that's Chad again, the phone is going in the garbage disposal." Although I'd rather stuff him down the disposal. Fortunately for my cell phone, it was my best friend, Samantha.

"Hi, Sam. You just saved my phone's life. If it had been Chad calling again, I was—"

"Are you kidding me? He's still bothering you? How can he seriously think you would ever get back with him? Best thing that ever happened to you was when he left you."

"I don't want to get all riled up, so no more Chad talk. He's not worth it. So what's up with you?"

"I got roped into joining a book club and the meeting's tomorrow. I mean, who has time to read books, let alone sit around with a bunch of people and talk about them? And then I thought of you."

That miffed me. She assumes I have nothing going on in my life other than reading. I watch a lot of TV too.

"I mean, you've always been an avid reader," she continued. "Even when you were beyond busy running the bookstore and nursing Chad through cancer, you still always had a book going. Remember back in high school when you decided to read every book that Dickens wrote?"

It's true. I'm a big Dickens fan. "Yeah, so?"

"So, this is a Jane Austen book club, and I haven't read any of her books, but I'm sure you have."

"Well, yeah. But it's been years."

"Will you come with me? Please? I have to work with these people, and I kind of said I've read her books, so I need you to cover for me."

I really didn't want to, but back in school, she really didn't want to play xylophone in the marching band, but I begged her to, and rather than hear about that again, I said, "What time?"

CHAPTER FIVE

SATURDAY · JUNE 15
Posted by Katy McKenna

"We have some newbies joining our book club today, so let's go around the room and introduce ourselves," said a prim, pink-cheeked woman with a faint English accent. "I'll go first since I'm hosting today. I'm Nora Baldwin. I'm a pharmacist at the hospital. Divorced and mother of fourteen-year-old Elizabeth." She pointed to a framed photo on the fireplace mantel. "I'm currently reading *Pride and Prejudice*."

Oh my God. When Colin Firth as Mr. Darcy looked across the room at what's-her-name, I thought I would pass out. What was her name? I should know this. I've seen the movie at least a hundred times.

The full-figured, forty-something seated on a tasseled ottoman spoke next. "I'm Melanie Ramos. Hospice nurse, married, and proud mother of two teenagers, Cassandra and Charles." Her star-tling amber eyes warmed at the mention of her kids. "I'm smack-dab in the middle of *Persuasion*."

"My turn!" squealed a barrel-chested man, swooping back his perfectly coifed sandy-blond hair. "I'm Justin Fargate. I know, my

name sounds like something straight out of a Jane Austen novel."
He giggled, covering his mouth. "No, seriously. It's really my name.
Thank you, Momma." He glanced at the ceiling. "I'm a nurse
anesthetist. Engaged." Justin squeezed the knee of the cute
Hepburn-ish brunette on the straight-back dining chair next to
him. "Right now I'm reading…" He pulled a book out of his man-
purse. "*Emma*. Love, love, love the movie version with Gwyneth."
Justin finger-quoted: "'My idea of good company… is the
company of clever, well-informed people who have a great deal of
conversation;' Jane Austen." He turned to his fiancée. "You're up
next, sweetie-poo."

"I'm Chloe Sarantos. I work in human resources at the hospital
and I'm engaged to this beautiful hunk of a man sitting next to
me." The blushing pixie cocked her head in Justin's direction. "My
favorite Jane Austen quote is, 'The most beautiful thing in the
world is a match well made.'" She sighed wistfully. "Justin and I are
reading *Emma* together and playing out the parts. It's so romantic."
She coyly peeked at Justin, and they covered their mouths,
giggling.

Please, somebody shoot me now, I thought as a wave of ick rolled
through me.

"Chloe's the one who invited me," Samantha whispered in my
ear. "Don't they make an adorable couple?"

"Yeah. *Adorable*."

"I'm Debra Williams," said the lady next to Samantha on the
sofa. The striking golden-brown-skinned woman had a riot of
gorgeous copper curls that I would kill for. "General practitioner.
Widowed—"

"Ohhhh," said Chloe and Justin, like this was news to them.

"—and first-time reader of Austen. I'm halfway through *Mans-
field Park*. I just love it. You know, I'm ashamed to say all I used to
read was Harlequin romances. But Jane Austen takes romance to a
whole new level."

I'd been eyeing the chunky person next to Chloe. I would not have pegged her as a Jane Austen fan. Brown hair cut into a short, no-nonsense do, a fuzzy upper lip, and dressed like a lumberjack.

"I guess it's my turn." She leaned forward, elbows resting on knees akimbo, speaking in a gruff tone. "I'm Chris, and I just finished *Northanger Abbey* last night. That's all I got."

The doorbell rang and Nora stood. "That must be Heather. She said she was running late." She patted her perfect russet chignon as she scurried to the front door and ushered in, of all people, my ex's child-bride and soon-to-be mother of triplets.

Sam clutched my arm. "Are you going to be all right?"

After my ex-husband's cancer battle, he had decided to get in shape. Heather had been his twenty-two-year-old personal trainer. In her defense, Chad had neglected to tell her he was married when they hooked up.

"I'll be fine." I've gotten to know her a little, and she really is a sweet space case and completely clueless that Chad's been hounding me to get back together. I screen my calls, but that doesn't stop the endless texts, e-mails, voice mails, Facebook messages. I need to figure out how to block his calls on my cell phone. The jerk is even sending me mushy Hallmark cards.

"Hi, everybody," said Heather. She flipped her strawberry-blond braids over her shoulders and set down a plate of cheese crisps on the coffee table. "Sorry I'm late. The bookstore was super busy." Then she noticed me. "Katy! It's super good to see you."

"Good to see you, too," I said, not sharing her enthusiasm.

She trundled her massive, perky pregnant self over to me, arms outstretched. "Give me a hug."

I stood and hugged her. Awkward.

"This is so cool. Wow. You're an Austen fan too. Chad never told me that." Her eyes swept over the group. "Oops. Sorry, guys. I'm married to Katy's ex."

"How cozy," said Justin, obviously relishing the weird dynamics.

I plunked into the corner of the sofa and Sam and Debra scooted over to make room for huge Heather.

All eyes were on me, so I figured it was my turn to speak. "I'm Katy McKenna. Divorced."

Nervous titters.

I glanced at Heather and threw a mean dig. "And former co-owner of The Bookstore Bistro."

She winced, and I immediately felt bad. "I'm sorry. That came out wrong. I mean, it's true, but it's fine. Really. I got the house and he got the business and all good things must come to an end although it really wasn't good, at least not in the end. Will somebody please shut me up?"

"What are you reading, Katy?" Nora held out a plate of fig and goat cheese canapés.

"Mmm. These look yummy." I stuffed a canapé in my mouth to stall answering. "Umm, I'm reading *Emma* too." I read it in my freshman year of high school, and I've seen every movie version since, so I figured I could fake it. "And I agree, Justin. Gwyneth was delightful as Emma, although I prefer the *Masterpiece Classic* 2009 version."

"Oh yes, with Romola Garai." Justin clapped gleefully like a little girl who's just blown out her birthday candles. "She was awesome."

I said to Sam. "You're up next."

"I'm Samantha Drummond. Maternity nurse and mother of two incredible children. Chelsea's fifteen and a sophomore at Santa Lucia High School—"

"Girl, you do not look old enough to have a fifteen-year-old," said Justin. "Just sayin'."

Sam smiled, unconsciously fluffing her short blond hair. "She's my husband's daughter, but I feel like I gave birth to her. Our boy, Casey, is four."

"What'cha reading, Sam?" I said, certain she wasn't reading anything.

She ignored me. "Nora, I must compliment you on this scrumptious tea." She picked up her delicate china cup and made a big show of savoring the brew. "Mmm. What is it?"

"Yorkshire Gold," said Nora. "I'll send some home with you."

I elbowed Sam's ribs. "You still haven't told us what you're reading." Then to everyone, I said, "Sam's really too busy to read books, but she has subscriptions to *People* Magazine and *Us*. Maybe she could give us an update on the latest Hollywood buzz." Sometimes I can be such a brat.

"Oooh." Justin scooted to the edge of his seat. "What are the Kardashians up to?"

Sam focused her steely blues on me. "Actually, I just started a book last night. A book you lent me."

I tried to recall what I'd loaned her. Must've been a while ago, because I was drawing a blank.

"What is it?" Chloe asked in a breathless tone, clutching Justin's hand.

Sam dug her dagger elbow into my arm. "*Fifty Shades of Grey*."

"Oh! Oh! Loved it." Justin clapped again. "Christian gave me goosies."

I wondered if they acted out that book too. *No. Don't go there.*

"Well, I can see our group is going to be very interesting with you two in it," said Nora. "Who's in favor of ditching the tea and having a glass of wine?"

"Me!" said me.

After we all had glasses of wine, we settled back into our seats and Chloe said, "I know this is completely off the subject but remember at our last meeting when we were talking about that guy in Iowa who strangled his pregnant wife in front of their two little kids—just because she was too tired to go Christmas shopping? And then he only got two years because the jury thought he was too drunk at the time to realize what he was doing, even though the prosecution was able to prove he'd been abusing her for years? And then he gets out a few months ago, gets custody of the kids, even though the kids begged the judge to let them stay with their grandparents? Well…" She paused, dramatically glancing around the group.

"Oh! I read about that in the paper this morning," I said. "He was found dead in the parking lot of a sleazy dive bar. Hit and run."

"Well I say good riddance to bad rubbish," said Debra. "Whoever killed that lowlife deserves a medal."

"I agree." Chris wiped cream cheese off her hairy lip. "If the courts can't do their job, then at least someone did. I hope they never get caught."

"Since we're talking about losers," said Melanie. "You all know I've never been a big fan of my brother-in-law, Travis. I know for a fact he's been abusive to my sister, Lisa, numerous times. But she always forgives him. Says he can't help it—which drives me bonkers. But she thinks she has to make the marriage work." She shifted her gaze to Sam and me. "Because their twelve-year-old daughter, Jenny, has a serious kidney condition and needs a transplant."

"Oh, that's terrible," I said. "Is she on a list?"

"Yes, if she lives that long, but wait'll you hear the next part of the story. The other day Lisa comes home after sitting for hours at dialysis with Jenny and finds Travis in bed with some bimbo. And Jenny saw them too."

Chris snorted. "Please tell us she finally got the balls to file for divorce."

Melanie nodded. "She has. And guess what he said he's going to do? He's changing the beneficiary on his life insurance to his girlfriend, and he's canceling his daughter's health insurance. Can you believe that?"

"He can't do that, can he?" asked Samantha. "Isn't there some law to protect her?"

"I don't know. But get this. He told Lisa he's moving to

Acapulco with his floozy to open a tattoo parlor, so she can forget about alimony or—"

"What a creep," shrieked Justin.

"—child support because he's never really believed she's his daughter. Let me tell you, that girl is his, and unfortunately, the poor kid has his Jay Leno chin."

"What's your sister going to do, Melanie?" Samantha asked. "Get a paternity test?"

"She can't work because caring for Jenny is a full-time job, so she's going to have to move in with us. Fortunately we have a big house, and I'm married to an understanding guy." Melanie took a quick sip of wine. "As far as a paternity test—what good will it do if he's already in Mexico? The whole thing's a mess."

"I understand divorce, but you don't divorce your children too," I said.

"It's difficult to comprehend how people can get away with stuff like this," said Debra. "You can't call the cops because technically there's been no crime, yet what he's doing is so deplorable."

"Bottom line, the man needs to be dead," Chris said flatly. "You know you're all thinkin' the same thing. He's a waste of air space, just like that guy Chloe was talking about. At least he got what he deserved."

CHAPTER SIX

Posted by Katy McKenna

"Hi, Katy," said Mom this morning via the phone. "I just spoke to your sister, and she's got her stuff packed and is ready for the move up here."

Emily is my twenty-two-year-old flaky half sister. I love her, but we're not close. By the time she was ten, I was nineteen and living in a dorm, doing my college thing, which didn't include hanging out with ten-year-olds. In retrospect, I guess I was kind of a flake too. It's not like she could have hopped in the car and cruised over for a visit.

In her sophomore year of college, she dropped out to pursue a career as the rapper LazyE. It was a very short-lived career. Now she's decided to become a writer, so she's moving home to mooch off the folks while she writes the next great American paranormal-fantasy-murder-mystery novel. Yeah.

"When's the arrival?" I asked.

"Next week. Kurt's driving down to help her."

"So he has to close the shop to help her move?"

Pop owns Pop's Fix-it Shop, located next door to Mom's hair salon. Entering the quaint appliance repair shop is like stepping back about seventy-five years.

"She needs his truck to move her futon and dresser." She sighed. "I just wish I didn't have to give up my craft room. But it was either that or my dressing room. Obviously, I can't do that. Not after all Kurt's hard work."

Both of those rooms were Mom's dream rooms for the eventual day when her children were no longer, never-ever going to live at home again. When I got married, I hadn't lived at home for several years so she felt safe turning my room into a dressing room. Pop built all the cabinets, and it looks like something you'd see on the Home and Garden TV channel.

After Emily's rapper career tanked, my sister announced she would never live in our bourgeois hick town again, so then Mom got her craft room/guest room.

During my recent divorce, I moved into the crafty guest room until escrow closed on my house, and now Emily's coming home. So my question is: Are you ever safe from your grown kids moving back in?

I have three bedrooms in my cozy bungalow—circa 1930s. The master, a guest room, and the third is an on-site storage facility that I intend to organize one of these days. I could offer the guest room, but there would go my swinging lifestyle. ;-)

Okay, nothing is currently swinging in the passion department, but there goes my privacy. I know I should offer, but I don't want to. Then again, it would give me a chance to get to know my grown-up little sister.

Instead, I said, "But won't it be fun having your little girl home again?"

CHAPTER SEVEN

TUESDAY · JUNE 25
Posted by Katy McKenna

"Hey, Ruby. What's up?" I asked, not wanting to hear the answer. A few years ago, she began checking the obits every morning, and if anyone she was even remotely acquainted with has passed, she calls to share with me.

"I tell you it's hell getting old. Beverly... you know Beverly, right?"

I put the phone on speakerphone while I finished buttering a slice of toast. "She's the lady who played Sandy in the Shady Acres production of *Grease*, right?"

"Right. Well, the poor dear broke her hip last night."

At least she's not dead. "That's a shame. How?" I unfolded the newspaper and glanced at the headlines while Ruby rattled on.

"She got up during the night to go to the bathroom and her diaper slipped down around her ankles and she tripped and—"

"Oh my God!"

"I know—"

"No, not that. I'm looking at the paper and Travis Baker died."

"And I should know who Travis Baker is?"

I relayed Melanie Ramos's story about her low-life brother-in-law.

Ruby snorted. "Sounds like he got exactly what he deserved if you ask me."

CHAPTER EIGHT

WEDNESDAY · JUNE 26
Posted by Katy McKenna

Late last night, while watching an old *Law and Order* about a Marine with post-traumatic stress disorder, I realized that's what I have. PTSD. I've been bumbling along, acting like nothing's happened, but in reality I'm falling apart.

Here's the short list of my life during the past couple of years:

- First, my husband's cancer battle.
- Then his betrayal.
- Divorce.
- Nearly getting murdered a few months ago.
- The police ride-along from hell.

Basically my life has been in turmoil, and I have been in total denial about the personal toll it has taken on me. Energized by my sudden epiphany, I poured another glass of wine and made a list to get my life back on track:

1. Throw out everything fattening and stock up on healthy food.
2. Join a fitness club.
3. Drink less wine. Starting tomorrow.

First thing today, I made a trip to Whole Foods and loaded up with organic veggies and fruit, healthy frozen vegetarian entrees, kale chips, and gummy vitamins.

Back home, I tossed out the cookies and taco chips, cleaned out the fridge, and finished the mint chip ice cream. It felt great checking off item number one on my list.

1. Throw out everything fattening and stock up on healthy food.

—————

Forever Fit's cavernous lobby was filled with buff, good-looking people sipping coconut water in their cute spandex workout clothes. A blue-eyed, bubbly blond greeted me at the reception counter.

"Hi. Welcome to Forever Fit Health Spa. I'm Brittany. How may I help you?"

"I'm thinking about joining a gym, so I'm checking out a few before I make a decision."

Brittany beamed. "Forever Fit is totally the best. When I joined, I was super overweight too." She made a boohoo face and shivered at the ghastly memory. "And you'll never guess what?" Brittany waited breathlessly.

"What?" *Hold the phone. Did she just say I'm fat?*

"We have a free trial membership."

Free sounded good.

"Would you like a tour of the facility? Jarod can show you around."

One look at stud-muffin Jarod and I was ready to sign up, but after the tour I was ready to move in. The indoor-outdoor,

Grecian-inspired, Olympic-size saltwater pool with waterfalls and slides. The gourmet health food bistro. The spin-bike movie theater. The day spa retreat, the coffee and smoothie bar, the rain-forest steam baths, the facial esthetician, the masseuse, the Himalayan rock-climbing wall, the zip line, the wine bar, and my favorite: toning beds you lie on and they work out your body while you snooze.

"I'm ready to sign up for my free membership, Jarod."

"Don't you want to see the exercise equipment, the aerobics room, the yoga studio, the squash courts, the weight-loss center, the—"

"Nah, I'm good. Feeling kind of tired from all this trudging around," I said, feeling fat and fatigued. "This place is huge. You should think about installing an escalator. Maybe I'll get a glass of wine and then take a look."

Translation: Maybe I'll get a glass of wine and sit down.

A local vineyard was hosting a wine and cheese pairing in the wine bar. The featured wine was Daou Celestus 2008, a blend of Syrah, Cabernet, and Petit Verdot.

The vintner eloquently extolled its virtues. "Note the lush aromas of dark fruits, licorice, and lead pencil, accentuated by the French oak." The skinny woman poked her long beak into her glass and sniffed.

We all sniffed along with her. I got the fruit and maybe a hint of licorice, but try as I might, no lead pencil, thank goodness. After appreciating how the ruby wine sheeted and stained the glass, she finally let us taste it.

"Are we all catching the smoky berry compote and candied violets?"

All I knew was it smelled good, tasted yummy, and paired well with the blue cheese and walnuts. If it weren't for Daisy and Tabitha, I never would have gone home again.

2. Join a fitness club.

CHAPTER NINE

Posted by Katy McKenna

My fitness plan for today was:

1. Eat a power breakfast in the Forever Fit bistro.
2. Get a massage or a facial—maybe both.
3. Take a steam.
4. Eat a light lunch.
5. Watch a movie.
6. Happy hour at the wine bar.

———

"Yaaay." Brittany, the counter clerk at Forever Fit, clapped happily, reminding me of Justin Fargate from the book club. "You came back."

You mean there are people who don't? I glanced at the wall clock. 10:14. "How late do they serve breakfast in the bistro?"

"10:30." She slapped a three-page application on the counter.

I flipped the pages. "All this for a free membership?"

"Yes, because we don't want you to sue us if you strain a muscle or something."

Like that's going to happen. I checked the clock again. 10:16. I set my purse on the counter and filled out the application, then scribbled my initials on all the lines she pointed out. "Are we good?"

"Almost," she said with barely contained glee.

What happy pill is this girl taking? I glanced at the clock. 10:22.

"Now all I need is a bank account number for the records," she said.

I fished through my purse and ripped out my debit card. 10:23.

Her lime-green nails tapped the numbers into the computer while my stomach rumbled. I was on a tight training schedule, and if I missed breakfast my whole day would be screwed up.

"All done. Yaay."

10:25. I grabbed my purse and was sprinting across the lobby when Brittany called, "You forgot your debit card!"

I spun around, tripped over my feet, and went down.

———

In the infirmary, the first-aid tech iced my swelling left ankle, wrapped it in a bandage, advised me to see a doctor, and told me to do "Rice Therapy": rest, ice, compress, elevate for the first forty-eight hours. She loaned me a crutch and I hobbled out to get an early lunch since I'd missed breakfast.

On the way to the bistro, I passed the front desk and noticed Brittany hunched over the phone. I caught a snippet of her whispered conversation.

"Why didn't you tell me before we..." Her narrow shoulders quivered as if she were crying.

I guess even Barbie dolls can have a bad day. I settled at a table in the bistro and propped my leg on a chair.

"Katy!"

I glanced around and saw book clubbers Nora and Debra waving. "Join us."

"Can't." I pointed at my ankle. "Come sit with me."

The ladies, attired in stylish workout ensembles, carried their coffees to my table and sat. "What happened?" asked Debra, giving me a quick once-over. Probably jealous of my comfy old sweats.

"Took a tumble. No big thing." Really didn't want to tell them I tripped over myself. I shifted in my seat with a groan. "Anyone got an ibuprofen?"

Nora rummaged in her purse and extracted a jeweled pillbox. "Let me get you a glass of water. Be right back."

"I had no idea you were a member here," said Debra.

"Just started the trial membership."

"You're going to love it. When you're better, you might want to try the boot camp class to get your metabolism jump-started."

"I'll check it out." *Is that her subtle way of saying I'm fat?*

Nora set a goblet of strawberry-infused water in front of me, and I swallowed two pills. "Will you be able to drive? If not, I'd be happy to run you home."

"My car's an automatic. And it's the left ankle, so I'll be fine." I grin-grimaced reassuringly, trying to get comfortable in my chair.

"Would you like me to take a look at it?" asked Debra.

"No. Seriously, I'm all right. Hey—no pain, no gain."

Brittany passed by our table looking like her puppy had died. Debra held out a hand to stop her. "Honey, what's wrong?"

Nora pulled out a chair and patted the seat. "Sit. Maybe we can help."

"No one can help me." She sat, swiping at her tears. "My life is ruined. My parents will never forgive me."

Debra handed her a napkin. "What could be so bad that they wouldn't forgive a sweet girl like you?"

"It's okay, honey," said Nora. "You can talk to us."

I picked up my purse from the floor. "Since we've only just met, maybe I should go so you can talk."

Brittany looked across the table at me with a woebegone face. "No. It's okay. You seem really nice." She turned her focus to Debra. "You know I've been saving myself for marriage, Dr. Williams. That's how I was raised." She showed us her silver "true love waits" ring on her left hand.

"Brittany's father is the minister at Ocean View Church in Cala Grande," Nora told me. "That's where I go. Lovely man. So inspirational." She pushed back the long strands of blond hair stuck to Brittany's wet cheeks. "Tell us what's wrong, honey."

"I broke the vow. I didn't mean to, it just happened. I went to a party and got a little wasted. No. Make that totally trashed." She shredded the napkin, rolling the scraps into tiny balls. "There was this guy there that I've liked for a really long time, but we've never hooked up or anything, and anyways, he kissed me, and…" She dropped her gaze to her lap and whispered, "We wound up having sex."

"How old are you?" I asked.

"Nineteen. I'm the youngest of four sisters," said Brittany, "and not one of them broke the vow. I'm the only one not married yet."

"Brittany, it's okay," I said, feeling motherly. "This isn't the end of the world. Really. These things happen. This doesn't make you a terrible person. Just human." *I doubt she's the only one in her family who's broken the vow.*

"No one ever needs to know." Debra patted the girl's shoulder. "Do you care about him?"

"I did. I really did." Brittany choked back a sob and cleared her throat. "I really thought he was the one. You know, like we were falling in love and would get married." She paused, mouth quivering again. "But he never returned any of my texts, so I finally realized he didn't feel the same way. It hurt, but that's not what I'm really upset about now."

She faltered, barely holding her emotions in check. "He just called and… and told me he's… HIV positive. Oh God, he literally laughed about it."

"Are you absolutely sure that's what he said, Brittany?" asked Debra.

The girl nodded as fresh tears erupted.

"But that doesn't automatically mean you'll get it." I glanced at Debra and Nora. "Right?"

"Of course not. And if it's been less than seventy-two hours since this happened, you may be able to take medication that could protect you from getting infected." Debra took Brittany's hand. "Honey, when did this happen?"

She covered her face with both hands, whispering, "Last Saturday night."

Debra removed her glasses and wiped them with the hem of her shirt, thinking a moment. "Okay. Here's what we're going to do." She put her glasses on and cupped Brittany's chin, lifting her face to eye level. "We have to wait at least two weeks from the time of exposure before an HIV test can provide accurate results. Then we'll get some bloodwork done. Once we do that, we can have those results back within half an hour. If we get a positive for HIV—"

Brittany moaned. "Am I going to die?"

Debra scooted her chair closer to Brittany and put her arms around the girl's slender shoulders, pulling her close. "Oh no, sweetheart. In the remote chance that you test positive, I'll refer you to an infectious disease specialist to handle your case. We can't cure HIV, but we can control it with antiretroviral drugs. I promise you, you can live a relatively normal life with HIV these days. Look at Magic Johnson."

"Who's that?"

"A famous athlete who contracted it in the early nineties. But let's not get ahead of ourselves. We don't even know if you have it."

"There's more." Brittany averted her gaze, then continued in a rush. "He also said I'm like the forty-fourth virgin he's... he's, you know. Since his diagnosis. He said when he hits a hundred, he's going to post our photos on Facebook and Instagram."

"Oh, Brittany. This is beyond belief," said Nora. "What a dreadful monster."

"He's got selfies of everyone, including me." She gazed, unfocused into the distance. "I thought he was a nice boy. I can't believe I wanted to marry him."

"What's this monster's name?" I was ready to go track him down and strangle him.

She wiped the snot from under her nose with the back of her hand and reached for another napkin to shred. "Jeremy Baylor."

"Jeremy Baylor?" Nora exclaimed, leaning forward. "Jeremy goes to our church. He's always seemed like a decent kid. Comes from a good family. This will destroy his parents." She reached across the table, stilling Brittany's restless fingers. "Honey. You have to report this to the police."

CHAPTER TEN

Posted by Katy McKenna

The book club gathered today on the sprawling redwood deck at Melanie Ramos's hacienda-style ranch house in the rolling oak-studded countryside. Crows squawked to each other from the trees and the aroma of dried lavender on the hillside infused the warm air.

I was sitting with my sore ankle propped on a chair, eyeballing a particularly nasty-looking chunky dip when Justin caught my eye.

"It ain't pretty, but you know you want it."

I dipped a Ritz into the mess and took a little bite of heaven. "Oh my God! What is this stuff?" I immediately double-dipped and shoved the cheesy-gooey-gloppy mess into my mouth. I dunked another cracker in and attempted to scoop the whole bowl into my mouth.

"Crack dip," he chuckled evilly, scrubbing his hands.

"Looks like you've corrupted another one," laughed Chris. "I used to be as skinny as a supermodel before crack dip came into my life, thanks to Justin."

Two words that do not go together. Supermodel and Chris. Could that happen to me? My dismay must have shown on my face.

"I'm kidding you," said Chris. "Man, are you easy."

I was double-fisting the dip when the glass slider leading into the house opened and a huge black Labradoodle scooted out and started making the rounds, begging for treats.

"Cassie!" yelled Melanie. "Why'd you let Tootsie out?"

A freckled little moppet about eight or nine years old stuck her head out the door. "She's really bugging me, Mom."

I was about to plunge a baby carrot into the dip when Tootsie knocked the plastic bowl off the table and started slobbering up the mess. "And now she's really bugging us!" Melanie scooped up the bowl and took it and the dog back into the house.

I refilled my wineglass and glumly chomped on the naked carrot stick. Melanie returned and the conversation shifted to the sudden death of her brother-in-law, Travis.

"Maybe there is a God after all." Chloe nibbled a crunchy bruschetta. "Talk about divine intervention."

"I seriously doubt this is God's work." Debra stopped to clear her throat. "Sorry. Allergies. But it is nice when the Grim Reaper gets the timing right."

"Sooner or later, we all gotta check out," said Chris. "I was in the ER when this guy was brought in, and I gotta tell you, he was packing a gut that was begging for a heart attack."

Melanie set down her wineglass, and Justin reached across the table to refill it. "I don't think I can talk about that awful person anymore." She lifted her glass. "So we'll toast to the bum instead." We raised our glasses and she continued. "Travis, wherever you are…" She glanced down. "As if we don't already know. Thank you for finally doing something right in your life and dropping dead. Amen."

Debra burst into a ragged coughing fit, and we all fluttered around her, offering water or slams on her back, but she waved us away. "It's just allergies."

When she settled down, Nora said, "This is just between us, right? Katy and Debra were with me when I heard this."

After she'd shared Brittany's awful HIV dilemma, Justin said, "He's got to be stopped."

"But Brittany doesn't want her family to know," said Nora.

"At the rate this guy's going, it won't be long before he's reached his goal, you know," said Sam. "Then everyone'll know. The whole thing'll go viral."

"This is all a little hard to believe," said Melanie. "What I mean is, and don't get mad at me, but is there any chance that Brittany has made all this up? You have to admit the whole thing sounds pretty bizarre. Especially about targeting virgins."

"It's a fair question, Mel, considering how absurd this all is. But I believe her," said Debra. "I've been her GP since she graduated from her pediatrician and have always known her to be a very honest, upbeat, grounded girl."

"Well, I believe it," said Justin. "Did you see on the news about the fraternity back east that was suspended because they had a Facebook page where they were posting photos of sleeping or drunk girls in various stages of undress and in sexually compromising positions? Without the girls' knowledge or consent, of course. There were comments like, 'I banged her, LOL.'"

"Remember the big story last year about the prep school where for years the senior boys had been taking freshman girls to a secret hideout and coercing them to have sex? Like it's some kind of badge of honor for the boy," said Debra.

"God, when did people become so incredibly heartless?" asked Chloe.

"My mom says it started with the Internet." Heather tipped back a few swallows of sparkling water, then belched and patted her tummy. "Excuse me, but we needed that."

Melanie stood to adjust the red umbrella shading our table. "So if he really is doing this, who's to say he'll stop at a hundred?"

"The minute he posts it, his sex life is over. No girl in her right mind will go near him," said Justin. "But he needs to be stopped before he infects any more girls."

"And before he posts their photos, or every one of those girls will be ruined," said Nora. "Can you imagine what the media would do to them? And their families?"

"But it's really not up to us, is it?" said Chloe. "I mean, what can we do? Brittany is the victim here. She's the one who has to report him."

"From what she said to us at the fitness center, she doesn't have the courage to do anything," I said. "She's just a kid who feels utterly helpless and hopeless."

"And when you're young and you feel like there's no hope…" Chris raised her plaid flannel sleeves to reveal faint white scars on both wrists. "Sometimes you do really stupid things."

We were stunned into silence.

"I was bullied from the time I was in third grade. Mom kept telling me it would get better when I got into middle school. She always said I would grow into pretty, that it just takes time."

"Middle school age is the worst. The kids can be so heartless," I said.

Chris bristled. "No offense, Katy, but good grief. You look like friggin' Anne Hathaway. What would you know?"

"Not then she didn't," said Sam. "She was the tallest kid in the school. Skinny, boney, gawky, pimply, buck-toothed…"

All eyes swung to me.

"…bug-eyed, dorky, shy…"

"Jeez. Why'd you hang out with me?" I said, feeling like a big creep with a terminal case of cooties.

"We were two of a kind, except I was short and chubby. But even though we were fringe-kids, we had each other, and thank

God we weren't bullied. Growing up is hard enough to do. I can't imagine going through that."

"And I couldn't imagine there would ever be a time it would stop. I thought this was the only answer." Chris pulled down her sleeves. "One good thing came of it, however. No one bullied me anymore. Instead I became invisible. And then in my senior year, the ROTC came to my school and that's when my life changed. Suddenly I had a dream, a place where I would belong. A future."

"You joined the army?" I asked the obvious.

She nodded. "Got my education, then fulfilled my commitment. Did two tours in Iraq and three more in Afghanistan in battalion aid stations in the combat zones."

"I'd say you more than fulfilled your commitment." My assessment of Chris had ratcheted up several notches.

"But I never did grow into pretty. Mom was wrong about that." She laughed. "But you two definitely did." Her eyes swept the group. "You all did."

"You should see Katy and me first thing in the morning." Sam waved her hands in denial. "Not a pretty sight."

You'd be amazed what waxing your mustache off and plucking that unibrow would do. But is there a tactful way to say that without sounding like a mean bully? No. "So you really believe Brittany might try to commit suicide, Chris?" I asked. "It's difficult to think of that bubbly Barbie-princess doing something like that."

"I don't know the girl, but yeah, I do. I guarantee it has already crossed her mind."

I remembered Brittany's words at the fitness center. *I'll be ruined; my family will be ruined. God, I wish I was dead.*

CHAPTER ELEVEN

MONDAY · JULY 1
Posted by Katy McKenna

Private Post

Keeping this post private. Ruby reads my
blog and she cannot know about this.

———

Pop called around lunchtime today. "Honey? Your mother needs you. She's had some bad news, and I'm just passing through L.A. now and can't turn around and go home. If I could I would, but your sister has to be out of her apartment by tomorrow morning."

Of course, I automatically jumped to the worse scenarios. Was Mom sick? Ruby had breast cancer in her fifties, and Mom is fifty-three now, so does Mom have cancer? "What is it, Pop? Does she have cancer?"

"No, nothing like that. But the story is hers to tell, not mine. Take Daisy with you. You know how much she loves her."

———

I barely got the front door unlocked before Daisy shoved her way through, searching for her grandma. From the kitchen window, I saw Mom sitting on the stone bench by the pond that she and Pop had built several years ago. Daisy had a paw on her lap and was kissing her hand. I pushed through the screen door and hurried to her.

"Pop said you need me." I sat, pulling her trembling body close. "What's wrong?"

"I've just had a bit of a shock, that's all."

"What is it, Momma?"

She scratched behind Daisy's ears. "You will be so disappointed in me, Katy."

"Mom, I could never be disappointed in you. Just tell me what it is, okay? You're scaring me."

A dove couple landed on a protruding rock in the pond and dipped their beaks into the water. Their soft coos seem to calm Mom a bit. "It's about my Uncle Ted."

"Grandma's brother? All I know about him is that she hasn't spoken to him in years. Nobody's ever told me why."

"This has nothing to do with any of that." A few moments passed while she watched the birds. "One night when I was six, I woke suddenly. I was lying on my stomach and warm hands were rubbing my back. My first thought was that it was Mom. She always did that when I was sad or sick. But when I came fully awake, I realized the hands were much too big and rough to be hers."

She paused, drawing a choppy breath. "I was uncovered and my pajama bottoms were down around my thighs. And then the big hands started rubbing places my mother's hands had never gone. Into my buttocks, under me to my flat little chest and then... into... my... vagina. The scary fingers would not stop digging into me. Rubbing, probing." Her desolate eyes met mine, wrenching my heart. "Katy, I hadn't even known about that part of my body until that moment."

"Oh, Momma. What did you do?"

"I didn't know what to do." The birds took flight and Mom watched them disappear. She stood. "I should fill the bird feeder."

I pulled her back down to the bench. "The birds can wait. You can't. Please tell me the rest. Please."

She sat, eyes closed, hands clenched in her lap. "I lay there for what seemed like an eternity. I knew it was my uncle making those awful sounds. I knew it was wrong. Terribly wrong, yet he kept doing it. And it hurt. My uncle was hurting me in my private places. Rubbing me harder and harder and moaning. I desperately wanted him to stop, but I was afraid to say or do anything, so I just lay there, frozen, so he wouldn't know I was awake." Mom clasped a shaking hand over her mouth, stifling a sob. "Oh God, Katy. I was so frightened. Finally I got an idea that I hoped would make him go away."

"What was it?"

"Katy, to this day, it was one of the hardest things I've ever done. I pretended I was waking up. I squirmed and yawned, made little fussy noises. And it worked. He stopped and I turned on my side, facing the wall, then reached down for the blankets and tried to yank them up. He was on top of the blankets, so the pulling forced him off the bed. I drew the covers up to my nose and curled into a tight little ball, then lay still again, barely able to breathe, pretending I was asleep. After a while, he went to the daybed across the room and pretty soon, I heard him snoring."

She looked at me and I could see the terrified little girl. "I lay awake all night, afraid he'd do it again, afraid for morning to come when I would have to face him."

"Mom? Would you like a cup of tea?" I knew the story wasn't done, but she was shaking so hard I was worried.

"I know it's a bit early bit I think a glass of wine would be better." She moved to the sectional sofa under the pergola and wrapped herself in a red fleece blanket, even though the temperature was in the high seventies. Daisy settled beside Mom, watching her with concern.

I brought out a bottle, poured us each a glass, and cuddled her to me. "What happened in the morning?"

"It's strange how my memory of his violation is so vivid after nearly fifty years, but the next morning is so sketchy."

"You were in shock."

"Yes, that would make sense. I do remember there were blood spots on my sheet and how much that frightened me. I was afraid I was going to die. And it burned terribly when I urinated. I didn't know what to do or how to tell anyone what had happened. I didn't even know the words to use. And I was so embarrassed."

"Grandma didn't notice the blood spots when she changed the sheets?"

Mom shook her head. "Saturday was always clean sheet day. That morning, I pulled the sheets off my bed and stuffed them into the washing machine before she could get to them."

"She didn't think that was weird?"

"No. She was impressed with her big girl. So from then on, I always took my sheets off."

"What happened after he... he violated you?" I said softly.

"I know I avoided him. I thought maybe this is what some grown-ups do. Maybe they wouldn't think it was bad. I mean he was my Uncle Ted. That meant he had to be a good guy. Maybe only I thought it was a bad thing. And then everyone would be really mad at me for all the trouble I would have caused."

"Oh, Momma." My heart ached for that frightened little girl.

"So I never told." She sipped her wine. "Those years were so hard. Family gatherings, the holidays, all ruined because he was always there with his family. They had two kids. Kathy and Gary. Kathy was older than me. Both nice kids, as I recall." She inhaled deeply. "Or we went to their house. That was worse, because I couldn't hide out in my bedroom. And I had to keep pretending nothing had happened. I always avoided him, especially when everyone was hugging and kissing hello and good-bye. Eventually they moved across the country. And then a few years later Mom had a falling out with him. So no more pretending for me. I could finally put it behind me. Until today."

"What happened today?" I asked, refilling her glass.

"For some strange reason, I felt compelled to search for him online. I have no idea why. But a mug shot came up. I haven't seen his face since I was a kid. But no mistaking it. It was him, all right, just older. And under that photo were several newspaper stories dating back over several months."

"What did he do to get arrested?"

"He was arrested on suspicion of molesting a child. His ten-year-old granddaughter. Tara's her name. Pretty name, don't you think? She told her mother and made a statement to the police. There's already been a trial, and he was found guilty, but he hasn't been sentenced yet. He faces a sex offender penalty ranging from probation to life in prison for molesting a child while in his care." She paused to drink her wine. "And he doesn't live across the country anymore. He lives in the Central Valley. Clover. That's just two and a half hours away. He's been there for over ten years. He and his wife. My Aunt Shirley. Unfortunately, Tara's father, Gary, passed away several years ago, and her mother has never remarried." She paused with a shaky sigh. "It's so weird. Gary was my cousin. He was several years younger; the last time I saw him, he was maybe five years old. I have no idea what happened to Kathy. Anyway, Aunt Shirley left Ted and has filed for divorce. Can you imagine finding that out about your husband after fifty-something years of marriage?" She took my hand, squeezing hard. "Katy. This is all my fault. If I had told, this wouldn't have happened to that innocent little girl."

"Mom, back then you were a scared little six-year-old. How can you possibly be to blame for what has happened decades later?"

"I don't know. I just can't help but feel responsible."

"Well, I do know. Even if you had told, it's not like the law would have punished him. It was a very different time back then."

"As an adult, I know that if I'd told my parents, he would have been banished from our lives."

"But your uncle still would have gone on with his perverted life, no matter what. Nothing, absolutely nothing would have changed that."

"You know, all these years, I have always hoped it was just a one-time thing for him. That maybe he'd been drunk. And I was the only one. That it never happened again."

She drained her glass. "I mean, the times I saw him after that, he seemed like a happy family man. He never acted like anything had happened. And my cousins never acted like there were problems. That's why I've held onto the idea that he was stinking drunk at the time." She slowly shook her head. "So I never, ever thought…"

We were both quiet for a moment, and then I asked, "How are we going to tell Ruby?"

"We're not."

CHAPTER TWELVE

TUESDAY · JULY 2
Posted by Katy McKenna

Private Post

I spent half the night wrestling with my conscience and finally concluded that Emily should stay at my house for a while. Mom's got enough on her plate right now and doesn't need any added stress. Before I changed my mind, again, I called Mom first thing this morning and offered my guest room.

"Are you sure you want to do this?"

No. "Yes, of course, I'm sure." *No, I'm not.* "It'll give us some time to bond. I should have offered sooner."

"Oh, honey. I really appreciate it. I'm so worried about telling Mom about her brother that I might not have enough patience for Emily."

Who does? "So you've decided to tell Ruby?"

"I don't really have a choice now. Sooner or later she's going to find out, and it's better if she hears it from me. I doubt she'd ever google him, but it could wind up in the local paper. But I want to hold off until after the Fourth of July weekend. And I do not want Emily to know about this."

"Okay, Mom. But you do know she's twenty-two now. Right? She's not a little girl anymore."

"I know. And in time I will tell her. But right now it's all I can do to muster up the courage to tell Mom."

"What time do you think Pop and Emily will get here?"

"He is trying to get out of San Diego before noon, so he doesn't get stuck in L.A. traffic. So maybe five. Five-thirty."

I glanced at my watch. *Only nine hours of freedom left.*

CHAPTER THIRTEEN

THURSDAY • JULY 4
Posted by Katy McKenna

Private Post

The hospital cafeteria is not my first eatery of choice, but Sam only gets a half-hour break, and yesterday I desperately needed to be talked down from killing my baby sister. Already.

"Emily didn't come home until four a.m. this morning?" asked Samantha. "Are you serious? On her first night in your house?"

"Four-o-eight to be exact, but who's counting? All her stuff is piled in the garage and in the living room, and no sooner does Pop drive away and she's calling her friends and tearing out of the house. She was still in bed when I left to come here." I shoveled a hunk of chocolate cake (my lunch) into my mouth, telling myself I would work it off at the gym when my ankle recovered. "So basically I've shared about three words with her since she moved in yesterday. Nice, huh?"

"That must've hurt your feelings," said Sam.

"Ya think?"

"And why is she staying with you?"

I told her about Mom's uncle, knowing Mom would be okay with that. Sam is family.

"God, that's so awful. Your poor mother, dragging that around all these years. That man should be castrated. That should be the automatic punishment for all sex offenders. But instead they usually get released so they can do it again."

"I think when it involves a child, it should be the death penalty."

"Whoa! You've always been against that."

"Changed my mind. This man got to live his whole life a free man. Who knows how many children he's screwed up? Going to jail in his seventies just means he doesn't have to worry about anything anymore. Free room and board. Three hot meals a day, clean clothes, free health care. The ultimate retirement home."

"I've always heard that child molesters do not fare well in prison. The inmates have a code, and someone like him is going to suffer."

"God, I hope so, but I'm guessing that because of his advanced age and the fact that he's probably not a flight risk, he won't be placed in a prison with hard-core murderers and gangsters."

"He'll still suffer, Katy." She reached over the table and placed her hand on mine.

"He hurt my mother." Tears threatened to spill and I tilted my head up, trying to contain them and save my mascara. "And his grandchild. And God knows who else. How could he?"

"He's a sick man."

Those words made me flash on my police ride-along. *"Please, Tanya. I'm begging you. Don't kill me. It's not my fault. I got a sickness. I need help so I can get cured."*

And Tanya's answer had been: *"That's a joke, Leon. The only cured pedophile is a dead pedophile."*

Sam checked her watch and stood, gathering her things. "Honey, I'm sorry, but I have to get back. I hate to leave you."

I dabbed my tears with a napkin. "I'm okay. I'll walk you back." I wrapped my cake in a napkin and stuffed it in my purse, in case I had a chocolate emergency later.

Today

It's fourth of July. It used to be one of my favorite holidays, but now I have a sweet doggy who is terrified of loud noises like fire-crackers. So, instead of shooting off fireworks tonight at my parents, I'll be sitting in the closet with Daisy panting on my lap, listening to soothing yoga music.

CHAPTER FOURTEEN

MONDAY · JULY 8
Posted by Katy McKenna

Private Post

I'm too angry about my sister's continuing selfish, rude behavior to even blog about it, so this morning I took a beginners' yoga class at Forever Fit, hoping it would cleanse my "chi" of my seething sister-hate. Brittany wasn't at the desk when I signed in.

The yoga studio was softly lit and sandalwood scented, bringing back childhood memories of strolling through Chinatown in San Francisco with my folks. A slate-backed waterfall trickled down a wall flanked by tall windows revealing a stand of bright green bamboo growing outside. Tranquil spa music soothed my rotten mood as I set my yoga mat as far away from everyone as possible.

An elderly woman with long silver hair glided to the waterfall. She placed her palms together in front of her slender chest and bowed. "*Namaste*. Greetings, everyone." Her kind eyes floated around the room. "I see we have a new pupil today."

Everyone turned to me and did the *namaste* thing again.

"My name is Moonlight." Her tranquil voice was barely above a whisper. "What is yours, dear friend?"

"Katy McKenna," I said too loud, my voice echoing through the room.

"Katy. We bring our hands together at the heart chakra to increase the flow of divine love. Bowing our heads and closing our eyes helps the mind surrender to the divine in the heart." She *namasted* me again, and I did likewise, not so much feeling divine love and more like feeling goofy.

"All right, class. Let's begin with child pose. Katy, you may want to remove your crocs."

We got down on our knees, put our heads to the floor, extending our arms along the floor behind us. Easy and it felt good.

Then lifted into cat pose—think of a cat hunching his back.

Then into cow pose—like a swayback horse. I was really liking yoga. The stretches felt wonderful and were easy-peasy.

Next we moved into downward dog. Not quite so easy.

Plank: hard, especially with my bad elbow and sore ankle.

Then back to downward dog, then lifted one leg up. Then back to plank. Only ten minutes into the class and I was sweating buckets.

Then a series of lunges. Was this really a beginner class? Seriously?

Cobra position finished me off.

Finally it was time for relaxation. Lying with bolsters under our knees and lavender-scented eye pillows, Moonlight played a glass Tibetan singing bowl….

———

"Katy? Katy, wake up. Class ended ten minutes ago."

I pulled off the eye pillow and looked up into Moonlight's ancient, beautiful face. I was groggy and it took a moment to connect the dots.

"You did very well for your first session, Katy. I look forward to our journey together."

So my question is: Is there a yoga class that just does the nap time?

On my way out, I stopped at the front counter to ask the hunky, bald receptionist about Brittany.

"All I know is she's in the hospital," he said. "Don't know why."

After I cleared the exit, I texted Sam at the hospital and asked her to see what she could find out. About an hour later she called. "It's not good," she said. "She's in the ER and it looks like she tried to kill herself."

"Oh my God! How?"

"Aspirin and alcohol. Debra's her family doctor and—"

"I know that."

"Anyway, she's with her now, and I was able to talk to her for a sec. They pumped her stomach and she's stable, but they're checking for internal bleeding, kidney and liver damage. Her parents are here, but they have no idea why she did this."

"Do you think Debra will tell her folks about Jeremy?"

"I doubt it. Brittany's over eighteen, and she was emphatic about us not telling her parents. As her physician, Debra cannot go against her wishes."

"But it's for her own good!"

"You don't have to tell me that."

"Then Nora, you, and I can talk to them."

"I'm not sure that's a good idea either. I work at the hospital where she's being treated. Nora too. I can't risk a lawsuit."

"Then I can."

"Katy, you can't tell them. It's too much and it won't change anything. They have enough on their plate right now without a complete stranger barging in and dumping this on them."

This evening, I typed Jeremy Baylor's name into the Facebook people search, then narrowed it down to Cala Grande and bingo! I could see why Brittany had been attracted to him. I had imagined him as a meth-addicted dude with facial tats and piercings, hands posed in a gang symbol.

Instead I was looking at a good-looking, clean-cut blond surfer. He hadn't locked down his privacy settings so I nosed around. Nice family photos, cute friends. Nothing came up that was even remotely connected to what Brittany told us. Nora had said he came from a good family, and she had always considered him a decent kid. Given what I was looking at, he appeared to be just that.

I was having second thoughts about Brittany. I mean, just because she told us he was a monster, did that really mean he actually was? Maybe she's a needy, unstable girl, desperate for attention.

And then I came across a picture of a cute girl a guy named Gabe had posted to Jeremy's timeline a few months ago with the comment: *Your numero uno, bro. LOL.*

CHAPTER FIFTEEN

Posted by Katy McKenna

Private Post

Around ten-fifteen this morning, Emily's bedroom door opened, sending Tabitha and Daisy streaking for the dog door. I was at the kitchen table paying bills when she slinked into the room, opened the fridge, and took out a quart-sized carton of Greek yogurt.

"You could at least say good morning," I said. *Oops. Bad start. Should have just said "Good morning."*

"So could you."

"You're right. Good morning. Did you sleep well?"

"No. The bed sucks." She opened the yogurt and leaned on the counter eating it.

Oh, gee. You poor thing. "I'm sorry. Maybe I can scrounge up another mattress pad for it. Are you going to work on your book today?" *Or look for a job?*

"I dunno."

"How far have you gotten? May I read it?"

"Pretty much just doing research right now." She sat at the table across from me. "You know, like watching shows like *The Walking Dead, Vampire Diaries. Almost Human.* I set the DVR to record a bunch of shows. I had to cancel some of your scheduled recordings. Hope you don't mind. But you know," she shrugged like a little smart-ass, "research."

I minded and I would readjust the recording schedule ASAP. "Have you read any of the *Sookie Stackhouse* novels?"

"No. What are those?"

"It's the book series that the HBO show *True Blood* was based on. I think you'd enjoy them. Sookie is a telepathic waitress and she's in love with a vampire and she—"

Emily held up her hand, shutting me up. "Don't really like to read that much. I'll just watch the show. You got HBO, right?"

"Nope."

"That sucks."

So does paying the bills. I closed my laptop. "If you don't like to read, how can you write a book?"

"I'm writing a series, not just a book." She twirled a section of her long, goth-black hair and yawned. "Maybe I'll go take a nap."

"I write," I said.

A faint smile curled her lips. "You do? What?"

Considering her look of derision, I should have kept my mouth shut. "A blog. About my life. Like a diary or a journal. You know. The everyday trials and tribulations." Like this conversation.

"Sounds really *boorriing*." She tossed the empty yogurt container in the garbage and headed out of the room.

"Hey. I've got stuff going on, you know." I stood, raising my voice. "Have you forgotten I was almost killed a few months ago? And how about my police ride-along? I would hardly call that *boorriing*."

From the living room, she finished me off with, "Blogging isn't really writing, you know."

Right then, I would have killed for ice cream. I rampaged

through my cupboards looking for a sweet morsel to sustain me, but I had been too thorough when I had dumped all my goodies a couple of weeks ago. What a dumb idea that had been. Then I remembered I'd saved my cake from my lunch with Sam in the hospital cafeteria last week.

Like a needy heroin addict, I dumped my purse on the kitchen table and unwrapped the dried-up cake. Napkin lint was stuck to it, but I broke off a petrified chunk and tried it. It wasn't that bad, but as I shoved the rest into my mouth, I caught my reflection on the toaster. That was bad.

My name is Katy Ann McKenna, and I'm a sugarholic.

———

Ruby called an hour later. "I got good news and I got good news. What do ya want to hear first?"

"I'll take the good news!"

"Your great Aunt Edith is coming for a visit!"

"When?"

"Sometime in the fall. We're going to have so much fun. We can take her to Hearst Castle…"

Hearst Castle? Really? The woman lives in the UK, the land of castles. Real castles.

"…and wine tasting and Disneyland. I can't wait for Ben to meet her."

"Maybe he'll want to go to Disneyland with you guys."

"Oh sweetie-pie, this is strictly a girl thing. You, Emily, Mary-beth. A fun girls-gone-wild trip."

Shoot me now. "What's the other good news?"

"Hold onto your hat. I have a job for you."

Oh please let it be ice cream tasting. No! Stop! I'm a sugarholic. If it's an ice cream job, I will have to say no. Just say no. Yeah, right.

———

Uncle Charlie's Clunker Carnival covers a few acres and along the street front is an ongoing carnival. Ferris wheel, merry-go-round, bounce house, calliope music, and carney food.

In every TV commercial, there's good old Uncle Charlie dressed like a clown, making balloon animals for a crowd of happy, hyper kids, flanked by shiny used cars.

"No cash? No problem. No credit? No problem. Bad credit? No problem. Uncle Charlie's got you covered with instant credit and no money down. So bring the kids for free ice cream and drive away in your brand new pre-owned vehicle today."

I parked my car on the street hoping to circumvent a bunch of clowns clustered by the cotton candy machine, but they were too quick for me. I saw them play a quick rock-paper-scissors and then one split from the pack, bearing down on me. I pretended not to see him and scurried toward the big striped tent where I figured I'd find the sales office.

"Let's make a deal," he hollered, catching up with me. "Name your price and we'll take that…" He paused, bending over to catch his breath while thrusting a sticky business card into my hand. "… old gas-guzzler off your hands. Send you home in a classy pre-owned Hummer." He pointed yonder to a shiny mustard-yellow Hummer. "In that baby, you'll be ready for anything. Hurricanes, tornados, the apocalypse, whatever."

I glanced at the card. "Really? That's your name? Mr. Chuckles?"

He straightened. "Nah. It's really Matthew."

Mr. Chuckles grinned, and I got the impression there was a cute guy hiding under the clown makeup and rainbow hair.

"Well, Mr. Chuckles, I'm not shopping today. Where can I find Mister, uh, Charlie?"

Matthew pointed to the big top. I thanked him and he said, "Everyone calls him Uncle Charlie. And don't ever get rid of your car. She's a classic."

I glanced at Veronica sitting primly at the curb in all her shiny orange glory. "Wouldn't dream of it."

The sales office had a large reception area, and I was told to wait with a crowd of other people. I selected a tattered *Time* magazine from a pile on a beat-up coffee table and took a seat on a worn-out leather couch. I would have preferred the People magazine, but I wanted to appear businesslike in case Uncle Charlie came out. I flipped to the back for the movie reviews. Finally I was called into Uncle Charlie's office.

"Good to meet you, Katy." He shook my hand at the door, then sat at his desk, gesturing me to sit opposite him in a leather chair. His wood-paneled office was a dusty clutter of memorabilia collected over thirty-something years in business. Clown paintings, bowling and softball trophies, framed yellowed newspaper clippings. "Did your temp agency fill you in on the job?"

"No."

He straightened his giant polka-dot bow tie. "We're doing a huge promotion, and what I need are some big, splashy posters, flyers, banners…"

The desk phone buzzed. "Uncle Charlie? A Ms. Levine is calling from the bank. Do you want to take this call?"

"Tell her I'm in a meeting." He shifted in his seat and yanked his bow tie with a grimace. "Where were we?"

"Banners."

"Oh yeah." He slapped the desk. "We're going to have a bunch of veterans compete to win a car and—"

The phone buzzed again. "There's a Mr. Smart calling about our web hosting. He sounds a little agitated. Are you still in a meeting?"

"Yes! In a meeting. Just take messages, June. And don't interrupt again." He yanked off his Bozo wig and swabbed his sweaty balding head with a handkerchief. "I'm sorry about that, Katy. I shouldn't get cranky with her."

"What do they have to do to win a car? Guess the winning number? Count jelly beans in a jar? Shoot bull's-eyes?"

"Nah, nah. Nothing hard. All they have to do is put one hand on the prize and keep it there the longest. Last man…" He caught my steely expression. "…or woman still got a hand on the car wins."

Pop did a stint in the Coast Guard. I could be his coach. Bring him water and snacks. A father-daughter thing. Could be fun.

"What car will they win?"

He led me to the window facing the lot and pointed at the Hummer. "She's a beaut, don't you think? Who wouldn't want that?"

Anyone with a bad knee, like Pop. No way could he hoist himself up into that thing. "A vet with a disability might have a problem with that."

He scowled, stroking his turkey neck. "Hadn't thought of that."

"So, no contest?" *And no job for me.*

"No, no. I've already contacted the radio and TV stations, and they'll be doing live remote broadcasts throughout the event. How fast can you get everything done?"

"When do you need it?" I already knew the answer. My work is the first thing a client needs and the last thing they think about. That meant he'll want it yesterday.

"The contest begins the 27th, but we'll want the banners up by the weekend."

"This coming weekend? Are you kidding?" I think I yelped.

"Is that a problem?"

"It's not only a problem, it's impossible. At least for me it is. I have to create a few thumbnail sketches for you to choose from." I ticked the steps off with my hands. "Then produce several pieces of finished artwork for the printers. Then they have to do proofs for me to approve, then…"

"Okay, I get ya. How much do you want to make this happen?"

"It's not about the money, Mister, uh—"

"Call me Uncle Charlie."

"It's about the time frame, Uncle Charlie. I'm just one person, working all by myself, and there are only so many hours in the day." My tone was borderline screeching at this point. "My suggestion for you is to go to one of those speedy sign shops. Maybe they can get it done in time. And way cheaper too."

"Nope." He slapped his desk again. "Has to be you. Ruby Armstrong, the boss at the Nothing Lasts Forever temp agency, spoke very highly of you. Said you're the best in town and worth every penny."

I closed my eyes, taking a long cleansing yoga breath. "If you move the contest date out another week, I'll do the job." *Now he will say "No way," and I'm outta here.*

Uncle Charlie looked at his calendar. "How's this. We kick off the contest on August second—that's a Friday."

I needed a visual, so I stepped over to his desk and looked at the calendar. "I can work with that." *Barely.*

Bzzz.

"WHAT, June?"

"A Ms. Kiger with the IRS is on line two and she won't take no for an answer."

"Katy, I better take this. We're having a little snafu with those jokers. Personally, I think they need to get their own house in order before harassing the little guys."

CHAPTER SIXTEEN

THURSDAY · JULY 11
Posted by Katy McKenna

While commuting through the dewy grass to my garden shed/office this morning to begin the Clunker job, I called Debra Williams to get an update on Brittany.

"She's doing okay, considering. Of course, I can't go into details with you. She was released from the hospital early this morning and is home now."

"Has she told her parents about Jeremy?"

"No. And I cannot get through to her. And because of that, I think she'll try again rather than face her problems."

I propped open the shed door, cleared away a cobweb blocking the entrance, and sat at my drawing board. The board is more of a desk these days because most of my work is generated on my big screen iMac. "Brittany has at least sixty years of living ahead of her." I switched the phone to speaker mode and woke up my computer. "A lot of wonderful things can happen in those years."

"You're right about that," said Debra. "I'm in my fifties, and when I think of what I would have missed. So many good things.

Of course in every life there are times when it feels impossible to go on. I don't often speak of this, but I'd like to share my story with you."

"Okay." I picked up a pencil and started doodling.

"Years ago, I was married and we had a little girl. My husband was an alcoholic, recovering, four years sober or so I thought." She gave a shuddering sigh. "Anyway, one day while I was working a sixteen-hour shift…" She hesitated, then rushed her words as if saying it fast would hurt less. "…he backed the car over Becky and killed her."

"Oh my God, Debra." I set the pencil down and reached for a tissue to blot my sudden tears. "How old was she?"

"Three. It was the worst day of my life. The only thing that could have hurt more would have been if I had been the one who killed her. Katy, I was so awful to him. I refused to forgive him."

"How could you have?"

"Eric wasn't a bad man. It was an accident. A terrible, tragic accident. I can't imagine his pain. Knowing he'd killed our baby."

"What happened to him?"

"He went to prison. I was glad. I wanted him to suffer for killing my little girl. But, Katy, he didn't belong in prison. Eric was a gentle, loving man, and to be honest, a better parent than I was. I was doing my residency. Working thirty-six hour shifts and exhausted 24/7. I should have realized he was drinking again, but I was too busy and too worn out to notice. If I had, they'd both still be here. Becky would be a grown woman about your age."

"What happened to him?"

"He served a three-year sentence, then wound up living on the streets up in San Francisco. One day he was found dead in an alley."

"Oh my God. When was that?"

"Over twenty years ago now. Hold on." She coughed several times.

"That sounds bad. You coming down with something?"

"Sorry about that. Allergies. I think the drought's making them worse." She cleared her throat. "Anyway, when he was sentenced, he told me to file for divorce. Said I was better off without him. Believe me, I had every intention of doing just that, but for some reason I never did. I guess deep down I still loved him. Then he was dead. I hate the fact that I never forgave him while he was still alive."

"If you could get through all that, then Brittany should be able to get through this."

"Katy, we all have our own level of coping abilities. And I wasn't a nineteen-year-old girl then. I told Brittany's parents not to leave her alone for a minute. Monitor everything she watches on TV, who she talks to, what music she listens to, and for God's sake, no Internet. I wanted to keep her under watch at the hospital another day, but they wanted her home. She'll be seeing a therapist, of course."

I stood, feeling restless, helpless. "That boy has got to be stopped. There must be something we can do."

"I agree. But I don't know what. If we go to the police, they'll want to talk to Brittany. I don't think she can handle that."

"But we can't just sit back and do nothing. I mean, knowing what we know and allowing it to continue. Doesn't that make us guilty too?"

CHAPTER SEVENTEEN

FRIDAY · JULY 12

Posted by Katy McKenna

Before I hit the sack last night, I checked Jeremy Baylor's Facebook profile and found this posted:

Parents out of town. Big party at my house on Friday Night. 6 until whenever. Bring eats, booze, and the ugliest girl you can find. 768 Wyndham Lane. Let's party!!!!

It was too late to call Sam, so I pasted his post into an e-mail, along with an invitation to crash the party with me.

———

Ryan Reynold's three-day stubble grazed across my eager lips while he delicately tickled my cheeks.

"Oh yes, my darling. Kiss me again…"

Ricket. Ricket.

He pulled away, leaving me breathless.

"No. No. Don't stop," I moaned. "Kiss me."

Ryan leaned in and nuzzled my lips, his beard scraping my

chin, his scratchy tongue slipping between my parted lips, his breath warm and fishy…

Ricket. Ricket.

"Ignore that damned text message alert, Ryan, and take me now."

"Meeeoow." I opened my eyes to Tabitha's raspy smooches.

"All right, sweetheart. I get it. Time to get up and feed you."

———

My iPhone was on the kitchen counter, still lit from a recent text from Sam.

Ok I will go to Jeremy's.

After I had a few swigs of caffeine under my belt, I called her.

"I'll go," Sam said. "But I think it's a total waste of time. We probably should just go to the police and let them deal with it."

"The police can't do anything about this. I mean, has a crime actually been committed here? And what proof do we have? Only what Brittany said to Nora, Debra, and me. The most they would do, if anything, is talk to Brittany and we both know that's not a good idea right now."

"While he continues to infect more innocent girls, just for the fun of it."

"That's why I want to talk to him before the party. Somebody needs to scare the hell out of him, and I don't want to do it alone."

She was silent.

"You still there?"

"Just thinking about what I have to do today. I have to run errands and then bake cupcakes for the book club meeting tomorrow. What're you bringing?"

Totally had spaced that out. "It's a surprise."

"Yeah, right. I'll pick you up at five."

———

"So don't want to do this." Sam was driving her Ford Escape slower than a sloth down Wyndham Lane. "Spencer's home and tonight is date night, and we haven't had a date night in a *looong* time, if you know what I mean, so we need to do this fast."

"Yes, I know what you mean, and oh, poor you. I haven't had a date night…" I finger-quoted. "…since before Chad got cancer. It's been so long that I'm actually considering letting Ruby set me up with this guy named Duke, who drives her senior Dial-a-Ride van."

"You win."

"There it is." I pointed at a tidy white rancher. "Seven-sixty-eight. Nice house. Looks quiet."

"It won't be for long." Sam parked the car across the street.

I pointed at a jacked-up red truck with a surfboard in the back, parked in the driveway. "That must be his truck."

We rang the doorbell and a dog started yapping.

"What're we going to say to him?" asked Sam, looking as nervous as I felt.

"We'll tell him we know what he's doing, and he has to contact every girl he's had sex with and tell them to get a checkup. And that we plan to inform his parents and…" I thought a moment. "The local news media. And he has to cancel this bash, or we will call the police and report underage drinking."

"That should do it," said Sam, watching the street for incoming teens. "Ring it again before I lose my nerve."

The dog sounded frantic, but it hadn't raced to the door like Daisy would have.

"That dog must be locked up somewhere. Hope it's okay." I peeked in the window by the door. "Maybe Jeremy's in the backyard."

"Or maybe nobody's home." She tugged on my arm. "Let's leave."

"We're here now, so we might as well go around and check."

"Why do I let you talk me into things like this?" Sam lagged behind as we crept down the driveway toward a gate at the end.

"Are we really doing this?" she asked, when we reached a white vinyl gate leading into the backyard. I unlatched the gate, holding the attached bell to keep it quiet as we stepped through. "I guess that's a yes."

We skulked across the lawn to a flagstone patio, halting at the edge.

"Jeremy?" I said, having second thoughts about this mission. "Hellooo. Jeremy?"

"Katy, no one's going to hear you whispering, you know."

"I feel like a trespasser."

"Probably because you are a trespasser."

I took a breath and yelled, "Jeremy! We need to talk to you."

"It's urgent!" screamed Sam. "A matter of life or death."

The dog's barking turned into a keening howl.

"This is now officially weird," Sam said. "We're outta here."

"That dog sounds like it's in trouble. Maybe hurt." I dashed across the patio to the sliding door and peered in.

"Be careful, Katy! The place might have an alarm. I really do not want to go to jail today. I still have to frost those damned cupcakes for the stupid book club!"

"Uh-oh. This is not good."

Sam was still rooted in the grass. "What?"

I signaled her over. "Come here and take a look."

"I'm fine right here. Just tell me."

"No. You need to see this."

Sam joined me at the window and looked in. "He's asleep on the couch. So what?"

"Look at all the beer cans on the floor."

"Okay, he must've got drunk and passed out."

"Before the party?"

"What can I say, Katy? The guy's a total idiot and obviously a terrible party host, too."

I locked eyes with Sam. "Are you thinking what I'm thinking?"

"Oh, I know what you're thinking, and no, he's not dead, Katy.

This is Santa Lucia, not *Breaking Bad*. You need to stop watching all your crime shows and watch my nice shows."

Nope. Not gonna watch the Real Housewives of... Anything.

Sam checked her watch. "It's past 5:30. Let's get out of here before kids start showing up."

"But we can't leave that poor doggy. It might be hurt, and that loser is obviously too trashed to do anything about it." I tried the slider and it opened. "Just let me make sure the dog's okay. Then we'll leave."

"Oh my God. You're going in? I can't believe you're going in!" She hesitated and then followed me through the door. "You go find the dog and I'll check the kid. I don't want to hear tomorrow that he was dying of alcohol poisoning, and we could have saved him. Although that's exactly what the little shit deserves."

I sneaked through the house, following the manic barking. "Hey puppy, puppy. Where are you?"

A door at the end of a hallway was thumping on its hinges as the dog tried to scratch its way through the wood.

"Please, please, please don't bite me." I opened the door and was nearly knocked off my feet by a Puggle plowing between my legs and making a beeline for his boy. Yeah, it was a he. No missing those cojones.

"Katy!" Samantha screamed. "Get out here!"

I raced through the house and found Sam giving Jeremy CPR. "What's going on?"

"Call 9-1-1!"

I grabbed the phone on the side table and dialed, but I was so flustered that at first, I couldn't remember where I was. After answering the dispatcher's questions, he said help was on the way. I hung up, went back to Sam, and felt Jeremy's neck for a pulse.

"Oh my God, Sam! I think he's dead!"

She pumped at his chest. "Can't. Stop. Until. Paramedics. Arrive."

The doorbell started ringing nonstop. "Yo! Yo! Yo! Party time! Open up, Jeremy!"

"Go away!" I screamed without thinking. "Party's off!"

"Yeah right. Open the friggin' door!"

"Oh, crap. I should have kept my stupid mouth shut. Now they know we're in here."

Sam glanced up at me. "We gotta get outta here." She kept compressing the dead guy's chest. "Start breathing, dammit!"

The back gate bell jingled. "Too late."

A crowd of boys lugging kegs of beer streamed into the yard followed by some incredibly homely girls. I grabbed a blue chenille throw draped over an easy chair and spread it over Jeremy just before one of the boys opened the slider.

"Hey! Where's Jeremy?" said a spacey-looking brunette, flipping his long hair out of his eyes.

Sam and I stood in front of the sofa shielding Jeremy, as the Puggle growled and wrestled to tug the blanket off him.

"He was here a minute ago," I said, all wide-eyed and innocent. "Right, Sam?"

"Yeah. Right. A minute ago." She glanced toward the kitchen. "Jeremy! Your friends are here."

"Are you like his mom or something?" He turned to the kids outside. "Dudes, his mom's here."

Sam's eyes narrowed. "I'm not his mom, you little twerp!"

Another idiot joined him. "Sweet. Hot older women."

First dude hollered to the others on the patio, "Jeremy said this was a 'bring an ugly girl party,' but there's cougars here too."

That's when we heard the sirens out front. And that was a good thing, or there might have been more dead bodies because those ugly girls were starting to foam at the mouth.

"Oh shit, we are so busted!" said Dude Number One.

In more ways than one, I thought, as the girls advanced across the patio.

———

The paramedics declared Jeremy dead. Although I already pretty much knew he was dead when we found him, having it confirmed really freaked me out and I began to tremble and feel lightheaded.

The patrol officers, who arrived with the paramedics, ordered everyone to wait outside, with a stern warning not to leave the premises until they released us. Sam, seeing my distress, helped me to the patio table, and we sat. The Puggle had practically glued himself to my legs, so I lifted the quivering dog onto my lap.

Bailey, the dog's name according to his tag, feebly licked my hand. "It's okay, little guy," I murmured in his floppy ear. "I know this is awful, but your boy wasn't a very nice person, was he?"

"Katy," Sam hissed, throwing me a warning glare that screamed, *Shut up!* "Someone might hear you and take that wrong."

"Take what wrong?" said a familiar voice behind us.

I swiveled to see Police Chief Angela Yaeger stepping out of the house. "Angela! What're you doing here?"

"I'd rather hear what you're doing here. Did you know the deceased?"

How to answer that? I glanced at Sam and got nothing. I would have to go with the truth and let the chips fall where they may. "No. But we knew *of* him."

Before Angela could reply, Sam blurted, "I'm Samantha. Katy's best friend. Are we going to be arrested? Because if we are, I need to call my husband." She looked at Angela with pleading eyes. "Please don't arrest us. I'll lose my job if I'm arrested for murder."

Angela sat at the patio table facing us. "How do you know it was murder, Samantha?"

Sam looked sick. "I… I just assumed. You know, all the police. You. Us. Here. Him." Her eyes were spinning like pinwheels.

Angela half-smiled, shaking her head. "Well don't *assume* anything. There will be an autopsy…"

The word "autopsy" gave me the heebie-jeebies. And then I

realized that Sam and I could be in a whole lot of trouble. So much for being a Good Samaritan.

"...and then we'll see where we are. When a young kid is found dead for no apparent reason, it does raise a lot of questions."

"What about all those beer cans? Maybe he drank himself to death," Sam said. "It happens all the time."

"It doesn't look like that. No vomit for one thing and not enough cans." Her gaze shifted to two business-suited men conferring on the lawn. "We'll leave it to the homicide detectives, who'll want to talk to you before you leave. But I would very much like to know why you two are here."

Her gaze shifted to me, making me squirm. "When I heard your name over the dispatch, Katy, I got real curious and decided to check it out for myself. What gives? You two like partying with children?" Her gaze swept over the throng of teens sitting on the other end of the patio, watching us.

Cradling Bailey, I dragged my chair around the table, closer to Angela. "I don't want those kids to hear me," I whispered.

I spilled everything we knew about Jeremy. His plan to expose one hundred virgins to HIV and post their photos on Facebook and Instagram. What he'd already done to Brittany and so many other innocent, young girls. Everything. Right down to this mean-spirited party. Angela listened in stony silence, lips pursed, occasionally shaking her head.

"Hey! Can we go now?" one of the boys hollered with cool-dude swagger.

Angela twisted in her seat and shouted, "You! Shut up and sit your ass back down."

An officer pushed the stunned boy back into his seat. "Nobody is going anywhere, smart guy, until we've questioned every one of you. Clear?"

The brat slumped in his chair and whined, "Why? I haven't done nothin'."

The cop got in his face. "So those beer kegs just walked in here on their own, huh?"

Angela rolled her eyes at us. "So glad my daughter is grown up and out on her own."

I caught the freaked-out expression on Sam's face and knew she was thinking about her hormonal fifteen-year-old stepdaughter, Chelsea, who was too cute to be invited to this party.

"Well, ladies. It's been a long day." Angela pushed away from the table and stood. "And I'm going home to put my feet up and have a nice glass of wine with my hubby. But you two have to stay until the detectives speak to you. I cannot hinder their investigation by extending special privileges, but I'll make sure they talk to you first. That's the best I can do."

———

Two hours later, we were released. We'd been advised not to speak to the media, but having two burly cops escort us through the pressing crowd of ravenous media vultures in the driveway made me feel like a criminal. And that's exactly what we looked like on the late-night news. Guilty with a capital *G*. Thank goodness our names weren't released or those reporters would be camped out on my doorstep right now.

CHAPTER EIGHTEEN

SATURDAY · JULY 13
Posted by Katy McKenna

"Sam and I found Jeremy Baylor—dead!"

"Oh my God! That was you two on the news last night? You both looked so guilty with your faces covered." Justin shooed us through his front door. "Let me get you poor kids inside." He led us into the living room where the rest of the book clubbers were already seated. "Everyone? You are not going to believe what Katy just told me."

"We heard," Chris grumped. "Probably the whole neighborhood heard."

Justin situated us in a pair of worn leather chairs flanking an antique tea table. "Chloe, sweetie-poo, why don't you pour the girls a glass of wine while I plate some food." He took Samantha's cupcakes and my quinoa salad à la Trader Joe's and scurried to the kitchen, calling over his shoulder, "Not a peep from anyone until I get back."

Following his order to the tee, we sat in silence. It was a little awkward, especially since I was dying to dish. I know that's awful, considering the subject matter—but considering who the subject was, can you blame me?

Chloe gave me a glass of Chardonnay. Between ladylike sips, I glanced around the room at the other club members, exchanging smiles, nods, and a few dramatic eye rolls.

"Here you go, ladies," sang Justin, swishing into the room and setting plates laden with delectable eats on the oak coffee table. He sat next to Chloe and sampled his wine. "Ooo. Superb choice, Chris." He swiveled to us. "Sooo… you walked into Jeremy's house and found his body?"

Debra blew out an agitated groan before I could open my mouth. "Before you share your story, Katy, I need to tell you all something, and it can't wait." Her voice wobbled and she tilted her head down, hands clenched in her lap. "Brittany died early this morning."

———

After hearing about Brittany's senseless suicide, the last thing I felt like doing this afternoon was working on the Clunker Carnival job. All I wanted to do was lie on the grass in the warm sunshine with Daisy and watch the clouds drift by, and cry for that sweet young girl. And so I did.

Her pointless death has stunned me to my core. How I wish I could reach out and shake Brittany to her senses. And tell her that what seems hopeless now will become a memory that will fade in time. Just one of so many memories yet to be made. Good and bad.

But I can't. Because that dear, beautiful girl now lies cold in the morgue. There will be no new memories. No true love. No children. No joy. And I can't stand that.

I barely knew her and yet the ache inside me is crushing. I

cannot bear to think of what her family is going through. The questions, the self-blame, the anger, the agonizing what-ifs.

Now Brittany is a tragic memory that will fade in time.

CHAPTER NINETEEN

SUNDAY • JULY 14
Posted by Katy McKenna

There was a short update in today's paper about Jeremy Baylor's death. Basically all it said was:

The Santa Lucia county coroner, Dr. Irvin Kempler, confirmed the manner of death is pending a toxicology report. Kempler said he has asked for the report to be expedited, and he hopes to have those results sometime next week.

I spent the entire day grinding out the uninspiring Clunker job. Now all I want to do is crawl into bed with a glass of wine, a bag of kettle corn, and watch a couple of episodes of *Grey's Anatomy* on Netflix. I just started watching, and I think there are twenty or thirty seasons! So that should keep me entertained for a while.

CHAPTER TWENTY

MONDAY • JULY 15
Posted by Katy McKenna

After several grueling hours of work this morning, I called Uncle Charlie to set up an appointment to go over my proposed designs. He said he was free all afternoon, so I gathered my things and hopped into the car.

After a quick makeup check in the rearview mirror, I began to back out of the driveway. Looking both ways for oncoming traffic, I spotted Josh sitting on his porch with my sister. They were laughing and appeared to be thoroughly enjoying each other's company.

Preoccupied, I narrowly missed crashing into a U-Haul van parked across the street from my driveway. As I passed Josh's house, they waved and I merrily waved back like I didn't have a care in the world—except that my rotten sister was getting cozy with my Viking. When I swung around the corner, I pulled over to ponder this new development.

He's way too old for my sister. He's also way too good for my sister. What if they start dating? Or are they already? And then, what if she doesn't come home one night, and I know she's next door having crazy hot sex with my Viking? That should be me—not her! I want some crazy hot sex. How dare she? I hate her so much.

CHAPTER TWENTY-ONE

TUESDAY • JULY 16
Posted by Katy McKenna

A little after seven this morning, I sat snarly-haired and makeup-free on my porch swing, savoring a hot mug of French Roast, camouflaged from view by the trumpet vine draped along the eaves.

Daisy lay unconscious at my feet, and Tabitha was perched on the railing chattering at a pesky blue jay. Across the street, a ragtag crew was unloading the big U-Haul I'd almost slammed into yesterday. An eclectic array of shabby-not-chic furniture sat on the cracked and weedy driveway.

I hadn't lived in the neighborhood when the former owners had vacated due to a foreclosure over a year ago. There's a broken front window, the dehydrated yard gave up and died months ago, and the paint is peeling. It looks like a spooky crack house. Really great for our neighborhood property values. With hope, the new owners will spruce it up.

I spent most of the day working on the Clunker job, breaking in the late afternoon to make a granny catch-up call—with an ulterior motive.

"Hey, Ruby. How's the new job going?"

"Great," she snickered.

"And your boss? How's he adjusting to you?"

She snickered again. "Oh, he's great too. Hold on." She told Paul to say hi to me, so I figured she was at the office.

"Hi, Katy. Wazup?" said Paul.

Okay. That was weird. Then a woman's voice asked if he wanted another Long Island iced tea.

"I'll take another one too," said Ruby, then came back on the phone. "Paul joined our poker group here at Shady Acres, and the girls just love him."

Paul hollered, "Ladies? I'm goin' to the can. Don't touch my cards."

Ruby continued. "We need to lower the stakes before the poor guy goes broke. Anyhoo, what's up with you?"

"Have you talked to Emily lately? I never see her, so I thought maybe she's been hanging out with you. I know how much she loves her favorite granny." What I wanted to say was, *Wouldn't it be fun if Emily moved in with you?*

"Well, of course I'm her favorite. Kurt's mother is the most negative, miserable woman on earth, so no competition there. Hold on, honey. Cindy's pestering me."

Her friend said, "I just want to know if you're still in the game."

"I'm still in, but we have to wait for Paul to get back. So, Katy —is Emily stirrin' up trouble for you? You want me to have a little chitchat with her? I can always threaten to take away her inheritance."

She must be drunk. "What inheritance? I'm getting your shoes, remember."

"I've been really raking it in with the poker. I'm playing online now, too. Even thinking of going pro. You know, hit the local card rooms, and then when I'm ready—Las Vegas baby! Maybe take a road trip with the gals. Vegas will never know what hit it. You should come too. You can see at night, so you could be the designated driver. Woo-hoo!"

The Shady Acres poker gals all woo-hooed, too. Three in the afternoon and they were snockered. "How many have you had, Grandmother?"

"Sweetie pie, it's not like I'm driving anywhere, so relax."

"And what does your boyfriend think about your poker career?"

"Well, Mother. Ben doesn't need to know everything about me." She belched. "Gotta keep some of the mystery going, don't ya know."

CHAPTER TWENTY-TWO

THURSDAY · JULY 18

Posted by Katy McKenna

This morning, I was feeling neighborly, so I decided that after I completed the Clunker job, I would bake something sweet for my new neighbors. I have a sugar cream pie recipe that is to die for, so I thought my new friends would love it. Unless they're diabetics.

———

After e-mailing the Clunker files to the printer, I closed up shop and commuted through my dandelion-infested lawn to the kitchen for the pie-making session.

Then I remembered I'd turned the house into a sugar-free zone when I'd decided to be a health nut. What a dumb idea that had been. And then I got a brilliant idea. I would go next door and borrow sugar from Josh. While there, maybe I could find out if there's something going on between him and Emily.

I slapped on another coat of mascara and changed into an

upscale version of my daily uniform of comfy jeans, tank top, and flats: silky tank top, chandelier earrings, and stiletto sandals.

Before going, I leashed Daisy for the visit. I figured that when Josh opened the door, she'd barge right in with me in tow, and I'd finally get to see the inside of his house.

I knocked on his front door, holding a plastic measuring cup and a plastic bag, while Daisy sat next to me, barely able to contain her joy at seeing her boyfriend. A minute later footsteps approached and Daisy's tail thumped the wood porch in rhythm with my heartbeat.

The door opened (cue up the celestial music here) and there stood Josh in all his Viking glory. "Hey, Katy. I was working out in the back. Hope you didn't have to wait too long." He looked a little sweaty. Suddenly I was feeling a tad dampish myself.

I swallowed hard, trying not to hyperventilate. I hadn't beheld his brilliance up close since my visit with Ruby to his office. And then I'd been slightly distracted by his fancy coffeemaker. Does that make me fickle?

I wondered if he had one at home, too. Maybe he'd make me another macchiato and we could curl up on his couch in front of the fireplace, sipping our steamy beverages while gazing deep into each other's eyes, and listening to cool jazz while the heat from the crackling fire warmed our naked skin…

I mentally slapped myself back to reality. "Hi." I thrust my cup at him. "I need some sugar."

He grinned devilishly. "Who doesn't?"

"I meant…" I swallowed my drool. "May I borrow a cup of sugar? I'm going to bake a sugar cream pie for the new neighbors and I'm all out."

Daisy lost patience with our exchange, stood on her hind legs, and threw her arms around Josh's neck, smacking a wet one on his lips. He stumbled back against the doorjamb and embraced her. "Whoa, girl. Nice to see you too."

Done with Josh, Daisy dragged me into the house and headed

straight for the kitchen, where I discovered my turquoise cardigan hanging over a chair.

Josh caught up with us, chuckling at our mad dash. "I guess I better give Daisy a treat, or she'll never kiss me again."

At the word "treat," her butt dropped to the tile floor and she held out her paw to be shaken.

"I don't have any doggy treats," he said as he opened the refrigerator, "but how about a little piece of cheese?" She was totally on board with that. He turned to me. "Is that okay, Momma?"

I gulped. "Sure, fine with it. Go for it. Yup." Shut up, Momma!

He opened a pack of sliced cheddar, broke off a piece, and slipped it into her mouth. "Here you go, sweetheart." He shook her paw, rubbed her neck, and glanced my way. "You want some cheese too?"

I snapped my gaping mouth shut. *What is it about this guy? Everything.*

"I'll get that sugar for you, Katy." He saw me eyeing the sweater. "Your sister left that here yesterday. She must've forgotten about it when things got a little steamy in here." He took the measuring cup. "Did she tell you what happened?"

I yanked my sweater off the back of the chair, strangling it into a chokehold. "No. Haven't seen her lately."

"Well, I'll leave that story for her to tell." He scooped sugar into the plastic bag from a glass canister on the counter. "I wish I could offer you a cup of coffee." He waved his hand toward a sleek, black Nespresso machine sitting on the counter. "I know how much you enjoyed your macchiato in my office, but I was just about to grab a shower and go out. I have a date with a very special lady." Wink, wink.

Oh my God. Was the jerk already cheating on my baby sister?

Josh glanced at his wristwatch. "Gotta get a move on." He guided Daisy and me to the front door. "When you give Emily her sweater, tell her we'll have to do it again. Real soon. Tell her it'll be way better next time."

I shambled down the sidewalk toward my house, oblivious to my surroundings, dragging a reluctant Daisy. Halfway there, she halted, staring across the street.

Three guys were sprawled on a tattered sofa, swilling beers. "Sweet Home Alabama" screamed from a giant boom box on the rickety porch steps. A ripped dude wearing a sweat-stained trucker hat hovered over a rusty oil-drum grill, brandishing a skewered foot-long at me with a big goofy grin made goofier by a missing front tooth.

The neighborhood property values just took another dip.

CHAPTER TWENTY-THREE

Posted by Katy McKenna

Friday, July 19

After a very late night, thanks to my new neighbors' endless replays of "Sweet Home Alabama" and a sugar-high from the pie that never made it across the street, I was not a happy camper when my alarm blasted me into the world on Friday morning. I wanted to pitch it against the wall and go back to sleep, but Daisy and Tabitha had other plans. Like getting up.

I resisted their pestering and tugged the covers to my chin, trying to recall why I'd set the clock for the ungodly hour of seven thirty and then it dawned on me: last night, after my third piece of sugar cream pie, I'd promised myself to go to the beginner Zumba class at Forever Fit.

───

As the class sambaed and mamboed back and forth, spinning,

dipping, lunging, and leaping in a perfectly choreographed rhythm that could have won them a spot on *America's Got Talent*, I stumble-bumbled along about three steps behind, huffing and puffing and slamming into the elderly women on both sides of me. How could I be the only one in the beginner class who didn't know the steps? What are the odds?

As soon as there was a water break, I eased myself out of the room and wheezed my way to the bistro for a healthy brunch. Three bites into a luscious asparagus and mushroom omelet, the other chair at my table for two slid out and Chad-the-Cad plopped down.

"Only a sexy girl like you, Katy, could pull off those baggy gray sweats, although I'd rather be the one pulling them off." He picked up the spoon by my plate and helped himself to a hefty bite of omelet. That was one of the many infuriating habits of his that drove me bonkers when we were married. "Why haven't you returned my calls or texts or e-mails?"

"Chad. You're married. Remember?"

"To the wrong woman."

"Your choice. For what it's worth, I happen to like Heather, and I don't want to see you hurt her like you hurt me. Actually, this would be far worse because I wasn't pregnant with three of your kids."

"How do I even know they're mine?" He sipped my water. "I mean if she was willing to screw around with me while I was a happily married man, who knows?"

I was dumbfounded. Chad had just hit an all-time low. Again. "Maybe she wouldn't have if you'd bothered to tell her you were married." I shook my head in disgust. "Why am I even talking to you? I am so thankful you left me for her. Saved me the trouble of leaving you. You're her problem now."

"You know you don't really mean that." He leaned in with his spoon for another bite and I smacked his hand away with a vision of nailing it to the table with my fork.

"Ooo. Feisty. Me likey."

Gag.

"Katy, Katy, Katy. When're you going to give up and give in to your heart? Last time I saw you, I said I would win you back. You know I always get what I want."

There was a time when I thought Chad was drop-dead gorgeous, and maybe he still is in the eyes of a lover, but now all I see are his glaring imperfections. Thinning hair, expanding waist-line, a few zits, and crooked nose. Not to mention he's a total sleazeball.

"I just hope you get what you deserve." I scanned the lobby, searching for someone to save me, and as luck would have it, there was no one. I pushed back my chair, picking up my plate.

He laid a pudgy paw on my arm. "Where are you going, baby? We're not done talking." His eyes X-rayed my boobs. "Remember how good the sex was?"

I jerked my arm away and caught the eye of the waitress and pointed at my food. Chad may have killed my appetite, but I wasn't leaving it behind for the vulture.

"Do you need a box?" She scurried over with one.

"Yes, and my bill, please."

"Put it on my account," said Chad-the-Big-Shot.

"Fine by me." I dumped the omelet in the box, snatched my purse off the back of the chair and beelined for the exit.

When I was clear of the club entrance doors, I chucked the food into a trash bin and ran to my car. My hand shook as I jammed the key in the ignition. No more Forever Fit for me. Chad had ruined that, too.

———

After my run-in with Chad, I was in no mood to deal with Emily's everything's-all-about-me attitude when I got home. As usual, she was sprawled on the couch in her ratty flannel robe watching one of her "research" shows.

I snatched the remote out of her hand, clicked off *Ghost Hunters*, shoved her legs out of the way and flopped on the couch. "I need to be alone."

"God, what is your problem?" said zombie-sister.

"Like I just said. I need to be alone." Daisy bounded into the room and leaped into my lap. "It's okay, baby. Momma's home." I wiped off the dust bunnies she'd collected on her head while hiding under my bed from Emily.

Emily stood with hands on hips. "So where am I supposed to go?"

"I don't know. Maybe your boyfriend's house?"

Her eyes bulged with pissy teenage attitude. "What boyfriend?"

"Josh."

"Josh? The guy next door? Why would you say that?"

"Oh, please. Spare me." And then the dam burst. "I... I... can't..."

Emily sat down and drew me into her arms. "God, Katy. What's wrong?"

I wept against her shoulder like a baby while my little sister rocked me, murmuring motherly platitudes. When I could coherently string my words together, I told her what had happened at the club and how Chad had been practically stalking me these past few months.

The rest of this post is private.
I do not want Mom and Ruby reading it.

"Katy, I wouldn't call that practically stalking you. He *is* stalking you. God, he is such a slimy scumbag. Even worse than I thought. After everything he's done to hurt you, how can he even begin to think you would ever take him back? God, how I hate that bastard." Her voice turned icy. "I really hate him, Katy."

I looked at her, thinking that seemed a little over the top, especially since she'd moved to San Diego before Chad had gotten cancer and the marriage fell apart. "Wow. I had no idea you felt like that."

She dropped her gaze. "There's something I've never told you. About Chad."

I really did not want to ask. "What?"

"You know when I moved away?"

"Yeah." I tried not to smirk. "Your rapper career wasn't going well, and you said you didn't want to live in this bourgeois town anymore."

"Okay, I admit that was all pretty ridiculous. But it wasn't why I left." She stared at the silver bangle on her wrist, slowly rotating it. "Remember when you and Samantha went on that spa weekend up in Big Sur?"

"Of course. But what does that have to do with Chad?"

"Well…"

"Please, Emily. Just say it."

"He called and asked me to come over and help him hang a painting. Said he wanted to surprise you when you got home."

"Go on."

"When I got to your house, he was really cool. Asked about my future plans. Like a big brother, you know. Anyway, we visited for a while, and then he showed me the painting and told me he wanted to hang it in the bedroom so it would be the last thing you saw when you went to bed and the first thing you'd see when you woke up in the morning. I thought that was so romantic. So we went into the bedroom."

I clamped a hand over my mouth, hoping that where my thoughts were going was not where she was going.

"When we got into the bedroom, the only wall that didn't already have art on it was over the bed, so he asked me to stand on the bed and hold up the painting, while he looked at it from across the room. He kept telling me to move it up, move it down, move it over. Then he said, 'Let me help you,' and he got on the bed behind me and reached around me and... and... I am so sorry, Katy."

"Oh God. You had sex with him? Oh my God, Emily!"

"No! God no. I would never do that. You have to believe me. No."

"Then *what*?"

"It all happened so fast. He slid his hands under my shirt and grabbed my breasts and kissed my neck." Her eyes swept the room, avoiding mine. "I could feel his... his thing pressing into my back. For a moment I was so stunned I just froze. Then I dropped the painting and he pulled me down on the bed, telling me how much he wanted me. Had to have me. That you didn't really understand him." Her eyes met mine. "Oh, Katy. It was so awful."

I was shaking hard, feeling light-headed, barely able to draw a breath. Chad cheating on me with his trainer had cut me deeply, but this was ripping me apart. "Did he..."

"Oh, he tried, but I think my screaming was a real turnoff. That and I punched him in the throat like Pop taught me." A faint smirk crossed her face. "Then I ran out of there like hell."

Thinking of Chad clutching his throat, staggering and gasping for air made me feel a little better. "Good for you, but why didn't you tell me?"

"Because he chased me to my car and wouldn't let me open the door until I promised not to tell you. He said it would break your heart and then you'd hate both of us. That he didn't know what had come over him. He was literally crying and blathering about how much he loved you... and I believed him. What else could I do, Katy? You loved him so much. How could I ruin that for you?"

I smoothed back her long dark hair and gazed into her dribbly gray eyes, maybe actually really seeing her for the first time. "*He* ruined it. Not you."

"Well, I was nineteen. What did I know?"

"So instead, you moved away. Oh, Em. How awful for you." The realization that she did that for me overwhelmed me.

"I think in the end it was probably a good thing I left. It helped me figure out who I am. I don't know if I could have done that here." She stood, mopping her tears with her robe sleeve. "How about a glass of wine? I could sure use one."

"There's an open bottle of white in the fridge."

While Emily poured the wine, I went to my bedroom to get a bag of kettle corn that I'd hidden from her. There was no way I could eat anything, but suddenly I felt like sharing. I removed it from the top shelf in the closet, and when I turned back to the door, my eyes pinned on the painting over my dresser. The colorful abstract of a local vineyard in the late afternoon sunlight was my favorite. While I was packing up the house that Chad and I had shared, I'd found it in the attic, hidden behind a stack of boxes. I thought it must have been a wedding gift that had gotten misplaced in the shuffle when we had moved in several years before.

"Em?" I called, still locked on the painting. "Can you come in here, please?"

"I'm right here." She stood in the doorway, holding two glasses of wine. "And yes to the question you're about to ask. That's the painting." She set the glasses on the dresser. "I knew it was in here, but it makes my flesh crawl to look at it, so no way would I have ever found that bag of popcorn you must've stashed in here."

I lifted the unframed painting off the wall and marched through the house and out the french doors into the backyard and tossed it into the metal fire pit on the lawn.

———

"I still can't believe you burned it. It had to be valuable," said Emily, sipping her fifth or sixth glass of wine.

It was dark and we were both bundled in blankets, watching the glowing embers in the fire pit. Soft strains of Lynyrd Skynyrd's

"Free Bird" floated through the air from across the street. I leaned out of my Adirondack chair and tossed another log on the crackling fire.

"It was actually a giclée, but I would have burned it even if it had been a Rembrandt."

"It felt good watching it burn," said Emily.

"It would have felt better if it had been Chad we torched."

"Are you going to tell his wife?"

"She's about to have triplets, and she'd probably go into labor if I told her now, but I can't *not* tell her. Can I?"

"Everything would have been so much different if I'd told you instead of bailing like I did. You would have left him, instead of nursing him through cancer and—"

"Don't do that to yourself." I thought of Mom's guilt over not telling her parents what her uncle had done to her. "None of this is your fault."

We sat for a while, comfortable in the quiet of each other's company. I tried to banish all thoughts of Chad, which got easier with each glass of wine. *I'll deal with him tomorrow.*

"You said moving to San Diego helped you figure out who you are. So, little sister, who are you? Besides a total pain in the neck, of course. And your big sister is saying that with nothing but love."

Emily picked up the half-empty bottle on the table between us, drained it into our glasses, and added it to the growing pile of empties by her chair.

"I don't think I can drink anymore, Em. That's like our third bottle."

"Fourth, but who's counting. Time for a toast."

I lifted my glass, ready to clink and she said, "My friend said that when you toast someone you must always look them directly in the eyes or it's bad luck."

"Okay." I stared into her eyes, although the flickering firelight and the previous several glasses of wine made focusing difficult.

"To my big sister, whom I've always looked up to and not just because you're way taller than me," said Emily.

That statement made me feel like a real jerk, and I silently vowed to work on my big-sister act. We clinked our glasses just as "Gimme Back My Bullets" hit the evening airwaves.

"What a perfect song choice. Lucky for Chad, I don't have a gun, although Pop says he's getting me one."

"I don't think that's a bad idea considering what happened a few months ago, when you came home to that lunatic waiting for you in the house. How scary for you." Emily reached out and rubbed Daisy's neck. "You saved your Momma that day, huh girl?"

Dogs have an uncanny sense about people, and I think Daisy felt the shift that had taken place in our household.

"You still haven't answered my question, Em. Who are you?"

Emily raised her glass again. "Another toast, or maybe it's more like an announcement."

I lifted my glass in expectation, and we locked eyeballs.

"I'm Emily Rose Melby. Not a rapper, maybe a writer, and very definitely gay."

CHAPTER TWENTY-FOUR

Posted by Katy McKenna

Private Post
Saturday, July 20

"*Nine-forty-eight?* Rats!" I had an 11:15 appointment at the printers. I leaped out of bed and nearly lost my balance as a wine-induced migraine slammed me full tilt, sprawling me back onto the bed, groaning in agony.

Daisy nuzzled me, whimpering. Was she worried about me dying? Or was she worried that she might starve to death if I died?

"I'm getting up, Daisy." I struggled to a sitting position and twinkly stars danced in my vision. "But it's going to take a while."

Eyes shut against the blinding light in the house, I groped my way to the kitchen. I opened the cabinet by the sink and grabbed the ibuprofen bottle, intending to start with four, but I couldn't open the damned bottle.

"Stupid, shitty, dumb, stupid childproof cap!" I banged the

plastic container repeatedly against the edge of the tiled counter. "I hate you! I hate you so much!"

"Ooohhh, pleeease. Be quiet. Shhh."

I squinted at my sister, sitting with her head resting on the wooden kitchen table.

"I couldn't get it open either," she moaned. "We need a toddler."

A rhythmic thud began pounding the walls and rattling the windows. "Gimme Three Steps" was blasting at a decibel that would have muted the sound of a jumbo jet landing in the street. A moment later the music was accompanied by the revving thunder of a Harley. Broooom-brooom-vroooommmm. I actually felt the gray matter jiggling like gelatin in my skull. Not a good feeling.

Emily lifted her head, pushing her matted black hair out of her pasty, mascara-streaked face. "We are doomed. Doomed!" She hauled herself erect and lurched zombielike toward me. "Must kill them. Kill them now!"

"Yes! Let's kill them." I flinched with every word. "Then I'll make coffee."

We propped each other up as we staggered to the front door. Emily struggled to focus her rheumy eyes on me. "You look gross."

"So do you."

We halted at the porch top step, blinking in the glaring overcast and waited until there was a lull in the engine revving, then I shouted. "HEY! YOU!" Yelling hurt.

The guy on the Harley waved at us. Two other men shouted, "Woo-hoo! Let's party!" while making lewd grinding motions and brandishing beers.

I said to Emily, "You know, beer would probably help our hangovers."

"Maybe settle our tummies, uh? Uh-oh. I think I'm going to—" Emily spun away and hurled into the red geraniums flanking the steps.

That's when I realized I didn't have my pajama bottoms on—

panties, yes. Just no PJ bottoms. And that's when Josh decided it was a good time to come outside and yell at the new neighbors but was instantly sidetracked by his other neighbors. The tipsy sisters.

———

I knew I was in no condition to drive myself to the printers, but I had that darn Clunker deadline and couldn't wait until Monday, so I had to enlist Ruby's help.

"Baby, you're looking a little green around the gills," said my astute granny as she strapped me into her tiny Spitfire. "You sure you can't put this off until Monday?"

"I can't. I have a deadline."

Ruby revved her engine and we peeled out, hauling ass down Sycamore Lane. The top was down, and I was hanging out the window, trying not to puke. "Can you drive a little slower? Please. Like really, really slow. Especially around the corners."

"You got it, sweetie." Ruby slowed, shifting to third gear. "I still can't get over it," she shouted over the engine with nasty glee. "You and Emily. Bonding over—how many bottles of wine, did you say?"

"Four, maybe five." My stomach rumbled in agreement. "We might have done a few shots too."

"You're a lightweight. You should have done what I always do before I drink. Take an antihistamine and a vitamin C with about a quart of water. And always drink one glass of water per glass of alcohol."

"I guess I'm not a pro like you." I burped a little bile and held my breath, willing the upchuck to go back down. "I was living in the moment and didn't think."

Ruby swung into the print shop parking lot and stopped. "Hold on." She jumped out and came around to my side and opened the door, offering an arm. "Come on, old girl."

I clung to her as she hauled me out of the little car and helped me to the door. Inside, she guided me to the counter where a young woman with several lower lip piercings gawked at us.

"Hello, I'm Ruby Armstrong. Ms. McKenna's caretaker. She's here to look at paper stock for the Clunker Carnival job."

"You're a little late." She glanced at the wall clock. "Like about two hours."

I laid my head on the counter, moaning.

"I'm sorry about that," said Ruby. "She suffers from PPS."

"Oh God. Why me?" I wailed. "What did I do to deserve this? I'm too young to die."

The girl backed away from the counter. "Oh my God. That's awful. Is it like contagious?"

———

Several hours later, after a long snooze, I opened the front door to Ruby and Mom. "Hey, kiddo. How was your nap?" hollered Ruby with a devilish grin. "Ready to party some more?"

"Wow, you look like hell." Mom breezed through the entry clutching a cloth grocery bag. "Must've been some shindig. I hope you can keep food down because we brought dinner."

I shut the door and leaned my forehead against it. "I can't eat. I'm suffering from PPS."

"And what, exactly, is PPS?" asked Mom. "I get so tired of everything being just initials these days. I never know what anyone is talking about."

"Post Party Syndrome," said Ruby.

"Oh. Your hangover. That's why we're here." Mom headed to the kitchen.

"We've got dessert too." Ruby rustled the bag in her arms. "We figured you'd need some mint chip ice cream."

"We brought wine too," called Mom from the kitchen. "We know how much you girls love your wine."

Emily had staggered out of her bedroom in time to catch that last sentence. "No. No wine. Never again."

"Famous last words," said Ruby. "Don't worry, the wine isn't for you. Your mom's just being nasty. We brought ginger ale for you."

The tipsy sisters wobbled into the kitchen as Mom dumped homemade minestrone soup in a pan and popped a french bread baguette in the oven.

"I don't think I can eat, Mom." I sniffed the soupy aroma filling the kitchen. "That stinks. I need some air."

"I'll tell you what stinks." Ruby wrinkled her nose. "You two could use a shower. You smell a little ripe. Why don't you do that while the food warms up? It'll make you feel better."

Willing to do anything to get away from the smell of food, I said, "Good idea," then dragged Emily to the living room and out into the backyard. Sucking in deep gulps of cool fresh air calmed my lurching belly. Back in control, I asked Emily, "Are you going to tell them that you're, you know."

"A les-bi-an? It's okay, Katy, you can say it."

"I know, it's just I've never thought of you as a lesbian. You wear makeup."

"Seriously? If I didn't wear makeup, you would have known?"

"You know what I mean. No need to get your panties in a twist." I admit I was having a little trouble accepting this new revelation, and my befuddlement, coupled with acute wine poisoning, was making my mouth run off.

"This is fairly new for me too. You just don't wake up one day and say, 'Gee, I think I'll be a lesbian now.' It's taken me a long time to come to terms with it and embrace it, but Katy, I am so happy. I feel like… like me. Truly me. Finally."

"Do you have a friend?" I asked.

"You mean girlfriend? I did, but we broke it off. That's the real reason I wanted to come home. I hated keeping her a secret from you guys and it's one of the reasons why we split up—the fact that

I wasn't ready to be open about it. It really hurt her last Christmas when I wouldn't bring her up here to meet the family."

"That must have been hard. I wished I'd known. So how're you going to approach this with Mom and Grandma?"

"I've rehearsed endless speeches, but I think it went pretty well with you last night. You know, just blurting it out."

"Yeah, but we were blotto."

———

After Mom had tucked us in on opposite ends of the couch, I slurped her delectable soup, waiting for Emily to drop her bombs. She decided to lead in with the Chad molestation story, which undid both Mom and Ruby. Especially Mom, who has her own secret to tell her mother.

While listening to Emily's story again, my thoughts drifted back to the day I met Chad at a ski lodge in Tahoe. It was a sunny spring day, and I'd just endured my first and last ski lesson and was trudging across the sun deck to the rental shop, jockeying skis and poles. I didn't see Chad lounging with his feet flung out until I tripped over them and fell in his lap, and later into his bed…

"Katy? Katy?" Emily poked me. "Earth to Katy."

"Hmm?"

"You going to tell them about Chad stalking you?"

"What's that supposed to mean?" asked Ruby.

"He's stalking me, but it's not like he's *stalking* me, as in get a restraining order because he might kill me. He just won't leave me alone. He calls, he texts, he e-mails me. He wants to get back together, if you can believe that."

Ruby stomped to the kitchen, and a moment later a cork popped.

"Don't do what we did," I said to Mom. "You do not want PPS."

"This isn't exactly a party." Mom chugged her half-empty glass.

"I don't have any clients tomorrow, so a few glasses won't hurt me. I'll call Kurt to come get us."

"And we took an antihistamine." Ruby set the bottle and a glass of water on the coffee table. "Don't forget to drink water, Marybeth."

I continued with my Chad dilemma. "My quandary is, should I tell Chad's wife? I was already wondering this before Emily told me her awful story."

"You said this girl is a sweetheart," said Ruby, "so she needs to know what kind of a schmuck she's living with. I just wish he'd get hit by a bus. She could collect the insurance, and be way better off."

Like Melanie's sister losing her horrible husband in the nick of time, I thought, then looked pointedly at Emily, mentally urging her to make her big announcement.

"What's that look you're giving your sister?" Mom sat forward and squinted at me over her wineglass rim.

"Nuthin'."

"Oh please. I know that look. Is there something else we need to know? Is one of you pregnant?" She shook her head. "No, that can't be it. Not with all the wine you've consumed." She glanced at Ruby. "Getting any psychic vibes, Mom?"

My semi-psychic grandma wasn't tuning in on this. No way.

Ruby arched a perfectly penciled brow at Emily. "Maybe."

"Hopefully it's something good," said Mom. "Because I don't know how much more I can take."

"Let's have a toast!" I raised my ginger ale. "Emily, tell them how to toast."

She did and we clinked and she blurted, "I'm gay!"

"Well it's about damned time you said something," said Ruby. "I really didn't want to ask, in case the cards were wrong, but how often does that happen? Never."

Mom set her glass down, gaping at my sister. "When did this happen?"

Emily snickered. "Apparently when I was born. Just took me a while to figure it out."

Mom moved to the couch next to Emily, taking her hands. "Honey, is this because of what Chad did to you?"

Emily jerked her hands out of Mom's grasp and the sister I knew and could barely tolerate reared her snarky head. "God, I knew you wouldn't understand. This is why I never told you." And then, just as quickly, "I'm sorry." She took Mom's hand. "I realize that getting told your daughter is a lesbian isn't what you want to hear."

"Oh, my baby. All I want is your happiness."

"Amen to that," said Ruby.

CHAPTER TWENTY-FIVE

MONDAY • JULY 22
Posted by Katy McKenna

Private Post
Sunday, July 21

"Breakfast will be ready in a few minutes, girls." Mom ladled batter into the waffle iron. "Your dad's outside. Why don't you grab a cup of coffee and go talk to him."

We found Pop sitting out on the patio, tossing peanuts to a blue jay.

"Hey, girls. Meet my little buddy." Pop's friend hopped close to snatch a nut and then flew off to hide it in the yard.

We sat flanking him, and Emily didn't waste time getting to the point of the visit. "Pop? I have something important to tell you and here goes. I'm gay." Bammo. No preamble. No lead-in. Not even a toast. Just bammo.

The poor guy looked like he'd been sucker-punched. "Whoa. Did not see that coming." He set down his coffee cup and scratched his gray stubble. "You sure about this?" Then shook his head. "I'm sorry. Of course you're sure, or you wouldn't have told me." He stood and drew her into his arms. "You are who you are, honey. And who you are is who I love." He pulled back. "Have you told Mom?"

"Last night, but she said I should be the one to tell you."

Pop embraced her again, glancing at me over his shoulder. "How long have you known?"

"I just found out too." We group-hugged while Mr. Blue Jay screeched for more peanuts.

————

That's not to say it wasn't a little awkward at the breakfast table. We all worked on getting our waffles perfectly buttered and syruped, coffees refilled, sugared, creamed, stirred. Who would be the first to talk?

Mom. "Katy, I think I hear your phone vibrating in your purse."

I got up to check, and it was Chad. Again. There were seven messages on the screen, begging me to talk to him, text him. The phone vibrated in my hand and another text popped up. *You are my soulmate.* So I texted "*SCREW YOU*," turned off the phone, tossed it back into my purse, and returned to the table. "I have something to tell you too, Pop."

He looked a little panicky. "Are you gay, too?"

"Nope. Just permanently celibate. Might even join a convent." That got a little chuckle and then I told him about Stalker-Chad.

"That little shit!" Pop stood, knocking back his chair. "I'm going to have a chat with that son of a bitch and when I'm done with him, I promise you, Katy, he will not ever bother you again. You have my word on that."

"Sit down, Pop," said Emily. "Please. There's more."

Now it was her turn to finish him off with her Chad-the-Molester story. All eyes were on him, trying to gauge his feelings.

When she concluded, he sat stone-faced for several moments, then asked Mom, "Did you know about this, Marybeth?"

She looked grieved to admit it. "They told me last night, and I wanted—"

"God, Marybeth! How could you keep this from me? Is that why you and Ruby drank so much that you needed a ride home?"

"Don't be mad at Mom," I said. "We begged her to let us tell you. Believe me, she was not happy about that."

"Well, I sure wish I'd been told all this a long time ago, so maybe I could have done something. But no. Instead my youngest daughter thinks she has to move away because of this bastard, and my oldest daughter, who should know better, didn't bother to tell me that he's stalking her. I always thought he was a slimy weasel, and this just proves it."

"And to think you nursed him through cancer, Katy," said Mom.

Pop stood again and kissed each of us on the head. "I love you all, but I need to walk this off."

Mom looked up at him. "With your bum knee?"

"Okay, drive it off," he snapped, then caught her worried expression and softened. "I'll be all right, Marybeth. Maybe I'll go to the beach."

"Better take a jacket. It might be chilly."

He rummaged in the hall closet, then slammed out of the house without another word.

"We need to get a dog." Mom pushed her plate away. "Max used to go everywhere with him, and right now he could use a quiet friend."

"Is he going to be okay?" asked Emily.

Mom patted her hand. "Your dad and I each have our own way of processing things. I'm a pretty typical female and will talk it to death. He's a typical male and will brood it out." She reached out and squeezed our hands. "You are his little girls and his job is to protect you, and hearing all this has completely emasculated him." She gazed directly at me, and I knew she was thinking about Pop recently learning about her uncle molesting her. All his girls had been hurt, and there wasn't a damn thing he could do about it.

I cleared the table, and as I refilled our coffee cups, Mom blurted, "Oh no!" and jumped out of her chair, hurrying to the hall closet with us on her heels. On her knees, she placed her fingers on the fingerprint gun safe that is bolted to the floor and opened it. The safe was empty.

"Oh, Mom!" cried Emily, breaking down. "I never should have told him. This is all my fault."

"Stop it," said Mom, clamping her hands on Emily's shoulders. "Chad brought this on himself." She pulled my sister close and reached for my hand. "Katy, you better warn Chad."

I returned to the kitchen and ripped my cell out of my purse and turned it on, and there was Chad's answer to my "*SCREW YOU*" text: *YES-YES-YES!*

My call to him went straight to voice mail. I didn't think it was a good idea to leave a recorded message saying my dad might be gunning for him, so I said, "Chad, there are lots of people very ummm—upset with you right now, so watch your back."

I clicked off and tapped the phone against my chin. What to do? Call Heather and warn her? No, can't call Heather. Don't have her cell number. Call the Bookstore Bistro. I did and Chad answered.

"Hey, Katy. I saw your text message, and I liked it."

"Listen to your voice mail." I hung up.

Mom came into the kitchen with Emily sniveling behind her. "Did you get ahold of Chad?"

"Yes, he's at the bookstore. I couldn't tell him Pop may be gunning for him."

"You're right. Try calling your dad."

I did and heard his phone ringing out on the patio table.

"He's probably walking on the pier at Pajaro Beach right now, watching the seals." Mom gazed out the window, thinking aloud.

"Then he'll get a coffee at that cafe on the pier, and by the time he comes home, he'll have cooled down." She turned to me. "We all need to calm down. In twenty-nine years of marriage, he's never done anything violent."

"So what should we do?" asked Emily, still weeping.

Mom handed Emily a paper napkin. "Blow your nose and go home. No point in hanging around here. He could be gone for hours. I'm going to work this off in the yard."

Gardening is Mom's therapy. A much healthier therapy than mine: chocolate.

Emily and I climbed into Veronica and as we belted in, my sister said, "Maybe we should go to the bookstore. You know, just in case."

———

"Hey, Katy!" Heather waddled around the counter, wanting a hug. "Wow! It's super good to see you."

I caught the astonished expression on Emily's face. Heather's so big she should be in the *Guinness Book of World Records*.

"Heather, this is my sister, Emily. Emily, this is Heather."

"It's so nice to meet you. Chad has said such super things about you."

I poked Emily in the back, warning her to be polite. "Oh, that's sooo...super of him." She forced a super phony smile that blew right over Heather's head.

"Hey! How about I treat you to lunch in the bistro. We still have your favorite sandwich. The Katydid."

That actually sounded good since I hadn't eaten my breakfast, and it was pushing noon. But no. We were there on business. "Maybe another time. Is Chad around? I need to ask him something."

"No," she said with a boohoo face. "He left a little while ago."

Emily hung back while I did all the talking. "Will he be back soon?"

"I sure hope so. He's on the schedule and I can only be on my feet for short stretches of time now. But I really don't know. A man came in a little while ago, and they left together."

"A man with a buzz cut?"

"Yeah. How'd you know? Is there something wrong?"

Yes. "No. Why would there be?"

"Because you seem to know who that old man was."

First off, Pop isn't old. He's fifty-six and in great shape. Ruggedly handsome and aging well. But Heather is the same age as Emily, so I let it pass. "Just a guess." I pointed at the counter. "Looks like you've got a customer waiting, so I guess we'll get going."

"Should I tell Chad to call you?"

"Sure. Thanks." We hugged again and she trundled off to the register.

Emily appeared to be mesmerized by what had just transpired, so I took her arm and guided her out the door.

"Wow. That was surreal," she said out on the sidewalk.

"Every meeting with Heather is surreal. But forget about that. I think Pop is out to avenge his daughters. He's always said if anyone ever hurt us it would be the last thing they do."

I called Mom on speakerphone as we walked back to the car. "Mom, we went to the bookstore just in case Pop showed up."

"And did he?"

"He'd already been there and left. With Chad."

Silence on her end.

"Mom?" said Emily. "You still there?"

"I'm here. Just thinking. He probably just wants to warn Chad. Give him a good talking to."

"What about the gun?" I asked.

"Let's not get ahead of ourselves. Your father's mad, but he's not going to shoot Chad in cold blood. In fact, the more I think about it, having a face-to-face with Chad is a good thing for Kurt. Scare the heck out of Chad, and he'll feel like he's protecting his babies."

———

A couple hours later, Mom called me at home. "Your father's sitting in the hot tub having a beer."

A warm rush of relief unknotted my gut. "How is he?"

"Quiet."

"What about the gun?"

"I haven't asked yet."

"Mom!"

"How's it going to sound to him? 'Hey, Kurt, I just happened to check the gun safe right after you left and your handgun was gone.' Katy, there is probably a very good explanation for it and… Oh, crud. I have to ask."

A few minutes passed and she called back. Emily was next to me, so I put the call on speaker. "I'm outside with your father, and I'm handing the phone to him."

"Hey, Katydid. You can stop worrying. Your old man's not a murderer. My gun's at the shop getting repaired. I still plan to teach you how to shoot, you know."

"Did you talk to Chad?"

"Nope. I got a coffee and sat in my car at the beach."

"Okay, Pop. Try to relax. I know we unloaded a lot on you this morning. Can I talk to Mom again?"

"Bye, honey."

Mom came on the phone. "Katy?"

"Go back in the house, Mom, before we talk." A few moments passed, then the screen door slammed. "All right. I'm in the house."

"Pop just lied to me. He said he didn't go to the bookstore, but we know for a fact that he did."

"Your father has never lied to me, and if he says he didn't go, then he didn't go," she said. "Enough, Katy. This is your father we're talking about. I have to go now." She hung up without saying goodbye, which I guess means she hung up on me.

"Pop's lying," said Emily. "What should we do?"

"I'm calling the bookstore."

I prayed Chad would answer. Then I would have hung up, knowing he wasn't dead. But instead, Heather answered. "Hi, Katy. Chad's still not back." She moaned a low, grinding groan.

"What's wrong? Did you have a labor pain?"

"No, heartburn. Not fun. I would really like to get out of here and put my swollen feet up. This is really so thoughtless of Chaddie."

Oh, Pop. What have you done?

CHAPTER TWENTY-SIX

MONDAY • JULY 22
Posted by Katy McKenna

This morning, my sister and I huddled under a blanket on the sofa, watching the local morning news, terrified we'd see Chad's face fill the screen as the newscaster announced:

"Local man missing. If you have any information, please contact the police."

Or worse: A video of a bagged body being loaded into an ambulance: *"A body was discovered under the pier at Pajaro Beach last night by a passing jogger. The deceased was male and had no identification. He is described as Caucasian, late thirties to midforties, paunchy, thinning hair, crooked nose, zits…"*

Or even worse: A video of Pop being hauled away in handcuffs: *"Kurt Melby, retired police officer and owner of Pop's Fix-it Shop, was arrested this morning for the brutal murder of Chad Bridges, owner of The Bookcase Bistro. The victim leaves behind a wife, pregnant with triplets…"*

Then a clip of Heather sobbing: *"He was such a good man,"* before doubling over in labor pains, screaming, *"Oh gosh! I think my water broke!"*

The landline rang, announcing, "Call from Ruby Armstrong." Emily reached for the phone on the coffee table.

"Don't answer it," I said, thinking, *What if she's calling to tell us Pop has been arrested?*

"It's Grandma. I have to answer it." She hit the speakerphone button. "Hi, Ruby."

"Hi, sweetie. I'm calling to tell you something about your father. Now please, I want you to stay calm."

"Oh God." I shoved my face into a throw pillow to muffle my voice. "I knew it. I knew it. He killed Chad."

"Your mother asked me to tell you that she had to take Kurt to the ER late last night."

"What? What?" I screamed, tossing the pillow across the room.

"Now don't get upset, but he had some chest pains."

"Oh my God! He had a heart attack?" Suddenly woozy, I stuck my head between my knees. "Is he dead?"

Emily rolled into a ball on the couch, whimpering, "Daddy, Daddy," while Daisy tried her best to mother us both.

"Jeez, Louise! You two are really something. He's alive and it wasn't a heart attack, so both of you just simmer down. He's going to be fine. It turned out to be angina."

"What's that?" I straightened, inhaling deep and slow to oxygenate my spinning head.

"I looked it up on WebMD and, well, hold on a sec and I'll read it to you. Now where did I put my glasses?"

"Check the top of your head," I said.

"Bingo. Okay, let me get back to the site." Her acrylics tapped the keys. "Okay. Here it is. Ready?"

"Yes." I found a nail that needed trimming and furiously gnawed on it.

"Angina is a blockage—"

"Hold on, Grandma," I said.

My sister was borderline hysterical and hadn't heard anything past the words "heart attack."

"Emily. He didn't have a heart attack, so shut it. I can't hear Grandma."

She hiccupped and clapped a hand over her mouth as Grandma continued. "A blockage in the heart blood vessels that reduces blood flow and oxygen to the heart muscle itself, causing pain but not permanent damage to the heart. Chest pain from angina can be triggered by exercise, excitement, or emotional distress and is relieved by rest."

Emily wiped her runny nose on her pajama sleeve and whimpered in a tiny voice, "But he's not dying?"

"No, kiddo. He's not dying. He's going to get a full workup at the cardiologist's, and oh, there was something else."

"What?"

"He also had a couple of little bones fractured in his right hand. Marybeth said it was swollen so he'd been icing it last night. He slammed the car door on it yesterday at the beach. The poor guy. Talk about having a bad day."

"That had to hurt," I said, wondering, *Did he break those bones beating up Chad before he killed him?* "Is he home now or should we go to the hospital?"

"He'll go home this afternoon, and when he gets there he'll need to sleep. Maybe you kids could take some dinner over later."

"I could go to Suzy Q's and get him something really healthy. No fat, no carbs, no gluten, no sugar, no meat."

"No flavor. Gee, that sure sounds good," she snorted. "Take him a pizza. I imagine the doctor will put him on a strict diet, so give the guy one last treat."

"I can get him a healthy pizza, like the one I always order at Klondike Pizza. A vegetarian with light cheese."

"Honey, save that for later and get him that roadkill pizza he loves with extra cheese, the way he likes it. Right now, your father probably feels like roadkill, poor thing."

After we had hung up, I went online and read the angina

description, stopping at the words: chest pain from angina can be triggered by emotional distress.

It would be very emotionally distressing to beat up and kill your daughter's ex-husband.

And then it dawned on me. Chad hadn't texted or called since yesterday morning.

CHAPTER TWENTY-SEVEN

TUESDAY • JULY 23

Posted by Katy McKenna

I've got good news and bad news. The good news: Chad's still alive. The bad news: Chad's still alive. I got the scoop when I finally worked up the courage to call Heather at the bookstore today. The fact that she answered the phone confirmed that Chad's still in the land of the living.

"How're you doing, Heather?"

"Oh, kinda tired. My feet and hands are super swollen. Even my face. And what's really weird is I have morning sickness again, all the time. I thought I was done with that after the first trimester."

"It doesn't sound like you should be working. Can you go home?"

"I wish. But no. Chad left for Las Vegas super early this morning to play in a golf tournament with some old college friends. I've known about the trip for a while, just didn't know I'd be feeling like this." She paused to holler, "I'll be right there!" and then came back on the line. "You know when you were in here looking for him on Sunday? Well, it turns out the old guy he left with was his golf teacher, and according to Chad, he needed to work on his chipping and putting. Just wish he'd told me, 'cause I got super worried. Sometimes Chaddie can be such a scatterbrain."

———

This afternoon, I went to the printers, picked up the Clunker job, and headed to the dealership. I pulled into the lot and parked as close to the office as possible.

I was hauling the boxes from the back of my car, when another pair of hands reached in. "Let me help you with that."

I turned and fell into the big brown eyes of Mr. Chuckles-Matthew. Without clown makeup, he was drop-dead-divine. Maybe twenty-four, twenty-five. Tall, olive-skinned, dark, wavy hair, curly ends brushing his collar.

"Matthew?"

"I'm surprised you recognize me without my clown wig."

"Your voice." *And your smile. And your big brown eyes.*

He grinned, probably reading my mind. "Where are these boxes going?"

"I'm delivering them to Uncle Charlie."

"Then follow me."

I followed Matthew to Uncle Charlie's office. He could have stepped into oncoming traffic, and I probably would have followed.

Uncle Charlie's secretary stopped us before Matthew opened his door. "Don't go in there. He's in a meeting." June flashed a "yikes" face and said, "IRS."

Uncle Charlie's angry voice boomed through the glass door. "What do you mean, penalties and interest? You can't squeeze blood out of a stone, you know. The economy is killing us."

"Where can I set these boxes, June?" asked Matthew, glancing around.

"Put them in the corner behind my desk. I'll make sure he gets them."

Rats. I really wanted to give him the job. And bask in his praise. "May I leave my bill with you, June?"

"Yes," she said, taking it. "I'll give it to accounting and they'll send you a check."

Matthew cleared his throat, looking shy, sexy, and sweet. "Want to get a coffee?"

OMG. A coffee date—the gateway date to a dinner date. "Sure."

He led me to the lobby to one of those big chrome coffeemakers that you can rent for parties. Not exactly the coffee date I'd envisioned.

He filled a Styrofoam cup with the steamy, pale liquid, handed it to me, and poured another for himself. I dosed mine with sugar and powdered creamer and then we sat at a sticky table beside a sunny window that needed washing.

Sipping my scalding, atrocious coffee-wannabe, I peeked at him over the Styrofoam rim. The bright light forced me to reassess my earlier age guess. Maybe more like twenty-two or twenty-three. But so darn cute, I wanted to pinch his two-day stubbled cheeks. *Oh well. Too young for me. Rats.*

"So. Katy. I see you still have your Volvo."

"Yup. You told me to keep her. Remember?"

"Yeah." He chipped off a piece of Styrofoam and twiddled it between his fingers.

I watched his fingers, thinking salacious thoughts about what else they could be twiddling. *Get a grip, McKenna. He's a child and you can't have him.* "Do you work here full time?"

"Part time. Finishing my education."

"What are you studying?" I felt like I was conducting a job interview.

"Marine biology."

"This is certainly a good area to do that. With the ocean a few minutes away, and, you know, all of its…" His damned fingers were still twiddling. "…biology."

Matthew stretched out his long jean-clad legs, and I became fixated on the dark hairs on his tanned ankles. I decided that if he asked me out, I would say yes and to heck with the age difference. Ruby keeps telling me I need to get laid, so lay it on me, baby!

Matthew pulled his phone out of his pocket and checked the screen.

Oh puh-leeze. Am I really that boring? Forget you, buddy.

"Sorry," he said with a sheepish grin. "Just checking the time. I have to put on my clown makeup and get to work."

Forgiven. I stood, still clutching the vile liquid. "Then I better get going. Thanks for helping with the boxes and…" I waved the cup. "…the coffee."

He laughed. "If you can call it that."

I returned the laugh and picked up my purse, ready to exit but not rushing it. Waiting, waiting…

"Can I have your phone number?"

Yes! Imaginary fist-pump. "Sure." I acted all cool as he gave me his phone. I added my number to his contacts and handed it back.

"Okay if I text you later?" he asked.

I shrugged a whatever. "Sure."

He beamed. "Great. See you."

I nonchalantly strolled toward the door, resisting the urge to glance over my shoulder to see if he were watching. But that would have demolished my cool vibe, and if truth be told, I knew I'd be disappointed if he weren't watching.

Back in my car, I barely noticed the scorching leather seat as I headed to the closest Starbucks. A few minutes later, I was sitting on the patio, sipping a light mocha Frappuccino, extra whip, and reflecting on my possible upcoming date.

Halfway through my drink, my phone chirped a text from Matthew asking me to go to Farmer's Market on Thursday night. Santa Lucia's Farmer's Market is a sprawling affair, covering the main street downtown for several blocks. Lots of food vendors, crafts, veggies, and musicians. The perfect first date.

I let him wait a few minutes. Didn't want him to think I'd been staring at the phone, willing it to ring like a high school girl. Instead I texted Samantha. *Guess what? I have a date! 4 reals*!

CHAPTER TWENTY-EIGHT

THURSDAY · JULY 25

Posted by Katy McKenna

Part One

I had lunch today with Samantha at Suzy Q's. She's always late and I'm always early. I was seated by the front window when she slid into the seat opposite me.

"I'm all yours for an hour and a half, then I have to pick up Casey at preschool, take Chelsea to soccer practice, and run to the store."

A waitress stopped at our table and asked if we were ready to order.

"I'm going to have the kale salad and a side of garlic truffle fries with aioli," I said. "And I'm fine with just water."

"I haven't had time to look at the menu yet," said Sam. "But I'll have the kale salad too. And iced tea." She looked at me. "Wanna share your fries?"

Not really. "Okay."

The girl gathered our menus. "I'll bring an extra side of aioli."

Yeah, and an extra side of fries.

"I have some bad news," said Sam. "On my way over, I stopped by the hospital to get the *Crazy, Stupid, Love* DVD out of my locker that Chloe loaned me and found out that Heather's in the hospital."

"Did she go into labor? She still has a couple of months to go, you know."

"No. She has gestational hypertension."

"What's that?"

"High blood pressure. It's a serious problem, Katy. It could lead to preeclampsia, then possibly eclampsia and then she and the babies are in big trouble."

I pulled my phone from my purse and googled preeclampsia. "Oh my God. Heather and the babies could die."

"If it goes into eclampsia the babies will have to be delivered, or she could stroke out or bleed out. They all could die."

"That's awful. How long will she be in the hospital?"

"Her doctor needs to get her blood pressure stabilized, then she can go home."

"Will she need to stay in bed?"

"No, that used to be the recommended therapy but that can lead to blood clots. But she does need to stop working and take it real easy. The goal is to go full term, especially with triplets. Problems like this aren't uncommon with multiple births."

I shook my head. "And Chad's out of town. Can I call her?"

"Maybe later. I would think that Chad's on his way home."

"Don't bet on it."

CHAPTER TWENTY-NINE

FRIDAY • JULY 26
Posted by Katy McKenna

Thursday, July 25
Part Two

Matthew and I had made plans to meet downtown at 5:45, an easy walk from my house in the railroad district.

I did my usual what-to-wear panic, and let me tell you, dating someone a few years younger (okay, several years younger) adds another layer of pressure. I wanted to look younger, sexy, and edgy. A combination of all three probably wasn't going to happen.

No sexy shoes because I was walking and nothing looks unsexier than a woman trying to walk with aching feet. No tight jeans because I like breathing and eating. And I do not own anything that I would consider edgy.

So that left cleavage. I don't have any of that either, but I have an amazing pushup bra that will give anyone (according to the online reviews, it's the number one choice of drag queens) cleavage, so I put that on and topped it with a silky scoop-neck coral tunic.

I clipped my hair up in a loose mess and added a fresh layer of makeup and a pair of sparkly, long earrings. During my metamorphosis, my personal beauty consultant, Madame Daisy, sat on the bathroom mat watching the magic happen, her tail banging the floor with approval.

At the front entry, I adjusted my ginormous décolletage in the mirror and then broke Daisy's heart by telling her she couldn't go on my date.

She gave me her super sad look, so I turned on Animal Planet. "Look, sweetie, your favorite show. *Celebrity Dog Swap.*"

When I was half a block from our meet-up location, I saw Matthew chatting with some skateboarders dressed in beanies and hoodies. He looked sexy in dark jeans and a button-down. He waved when he saw me, and the kids skated off.

"Hey. You look incredible." His eyes slid to my big boobies. "I like your hair."

"Yours looks good too." I wanted to reach out and comb my fingers through it. "Are those kids friends of yours?" *Please say no.*

He laughed as if to say, "as if," then pulled out his phone. "Let's do a selfie." I wanted a photo to show Sam, so I held up my phone too and we grinned for a double selfie. I sent mine to Sam so she could drool with envy.

Matthew took my hand and we strolled down the street, stopping to listen to a reggae band. Swaying to the music, all I could think about was my hand cradled in his. At the puppet show, he threw his arm around my shoulders and my knees went rubber.

"Why don't we go sit down over there?" I panted, pointing at a group of tables in front of a yogurt shop.

Matthew led me over and pulled out a chair for me. "Would you like a yogurt?"

"No, thanks. A water would be good though."

While he was inside the shop, I noticed the skaters across the street about three doors down, flipping their boards and goofing around, surreptitiously glancing in my direction.

My phone chirped a text from Sam. *OMG, he's hot!! Have fun!!*

"Here you go." Matt gallantly opened my water and set it on the table.

"Thank you. Got a little headache." Actually, I had killer cramps, which is so typical. Haven't had a date in eons, so of course…

I slapped my overpacked mini cross-body bag on the table, unzipped it, and several super-duper tampons exploded across the table. I snatched them up, found the ibuprofen, and jammed the tampons back into the purse.

"You missed this one." Oblivious to my mortification, he handed me a tampon that had landed in the gutter. "Wanna get something to eat?"

Anything to move this date forward to the next scene. "What do you have in mind?"

"Pasta?"

"I love pasta. Do you have a particular place in mind?"

"I've never been to Bada Bing, but it's my parents' favorite restaurant."

"It's good." The food's not that good, more like just okay, but the ambiance is cozy and romantic.

———

The hostess seated us outside under the grapevine-covered arbor. An elderly man was doddering around the tables, badly playing an accordion. After the busboy set a basket of breadsticks on the table, poured waters and handed us gigantic menus, the waiter appeared.

"*Buonasera.* My name is Lorenzo. Would you like to see the wine list?"

"Sure," said Matthew with a big grin.

Lorenzo placed the bulky wine binder in front of my date. "I'll be back in a few minutes to take your order."

Matthew flipped a page or two, then handed it to me. "You pick."

"Do you want a bottle or a glass?"

"Let's share a bottle."

"Red or white?"

"I'm good with either, so you pick."

I have always assumed that when asked out on a first date, the asker pays, but maybe the rules have changed since I've been out of circulation. A part-time used car salesmen/college student can't be making much, so although I saw several local wines I love, I decided to go with the cheapest deal—a carafe of the house red. I figured a decent restaurant would have a decent house wine.

I went the same route with my dinner order. "I'll have the half order of fettuccine Alfredo."

Lorenzo nodded. "We have a *bellissimo* carrot bisque this evening." He kissed his fingers to accentuate bellissimo. "Topped with crème fraiche and a drizzle of truffle oil."

Ooo. I love carrot bisque, I thought, but instead said, "No, thanks."

He cocked a bushy black eyebrow and tried again. "Perhaps the lady would care for a salad to start?"

"No, thank you. Not really that hungry." I was ravenous.

He gave up and turned to my date. "And you, sir? What would you like?"

"I'll have the lobster and a Caesar salad."

I stared at him bug-eyed, thinking, *Seriously? Lobster? I ordered the cheapest wine and a half-order of cheesy noodles and you're ordering lobster?*

"Will that be the twenty-four ounce or the forty-eight ounce, sir?"

"The forty-eight ounce."

I glanced down at the menu for the price. *Crap! Market price. He must be loaded. Is it too late to change my order, or would that be tacky?*

"Very good, sir. Do you care for an appetizer?"

"Sure. I'll have a shrimp cocktail."

Of course, he wants a damned appetizer.

"Very good, sir." The waiter snapped me a chilly smile, then plucked the menus from our hands. "The busboy will bring your carafe of *house* wine."

Lobster, Caesar salad, and a shrimp cocktail? He damn well better give me a shrimp! I grabbed a crunchy breadstick and chomped on it. I was going to eat every damned breadstick in the restaurant.

The aging accordionist now stood by our table playing that super-romantic *Titanic* song, "My Heart Will Go On." He made up for his lack of talent with volume and a lot of winks at me.

"Wow, this place is really fancy, huh, Katy?" shouted Matthew. "No wonder my mom and dad like it so much."

The fuzzy-cheeked busboy filled our wineglasses and set the carafe on the table. I was about to sample mine when he asked for our IDs.

"Seriously?" I said. "You want to see my ID?"

"The rule is, if you look under thirty, we have to see your ID."

He thinks I look under thirty! I opened my purse on my lap under the table to avoid another tampon stampede and extracted my license. "Here you go." I flashed him a flirty smile while he glanced back and forth between me and the photo on my license, taken in my early twenties. He scrunched his brows, squinting at me.

"Yeah. It's me," I snapped. "My hair was a different style then."

"Whatever you say, ma'am." He handed it back and turned to my date.

He called me ma'am? How rude! "Your turn, Matthew," I said, tasting my rotgut burgundy.

"Uhh, this is a little embarrassing, bro, but I lost my wallet the other day. But she can vouch for me."

I try not to overuse the word "awkward," but it's the perfect word for moments like this. I had no idea what Matthew's exact age was, but I did know that I'd tried the old "I lost my wallet" gambit plenty of times when I was underage. It had never worked.

"Sir, I have to see a valid ID. Your moth…" He caught my freaked-out expression and continued. "…friend can't vouch for you."

"Dude. Come on. I'm twenty…" He glanced at me. "…five. This is ridiculous."

Fuzzy-Cheeks said, "If the Alcohol and Beverage Control people come in here and see you drinking, they'll ask for your ID, and if you don't have it, I'll lose my job and get a big fine. For all I know, this could be a sting."

Matthew gave him a pleading look, his tone sliding into whiny, "Oh come on, dude. Give a bro a break."

"Sorry, *bro*. Your food should be out soon." He picked up Matthew's wineglass and left.

"Katy." He held out his hand for mine, and I ignored it. "I really did lose my wallet, I swear."

What the hell was I thinking? Is he even old enough to go to an R-rated movie? I set down my glass and leaned forward on my elbows, speaking low. "Matthew? Exactly how old are you?"

"Do you mean my chronological age or my spiritual age, because I'm an old soul, Katy."

I gave him a withering look. "Guess how old I am."

"Well, you might be a little older than me." He held his thumb and index finger a smidge apart. "But age means nothing in the spiritual world. It's just a number on the calendar."

"Humor me, Matthew." I grabbed the last breadstick and munched, crumbs flying everywhere.

"Call me Matt."

"Just take a guess. Matthew."

He scrutinized my face, probably trying to come up with a

number that worked for both of us. "Twenty-six, twenty-seven? But really, Katy, it doesn't matter that you're an older woman."

"I'm thirty-one. And a half."

His eyes widened, and a faint smirk flitted across his pretty face.

"What was that look for?"

"My friends said you looked old enough to be my—"

I held my hand up. "The little twerps in the hoodies?"

He nodded, drinking his water and avoiding eye contact.

"I'm paying for this meal, aren't I, Matthew?"

The busboy reappeared bearing a Caesar salad that could have fed a family of four for a week. Lorenzo swooped in from behind, brandishing a colossal pepper mill.

"Would you like cracked pepper, sir?" The pepper mill hovered over the salad.

"Sure," said Matthew.

"No," I said, swatting at the pepper mill. "Wrap everything to go. We're leaving."

"I'll be right back with the bill." Lorenzo avoided my killer glare. "The busboy will wrap your food."

"Way to go, bro," said the busboy with a knowing leer.

I dusted the bread crumbs off my big boobs. "If you're thinking he's getting laid by this old lady, you are so wrong."

As my former boyfriend and I exited the restaurant, the accordionist trailed us to the door, playing "You've Lost That Lovin' Feeling."

CHAPTER THIRTY

FRIDAY • JULY 26
Posted by Katy McKenna

Thursday, July 25
Part Three

"Jeez, Louise, he's a dreamboat." Ruby scrutinized the Matthew-and-me selfie. "Well, at least something good came out of your date with the juvenile delinquent."

"And what would that be?" I asked because nothing good came to mind.

"My dinner. Thanks for bringing over this feast. I can't remember the last time I had lobster." Ruby eyed the colossal crustacean on her plate. "You sure you don't want any? This bad boy must weigh a couple of pounds."

"Forty-eight ounces. Market price and probably older than my date. And yes, I'm sure. Not into crustaceans. Looks too much like a giant prehistoric bug for my taste. I'll stick with the fettuccine."

"Your loss." Ruby drizzled melted butter over the lobster and popped a bite into her mouth. "It's a little late for me to be eating such a heavy meal, and I'll probably be up all night with heart-burn, but it'll be worth it."

She chewed in silence for a while (except for several mm, mm, mm's, and a few eye rolls), and then out-of-the-blue, she said, "You know I haven't spoken to my brother, Ted, in years, right?"

"Yeah. What about it?"

"I'm thinking it's time to let bygones be bygones. He's getting old and—"

"Isn't he younger than you?"

"Yes, but I stopped aging years ago, when I decided to go blond instead of gray."

"That and your facelift helped."

"Best money I ever spent." She stroked her smooth neck. "Any-hoo, I think it's time. I told you my sister is coming for a visit in the fall and it got me to thinking. This could very well be our last chance to all be together."

"You're not that old, Ruby." I pushed my crummy dinner around my plate. "I'm getting more water. The fettuccine is really salty." I went to the sink and filled my glass. "Keep talking."

"Well, none of us is getting any younger, that's for damned sure and I don't want to die regretting that I never tried. So, I have to do this. Bury the hatchet, so to speak."

I sat back down. "I've never heard why you had a fight with him."

"It wasn't so much a fight as it was a heartbreaking betrayal. My sister feels the same way." She set down her fork and wiped the buttery grease off her lips. "Years ago, when our mother was dying... You remind me of her so much, Katy. Anyway, Mom wasn't going to last much longer, and I called Ted, thinking he would jump on a plane and get there as soon as possible. I mean, who wouldn't? Edith flew out from the UK, for God's sake. But Ted said he and his wife were about to leave on a road trip. I begged, but he refused to change his plans. Said he'd been working long hours and really needed a vacation.

Mother kept asking, 'When is my little Teddy coming?' And I had to keep saying, 'Soon, Mom. He's on his way.' The last thing she said was, 'Tell Teddy his momma loves him.' At that moment I wanted to kill him."

"And you haven't spoken since?"

"Oh yes, we spoke all right. When Mother's will was read. All three of us were doing well by then and had no need for the little bit of money she had saved. Ted owned a heating and air-conditioning business. Gramps and I weren't wealthy like Ted, but we were comfortable. And Edith was living in England with her husband and had a thriving veterinary practice, so we were fine with Mother's decision to leave her money to the women's shelter. But Ted had a fit. He wanted to break the will, and Edith and I refused."

"How much money are we talking about?"

"Around $18,000. So $6,000 each before taxes. Wouldn't have made one bit of difference in our lives, but I'm sure it made a huge difference at the shelter."

"And so you never spoke to him again after that?"

"Right. Eventually, I boxed up his childhood mementos and sent them to him and that was that."

"When did this all happen?"

"Mom died when your mother was eleven or twelve, so, long time ago. Anyway, it's time to reach out. Who knows? Maybe he'd like to reach out, too, but thinks we'll never forgive him."

"But why would you want to? I mean, just because he's your brother doesn't mean he has to be in your life," I said. "Ask yourself this. If you met him at a party, and then someone told you what kind of a person he is—knowing what you had been told, would you want him as a friend?"

"Of course not, but—"

"But because he is blood related, you think he should be in your life?"

"No, but he is my brother." She set down her fork and reached across the table for my hand. "Sweetheart, I get what you're saying, and in theory I agree. But I need to do this. Like I said, I don't want to die regretting things that I could have done and didn't. There will be enough things that I'll wish I'd done but didn't or couldn't."

"Like what?"

Her face lit with an impish leer. "Like have a romp in the hay with Bruce Willis, Richard Gere, Morgan Freeman, George Clooney. Hmmm, who else?" She narrowed her eyes, thinking. "Oh, and Ryan Seacrest. He is so cute. That's my current list. Want to hear my old list?"

"Sure."

"No, you don't." She pulled back her hand and picked up her wineglass. "If it doesn't work out, then so be it. But I have to know I tried. I've talked to Edith about this, and she's on board. Now I have to locate him. But that shouldn't be too difficult with the Internet. Trouble is, my computer's on the fritz. It keeps freezing up."

"Do you want me to look for Ted?"

"Oh, honey. I would really appreciate that. Just think—with your help, maybe I'll get my baby brother back."

CHAPTER THIRTY-ONE

The bimonthly book club gathering was today at Chris's home, a quaint 1940s duplex, everything original. The yellow-and-black tiled kitchen is so out of date that it's back in style. I guess you call that retro-chic. I was amazed that she lived in such a cozy, cute house. From the way Chris dresses and acts, I'd pictured her living off the grid in a bunker.

"Looks like we're all here except for Heather," Nora said, as we gathered around the red Formica kitchen table to fill our paper plates from the potluck.

Sam uncorked a bottle of zinfandel and filled a motley crew of wineglasses. "She had a scare a couple of days ago and needs to lie low until the babies arrive. Gestational hypertension."

"Ooo. That's not good." Melanie tasted her wine. "But this sure is. Nice choice, Chris."

"I stopped by the bookstore this morning," said Chloe, "to get a Mother Goose book for my niece, and she was working. She said she'd try to get here and didn't mention anything about problems with her pregnancy, though she wasn't her usual perky self. Seemed kind of dragged out."

"She's not supposed to be working," Sam said, as we all trooped into the tiny living room.

I settled on the wood floor next to Sam. "Did you see Chad there, Chloe?"

"Sorry I don't have more seating," said Chris. "I really should move to a bigger place." She tossed a couple of throw pillows to Sam and me.

"Not a problem." I set the cushy pillow behind my back. "This reminds me of my college days, except the wine's way better."

"If Chad was at the bookstore, I didn't see him, Katy," said Chloe.

I shook my head, not surprised. "Last I heard, he was on a golf trip and my guess is, he still is."

"What a despicable person." Justin cuddled Chloe. "I will always take care of you, Pooh-bear."

"I know, Papa Bear," she cooed, leaning into him.

Oh, barf. Get a room.

"Not to change the subject, but what is everyone reading?" asked Nora, sitting prim on the fireplace hearth.

"Before we get into that," I said, noting her miffed look at me. "I'd like to share a couple of stories about my ex."

When I finished my nasty tale of sister-seduction and stalking, my audience was spellbound. "So what do you all think? Should I tell Heather?"

Chris shoved a hummus-loaded pita chip into her mouth and mumbled, "Hell yes."

"No." Debra held up a hand to squelch our gasps of disbelief. "Hold on till you hear me out. Yes, she needs to know but not in her present condition. Not with her blood pressure problems."

"What a mess," said Sam.

"She'd be better off if he just dropped dead," Chris said.

Garlic hummus clung to her mustache, making it uncomfortable to watch her while she spoke.

"You said that about Melanie's brother-in-law too," said Chloe, intent on scrutinizing the paper plate of food on her lap.

"And I was right, right?" She popped another chip gobbed with hummus into her mouth. "He's dead and she's better off. Just sayin'."

I tapped my upper lip, hoping Chris would get the hint. She didn't. Instead she ate another chip and smeared more hummus into her 'stache. I was mortified for her.

"She's right." Melanie focused her amber eyes everywhere but on Chris. "And my sister got Travis's life insurance policy, so she doesn't have to work and can concentrate on taking care of her sick daughter."

"My heart goes out to Heather, and I agree with everyone here that she needs to know, eventually." Justin leaned forward in his seat and tossed Chris a napkin. "Sweetie, you have a little some-thing-something." He touched his clean upper lip.

Chris wiped off the hummus, and you could feel the silent sigh of relief in the room. And then she reached for another pita chip.

"Don't hate me for saying this," said Justin, "but Heather knew he was a scoundrel when she married him, and now she is paying the price for her bad judgment."

"That's a little harsh, Justin." Chloe slapped his arm.

Justin crossed his arms over his burly chest. "But it's the truth." He turned to me. "And you, my dear, deserve a man who will cherish you, the way I cherish my Chloe."

"Thank you, Justin. Now tell me where I can find one." And then it struck me. *I need a man who's in touch with his feminine side. A man who can communicate his feelings and truly "get" me. A BFF with bene-fits and preferably in my age group. Oh my God, I need a "Justin."*

CHAPTER THIRTY-TWO

MONDAY • JULY 29
Posted by Katy McKenna

I was downtown stocking up on beauty essentials at Sephora and decided to drop by the police station and see if Chief Yaeger had time for a chat. I peeked in her open office door. "Knock. Knock. Got a sec?"

"Katy. So good to see you." Angela came around her desk and hugged me. She pulled back and took my hands. "Ready to sign up?"

"I don't know, Angela. Having that guy die practically in my lap really did a number on me." *Not to mention what it's done to my dreams.*

She waved me into the leather chair fronting her desk and returned to her seat. "Oh, Katy, I'm so sorry. You know, in all my years on the force I've never had as traumatic an experience as you had on your ride-along. In fact, due to your experience we've suspended the program indefinitely." She folded her hands on the desk, looking chiefly. "Now what can I do for you today?"

"I was wondering if the cause of Jeremy Baylor's death has

been determined yet." Another face that's been haunting my dreams.

She shuffled a pile of papers into a neat stack and set it aside. "The autopsy was completed, and first off, he did not have HIV."

"Are you saying Brittany died for nothing? Oh my God."

"What can I tell you? I guess he thought telling her he had HIV was a funny joke. You ever watch any of those prank shows on TV?"

"I have in the past, but so many of them are just plain mean. I guess I have a different idea about what funny is."

"You and me both. And they give kids bad ideas. I don't know if Jeremy was influenced by any of that, but I wouldn't be surprised."

I picked up the brass nameplate from her desk and traced the etched letters with my finger. "Well, he's not laughing now. But what about that kid who posted a girl's picture on Jeremy's Facebook? The one that said, '*your numero uno, bro.*'"

"I don't know. Maybe Jeremy told all his friends the same thing he told Brittany."

"How sad to think he thought it was funny. And it's even sadder if all his friends thought so, too. What is wrong with this generation?" As soon as those words popped out of my mouth I felt a hundred years old. "Wow. I sound like my parents."

"Wait'll you have kids. You'll be channeling your parents endlessly. It's in our DNA."

"Can't wait. Anyway, can you tell me the cause of death, or is that classified information?"

"Jeremy died from a lethal mix of cocaine, oxycodone, and alcohol." She exhaled an exasperated sigh. "There was one thing that was odd though. We never found the oxycodone bottle and the parents said there was none in the house. To their knowledge anyway. What do parents ever really know once their kids reach their adolescent years?"

"Probably got it from one of his friends or bought it on the street."

"That's what we assume. The coroner ruled it accidental, and there's no evidence to suggest otherwise, so we aren't pursuing it. The good news is, we don't have to track down his virginal conquests and ruin their worlds."

———

Walking to my car, my phone chirped a group text from Samantha: *Heather back in hospital. Serious.*

I stopped under a store awning and called her. "What's going on?"

"The idiot was on a stepladder at the bookstore and fell off. One of the employees called 9-1-1."

"What the hell was she doing on a stepladder?"

"And what the hell was she doing at work?" said Sam. "Right now her blood pressure's through the roof and she has high levels of protein in her urine, so it's looking like preeclampsia."

"Is there anything I can do?"

"Yes. Find Chad. He's not answering his phone."

"Is he back from Vegas?"

"According to Heather, he is. We're having a tough time calming her down. She wants *Chaddie*. And I want to kill him."

"I'll run by their house."

I knew where their house was located due to several drive-bys I did right after his marriage to Heather. Chalk it up to curiosity fueled with red-hot resentment. All I can say is the bookstore must be doing pretty darned well, or they are in serious debt. I'm betting the latter.

At the massive mahogany-planked double entry door that looked like it cost more than my house, I rang the bell. Its catchy gong-song echoed through the house. I rang again, tapping my foot to the beat on the terrazzo-tiled porch. No answer. I called Sam. "Has Chad shown up?"

"Nope. You need to find him, Katy. She's frantic, and if we can't get her stabilized soon, it's going to be bad."

"There's only one thing Chad loves more than himself and that's golf. I'll head to the country club and see if he's there."

When Chad and I were together, one of our many running arguments had been about joining the Santa Lucia Country Club.

"Katy," he'd say. "It's a great place to make business connections."

"Chad," I'd say. "We're not business moguls. We own a little bookstore that's barely making it and the country club is not in our budget."

And he'd counter with, "We can run it through the business and take the write-off."

———

At the club, I raced to the pro shop, thinking that if he was playing golf, he had to sign in first, and maybe somebody could track him down on the course. Along the way, I received several disapproving glances to which I responded, "Yeah, I know. I have jeans on. This is an emergency. Do you know Chad Bridges?"

Most just shook their heads, but one beer-bellied fellow pointed toward the putting green. "You look too smart to be married to the jackass, so he must owe you money too. Am I right?"

"Close enough. Thanks."

And there he was with his arms wrapped around a middle-aged, bleached blond helping her putt. How considerate.

"Hey, Chad!" I hollered from the edge of the green. "Your wife's in the hospital! You might want to wind up your golf lesson and get over there." I wondered if Blondie was the reason I hadn't received a sex-text from Chad for the past few days. *Maybe I should thank her.*

"You have a wife?" The woman jerked out of his grasp, brandishing her putter dangerously near his plonker. "You son of a bitch. I bet you're not even a real pro."

That statement drew a round of hearty guffaws from the audience lounging on the deck above the putting green.

"Baby, you got it all wrong," Chad said to his voluptuous protégée. "Yeah, I'm married, but it's over. I swear."

Blondie stomped off, yelling at the peanut gallery, "One of you guys order me a dirty martini. Make it a double."

Chad hoisted his golf bag to his shoulder. "Thanks a lot for making me look like an ass, Katy." He stomped away.

I tagged along. "If you're going to thank me for anything, how about thanking me for tracking you down, since you can't be bothered to answer your phone. As far as making you look like an ass, you sure don't need my help."

From my car, I watched him exit the parking lot, then followed to make sure he went straight to the hospital.

———

I caught up with Chad just as he was shoving through the knot of book clubbers loitering outside Heather's room. From within the room, I heard Sam say in her sunniest voice, "Oh look, Heather. Your hubby's here."

"Oh, Chaddie," cried Heather. "I'm so sorry. Please don't be mad at me."

Sam broke in. "Heather, let me take Chad away for just one minute to explain your condition to him. Okay, sweetie?"

"K."

Of course, I didn't get to listen in on what Samantha told Chad, but while she was talking, Debra filled me in.

"Things have escalated. Her OB thinks she's in eclampsia, which may be why she fell off the step stool. She was probably experiencing dizziness, blurry vision…" She blew out an agitated sigh. "The clerk at the store says she was seizing before the ambulance got there. That in itself is extremely serious, but the fall caused placental abruption."

"What does that mean?"

"The placenta has peeled away from the uterine wall."

That sent a shiver rolling through me. "Now what happens?"

"The babies need to be delivered as soon as Heather agrees."

"But it's too soon. Way too soon."

CHAPTER THIRTY-THREE

THURSDAY · AUGUST 1
Posted by Katy McKenna

Have not been in a blogging mood the past few days. Heather had a stroke. Oh, God, here come the tears again. The doctors are optimistic about her long-term recovery. Doesn't that sound like something a doctor would say when they really have no clue?

Two babies were stillborn and one very tiny guy is in neonatal intensive care. Eleven and a half ounces.

CHAPTER THIRTY-FOUR

FRIDAY · AUGUST 2
Posted by Katy McKenna

I am so sick of dealing with Chad, talking about Chad, posting about Chad. I really need this "Chad Chapter" in my life to be over. That being said, now I'll write the latest about, what else, Chad.

Last night, Sam told me he hasn't been to the hospital since the day after Heather's stroke and emergency C-section. After hearing that, I decided to try to knock some sense into the jerk's thick skull.

––––––

Chad's black Lexus SUV was in his driveway, but he didn't answer the door. I spied a surveillance camera aimed at me, so I waved, shouting, "I know you're in there, so you might as well open the door, 'cause I'm not leaving until you do!"

I waited a minute, then stepped behind the bushes fronting a window about ten feet from the door and peered into the gloomy house. I saw remnants of a "Happy Meal" on the coffee table. He likes to collect the toys.

Propelled by pissed-off adrenaline, I worked my way across the front of the house, looking in every window that wasn't draped. I continued around back, where not a single window was covered, so the peeping was easier. On the fourth window, I got lucky. Or rather he was getting lucky. And get this! It was Blondie from the country club.

My first impulse was to bang on the window, thus interrupting his banging. Then it came to me. Video. YouTube. Viral. Yes! Fist-pump. On the other side of the room, one of the french doors was cracked open, so I set my phone video mode to HD and slowly, ever so quietly, inched the door open. When it was wide enough to slip through, I focused on them and zoomed in for a nice hairy butt shot.

"Oh, Lisa, baby," Chad grunted. "Uh-huh. Yeah. That's it, baby. God, I love your big hooters. Jiggle 'em for your daddy."

That was my cue. "Speaking of daddies, shouldn't you be at the hospital taking care of your wife and baby? Huh, Daddy?"

They froze, then twisted to gawk at me. Priceless.

"What the hell're you doing?" screamed Chad, disengaging (for lack of a better word).

"Filming your infidelity for posterity." I zoomed in on his sweaty, enraged face. "Gosh, the lighting in here does nothing for you."

"Turn off that damned thing!" Lisa yanked the sheets over her big hooters.

I aimed the phone-cam on her flushed face. "FYI, he really likes it when you call him Big Guy."

She pointed a purple nail at me. "You're a crazy stalker just like Chad said."

I could see where me breaking in and filming their sex-fest might seem a little stalkerish, so I set her straight. "If I was going to stalk someone, Lisa, do you really think it would be him? Seriously?"

Lisa glanced at her chunky shag-buddy battling to disentangle from the sheets. "Maybe not."

"Chad, you know what?" I said.

He stopped wrestling the sheets. "What?"

I zoomed in on his limp tallywacker. "This video's going viral, Big Guy."

He flung out an arm to grab the phone, but I was too quick. Making my exit through the french door, still filming, I hollered over his threats to call the cops, sue me, kill me. "I'll send you the YouTube link."

I raced to my car, wishing I'd left the motor running for a fast getaway. I didn't think they'd chase me in their birthday suits, but there was the possibility they'd call the police.

Once I cleared the neighborhood, I started to giggle and shake. A strange sensation. What had possessed me to pull such a crazy stunt? I parked in a cul-de-sac to watch the video.

"Oh, this is good." Could I blackmail him with this? Not for money, but to force him to do his duty by Heather and his child. Just until she recovers. God knows, I wouldn't wish that sweet girl a lifetime tethered to the loser.

For safekeeping, I e-mailed a copy to myself and resisted sending it to Samantha. I wanted to savor the moment with her.

After a couple more viewings, I headed to the temp agency to check in with Ruby. Maybe she'd take me to lunch, and we could watch the video.

When I entered Nothing Lasts Forever, I did a double take. My fairy grandmother had magically transformed the dingy office into a respectable workplace with new furniture, window coverings, and a fresh coat of paint.

From Paul's office I heard soft murmuring, and my smutty mind instantly shifted into high alert, but I didn't whip out my phone to document the details. Instead I rapped on the opaque glass door. "It's me. Katy." I didn't want to open the door and be blinded by the sight of my granny canoodling with her boss.

"Come in, sweetie," said Ruby.

"I can come back later if you're busy."

The door swung open and Ruby waved me in, clutching a handful of playing cards.

"Hey," said Paul. "We were just talking about you."

Ruby stepped to the desk and slapped her cards down. "Gin."

"Not again. Katy. You need to take your job back," said Paul. "I can't afford your grandmother."

"You can't afford to lose me, bub," said Ruby. "How many new clients have I brought on?"

"She's right. I gotta keep her. At least until the new furniture is paid off." He glanced at his watch. "I promised the wife I'd take her to lunch at Bada Bing. It's her favorite. Say, you two want to join us? My treat."

"Katy, take a look at Paul's family." Ruby thrust a framed photo under my nose. "Good-looking kids, huh?"

I glanced at the photo, not registering the faces. "Yeah."

"How old did you say your boys are, Paul?" asked Ruby, still holding the photo in my vision line.

"Jason's twenty-one and Matthew is almost eighteen. Great kids."

Matthew? Matthew as in *the Bada Bing is my parents' favorite restaurant* Matthew? I looked at the photo again. Crap. It was him. Seventeen. Thank God I didn't sleep with him. Not ready to add pedophilia to my growing list of crimes. You can add "stupid" to the top of the list though. *Judge! I confess! I'm guilty of stupidity and I'm a repeat offender.*

"Thanks, Paul, for the invite, but we'll take a raincheck. I need to spend a little quality time with my brilliant granddaughter."

———

Over lunch at the Kale Kompany, I shared the Chad video with Ruby.

"Katy, I am proud to call you my granddaughter," she laughed, dabbing her eyes. "Play it again."

Chad's voice boomed through the speaker: "Jiggle 'em for your daddy."

"Wow. I can't believe you had the nerve. I also can't believe I loved that schmuck," she said, shaking her head. "Boy did he have me fooled. Are you really going to put this on YouTube?"

"No. Or at least, not yet."

"Oh darn. The gals at Shady Acres would love it."

"I'll e-mail it to you." I briefed her on my plan to blackmail Chad into doing the right thing.

She leaned back in her seat, appraising me. "Too bad Josh can't use a little help in his PI business. You're a natural. You're a bold, brassy broad, you know that?"

I slathered a few garlic carrot fries in mayonnaise and washed them down with iced tea, thinking, *More like impulsive, spiteful, stupid.* "Speaking of Josh. Have you seen him lately?"

"I've run into him a few times in the hall. You know what might be fun? We've got a senior prom night coming up at Shady Acres. You could invite him."

Oh yeah. I can just see Josh-the-Viking going for that. Besides, he's not my type anymore. I'm looking for a Justin Fargate clone. I bet he'd love going to the prom.

"You could double-date with Ben and me. And there's going to be a tango contest." Suddenly her eyes brimmed with tears.

"You look like you're about to cry. What's wrong?"

"Ronald."

"The retired gay mortician?"

"Yes. The contest was his idea." She shook her head. "But he's danced his last tango."

The waiter refilled our iced teas and cleared the table. As Ruby stirred sugar into her tea, she sighed. "He'd had prostate cancer for years and it finally got to the point where he needed to be in the hospital, and a couple days later—"

"He died?"

"Yup. Just like that. Heart failure." She snapped her fingers. "I thought for sure they'd get him up and dancing again. Did I tell you about Beverly and how she tripped over her Depend diaper when it fell down around her ankles late one night, and she broke her hip?"

"Yes. What about her?"

"Well, one thing led to another and the next thing you know, she's on a respirator, and then two nights ago, out of the blue, she passes. She'd already nailed the lead in our upcoming production of *Dream Girls*, so it's not like she had nothing to live for." Ruby drained her iced tea. "And now she's gone. Eighty-three years on this earth and all she gets is one lousy paragraph in the paper. And you know why? Because she had no family to write an obit about her."

"Don't worry, Ruby. We'll write a very nice obituary for you."

"I'm not worried about that. I already have a rough draft. We can work on it together."

Great. Can't wait.

"At the rate things are going, I won't have a single friend left."

"Ruby. It's to be expected. They were much older than you and sick. Their time had come. You know, the circle of life and all that."

"I understand all that, but we've lost nine residents just in the past month. If I get sick, do not send me to the hospital. It's a damned death trap."

CHAPTER THIRTY-FIVE

SATURDAY • AUGUST 3
Posted by Katy McKenna

Got a call last night from the schmuck. When I saw his name on the screen, I panicked. My first thoughts were, *What was I thinking? Why did I make that video? Could he sue me?*

I waited for the voice mail to start recording. "Katy. It's me. Listen, I've thought about what you did today, and I am begging you. Please do not put that video on YouTube. I will do anything you want. Anything. Just don't do this to me. And think about Lisa. This will destroy her."

I clicked on. "Do you honestly think I care about Lisa?"

"Oh, hi."

"Here's what you're going to do."

"I'll do anything."

"Yes, you will, Chad. And you want to know why?"

"I have a pretty good idea."

"Because now I own your flabby, hairy ass, that's why. If I say jump, you better be askin' how high." I was liking my new tough-guy persona. Bold, brassy. "You're going to take care of your wife. She had a stroke and lost two babies."

"So did I, you know. It's been… really hard."

He actually had the nerve to sound distraught. What a crock.

"Hold on a minute. I, uh, need to turn something off." More like I needed to turn something on. I rushed into the kitchen and opened my laptop sitting on the counter. Next, I opened Quick-Time and set it for an audio recording, then put my phone on speaker and turned up the volume. There's probably an app that will record cell phone conversations, but I don't have it.

"Okay, I'm back. You were saying?"

"I was saying it's been really hard for me too, you know. I lost two babies and my wife almost died." His voice quavered, but I wasn't buying it. "Lisa was just trying to comfort me, that's all."

Since I was recording the conversation I resisted saying, "Don't you mean Lisa's big hooters were comforting you?"

He continued, "I called Heather's mother and asked her to fly out here and help. She's recovering from surgery and is coming as soon as she's allowed to travel. Really bad timing."

"How inconsiderate of her."

"So, we're good? You won't post it? It would really hurt Heather. And I know you care about her."

"No, I won't post it. At least not yet. But Chad?"

"Yeah?"

"You're going to have to man up and give Heather what she needs. You owe it to her. You know what I'm saying?"

"You're saying that if I don't—"

"You'll wish you had," I said, and then I went all espionage on him. "I have the video ready to launch. All I have to do is go online and click the button. And if you think you can stop me by calling the police or suing me, just know this—there are copies out there already. You don't want to make me mad, Chad."

"Wow, Katy." His voice got husky. "You're really turning me on."

———

Apprehensive, I peeked into Heather's hospital room from the hall-way. Would she look different? Could she speak? Would she know me?

A plaid curtain was drawn around her bed. I started to back away, but then Debra and Nora stepped into sight.

"Oh look, Heather." Nora drew the curtain back and motioned me in. "Another visitor."

Heather's eyes lit up and she smiled. She looked fine. Well, not fine, but pretty darned good considering all she'd been through.

"She's coming along nicely, Katy," said Debra, sensing my trep-idation. "It was an ischemic stroke but a mild one."

I had no idea what an ischemic stroke was but didn't want to ask in front of Heather. "Does it bother her that we're talking about this in front of her?"

"Heather, does it bother you?" asked Nora.

"No. You're my friends."

Debra continued, fondly looking at the young woman. "Heather has a great neurologist and cardiologist keeping tabs on her. They expect a full recovery."

"But you have your work cut out for you, don't you?" said Nora.

"Got to get strong," said Heather with a misty smile. "For my baby."

I'd been afraid to ask, but since the subject had come up. "How's the little one doing?"

"Good." Heather looked motherly and proud.

"He's gaining weight fast," said Nora.

"We don't want to tire you out," Debra said to Heather, "so I'm going to take Katy down to the nursery and show off your little guy, okay?"

"I wish I could go too," said Heather.

"You can go after your neurologist looks in on you." Debra adjusted the window blinds to cut the glare in Heather's face.

Nora sat in a chair by the bed. "I'll stay and keep you company."

Debra walked me down the hall. "We're not really going to the nursery. It's neonatal intensive care, and I can't take you in there. I brought you out of the room, because I figured you might have some questions you weren't comfortable asking in front of Heather."

I nodded, appreciating her sensitivity. "So how is she really?"

"She's doing well, considering. The first few days were critical as far as another stroke occurring, but she's over that hurdle now. It's a good thing she was in the hospital when this happened."

"How has she taken the loss of the babies?"

"As you would expect. But I have to say, Heather is an amazing young woman. Ditzy but resilient. An optimist if ever there was one."

"And the surviving child is really doing well? Or was that for Heather's benefit?"

"He really is doing well." Debra smiled and then coughed several times, her hand pressed into her chest. Her smile became a pained grimace.

"Are you all right? That cough sounds bad. Like bronchitis. Should I get you some water?"

She waved my concern away and continued to sputter while she talked about Heather's newborn. "He's got a lot of growing to do, but there's no reason to expect any severe complications. This little one's meant to be here."

CHAPTER THIRTY-SIX

MONDAY · AUGUST 5

Posted by Katy McKenna

It's been two weeks since I delivered the Clunker Carnival job and still no check. When I called last week, they said it was in the mail. My house is two miles from the car lot, so I should have received it days ago—even if they sent it pony express. So I called again today.

Ring, ring. "Clunker Carnival. *Para continuar en español, pulse uno.* If you know the extension of your party, please dial it now. Otherwise, please listen to the following menu."

I listened, then pressed six for accounting. "We are experiencing an unusually high volume of calls right now. Your call will be answered in approximately twenty-two minutes. Thank you for your patience."

I had no patience, so I hung up, grabbed my purse, and stomped out the door.

Before stepping out of my car at the Clunker lot, I scanned the area for my teen date. Really didn't want to deal with that twerp again. The coast was clear, so I dashed to the office.

A chilly coastal fog was shrouding the car contest still in progress. The disheveled crew of survivors were hanging onto the yellow Hummer for dear life while a frizzy-haired radio deejay was doing his best impression of "excited to be here." A ragtag group of kids with drippy ice cream cones sat bundled in blankets on folding lawn chairs, fussing about going home.

"We'll go home when Mommy wins this damned car and not a minute sooner, so pipe down," shouted a skinny, bedraggled woman in desperate need of a shampoo.

Inside the building, I tapped on the accounting office window. A lone woman inside appeared fixated on her computer monitor and didn't look up. I tapped again, this time with my car key. Still no response.

I glanced around at the other folks waiting in the lounge area. All eyes were on me. Fresh entertainment.

"Give it up, girl," said a grungy, young redhead. "She is *not* gonna talk to you."

"Oh, she's gonna talk to me, all right." Remembering that I'm bold and brassy, I wedged my fingers between the sliding glass panels, inching one aside. "Excuse me, ma'am."

Still nothing. How rude.

"Hey! I know you can hear me. I'm here to collect the money you owe me."

Not even an eyebrow twitch. How could she not hear me? Unless she was deaf. Oh my God. She was deaf and I was being incredibly disrespectful. I stuck my arm through the window, waving to get her attention.

"Okay, lady," a baritone said in my ear. "Step away from the window."

"What?" I pulled my arm back and turned to face a short, portly security guard whose shirt buttons were straining to escape.

"Ma'am. We don't want any trouble here."

"Me neither." I looked back at Office Lady, now watching me, and hollered, "I just want my damned money!"

The guard kept his voice quiet and nonthreatening. "Please step away from the window."

I stepped away, and Office Lady poked her pinched, sour face through the window. "I think she has a gun and was going to rob me."

"That's ridiculous. I don't have a gun."

"Well, you were waving something at me."

"My hand." I waved my hand again. "I knew you saw me."

She ignored me. "You better check her, Malcolm, because it sure looked like a gun to me."

"Hold your arms away from your sides, please," sighed Malcolm, unclipping a black wand from his belt.

I crossed my arms over my chest. "Unh-unh. No way are you touching me."

"I'm not going to touch you. This is a metal detector. Just going to wave it around you." He leaned in and whispered, "Let's just make Tina happy, please?"

"Oh, by all means, Malcolm. Wouldn't want Tina to be unhappy. And don't worry about my total humiliation here."

"Thank you, and I sincerely mean that." He whooshed the detector through the air around me and declared me gun-free. "Are we good now, Tina?"

"Well, with those big beefy man-hands of hers, you can see why I thought she might have a gun." She shut the window and returned to her computer.

Man-hands? I glanced at my hands. They looked normal to me. Size seven ring finger, medium-size gloves. Josh once said my wrists are dainty.

"I'm warning you now, Malcolm. This could get ugly." I stepped back to the window, wedged it open again and announced in a super-friendly tone to mask the bloodlust boiling inside me, "Hi." I waved my big beefy hand at Tina. "It's me again. Katy McKenna. I'm here to pick up the check you said you mailed."

"What check?" she asked without looking up from her monitor.

I pointed out the lobby window. "I'm the one who made the posters for your contest out there."

The lobby audience turned to look out the window at the contestants freezing in the summer fog.

"But I haven't been paid yet. Just cut me my check, and I'll be on my way, and you can get on with whatever you're doing." *Probably watching cat videos.*

Tina stared at the monitor and tapped her mouse. "You're not going to be paid."

"What do you mean, I'm not getting paid?"

She pushed her chair back and came to the window looking exasperated. "Listen," she whispered, disappointing the lobby listeners and gagging me with her rancid tobacco breath. "We can't pay you. Clunker Carnival is filing Chapter 11 any day now, so technically we don't have to pay you."

"Yes, you do," I whined, pounding the little shelf under the window. "That's not fair. I did my work in good faith."

"Who said life is fair?"

I leaned into her, boldly announcing for all to hear. "Nobody pushes Katy McKenna around and gets away with it. You got that?"

Tina's eyes narrowed. "Bring it on, sister."

CHAPTER THIRTY-SEVEN

WEDNESDAY · AUGUST 7
Posted by Katy McKenna

Private Post

I was trying to determine what was a weed and what was a flower in my wildflower garden when Mom called with an update on her uncle. "Get this. He could have got life in prison, but due to his age and the fact he's never had any criminal charges in the past. Was a respected community member and a successful businessman until he retired, blah, blah, blah." She took a deep, shuddering breath. "Ted got three months house arrest and three years' probation."

"Are you kidding me? That's it?"

"That's it. Oh, he'll have to do an education program for sex offenders and some community service, but yeah, that's it."

Done with weeding, I sat in the grass against a gnarly old pepper tree. "You and I both know that you and his granddaughter weren't his only victims."

"I know. When you have a sickness like this, you don't wait nearly fifty years to do it again."

"What about his daughter? He must have molested her."

"We'll never know. Don't want to know."

"How did you find out about his sentence?"

"I've been checking the Fresno County Superior Court Facebook page. They post case information on it."

Daisy flopped next to me, resting her head on my lap. "Are you ready to tell Ruby?"

"I'll never be ready to tell her."

"I told you I'm supposed to be searching for him on the Internet. I can't keep putting her off, Mom. You have to tell her."

"I know. What really kills me is he's going to be loose out there. Free to continue preying on innocent children. Sex offender education is such a joke. He is a smart, educated man, and he knew exactly what he was doing, but I think this is like being a drug addict. He knows it's bad, but that's not going to stop him from doing it again. He needs to be in prison and... castrated! That's the only thing that's going to stop him."

CHAPTER THIRTY-EIGHT

THURSDAY · AUGUST 8
Posted by Katy McKenna

Around two thirty, I went to the hospital to visit Heather. I was about to enter her room when I heard Chad's voice and hung back to eavesdrop.

"So, babe, you sure you don't mind? I wouldn't have even considered it if it weren't about business."

"No. You should go."

Where the hell is he going? Another golf tournament? I pictured her giving him a valiant smile.

"It's just for a few days, but I have to leave now, or I'll miss my flight. Enjoy that *People* magazine I brought you. There's a good story in there about a big celebrity hip hop event at the White House."

"Hip hop at the White House?"

"Yeah. Remember the president was a big time rapper before he went into politics?"

"Oh. I guess I forgot. Thank you. Love you, Chaddie."

Heather probably expected a similar endearment in response. What she got was, "Yeah. Me too. See ya."

"Chaddie, wait. Have you visited Noah today?"

"I was just heading to the nursery to do that, but I have to hurry."

I scurried to the next room's doorway and waited for the scumbag to pass. He was moving fast toward the elevator, but I managed to slip in just as the doors closed.

"Hey, Chaddie. Whatcha doing?" I glanced at the other elevator passenger; a nurse in red polka-dot scrubs, clutching a clipboard to her chest. "I'm his parole officer. He's actually on house arrest. Indecent exposure. But since his wife's in the hospital, he's allowed to visit. Show her your ankle bracelet, Chad."

The door opened and Chad power walked toward the lobby entrance. I dashed ahead, blocking him. "Where're you going on your so-called business trip?"

He stopped, hands on hips. "It's none of your business, but I'm going to the Book Expo in New York."

"You own a used bookstore. Keyword—used. Why would you go to the Book Expo?"

"I want to expand the business. You know, go big."

"More like go broke. Barnes & Noble is two blocks from your store. Let them be big. You can't compete with that and you know it. What's really going on?"

He kept peering over my shoulder toward the glass entrance door. "I have to get going." He shouldered past me and out the door, hurrying to a shiny red Mustang. And guess who was sitting behind the steering wheel? The costar of my epic porn video.

I raced to the convertible and leaned my hands on the driver's door. "I just don't get you, Lisa. He's not even that good in the sack." I glanced up at Chad standing on the other side of the car looking like he'd love to throttle me. "Of course, it's not like he has that much to work with. You know what I'm saying? Big feet can be so deceiving."

She crossed her arms like a petulant child. "You never understood him, and neither does his current wife."

The harsh sunlight illuminating her forty-something face was unforgiving. Clearly she'd spent a lot of time in the sun.

You'd think if he were going to cheat on Heather he would at least be doing it with a young, gorgeous babe. Maybe he actually cares for Lisa.

CHAPTER THIRTY-NINE

FRIDAY • AUGUST 9
Posted by Katy McKenna

"This is delicious, Katy," said Emily, talking with a full mouth. "What do you call it?"

"Pasta Mama. I saw it on the food channel on an old *Best Thing I Ever Ate*. The celebrity chef swooned over it and it sounded easy, so I thought I'd give it a try."

"It's a keeper." Ruby refreshed her wineglass, then tossed back a tumbler of water. "The one problem with the drink a glass of water for every glass of wine idea is I need to tinkle all the time. Be right back."

The three of us were enjoying an early dinner on my patio. A warm breeze tousled the wind chimes hung in the pepper tree, adding to the relaxed ambience.

I salted and peppered a puddle of olive oil on my bread plate and dunked a chunk of warm baguette. "So how's the writing going, Emily? Got anything on paper yet?"

"As a matter of fact, I do. Though not on paper. What century are you living in?"

"It's a figure of speech, dork." I munched my bread, and olive oil drizzled down my chin. "So tell me about it."

Her face lit with enthusiasm. "It's about these two evil fairies that…" She tilted her head, brows furrowed. "Did you hear that?"

Feminine laughter floated over the six-foot cedar fence from Josh's backyard.

Ruby blew through the french doors bellowing, "Did I miss anything?"

I held up a hand to shush her, just as the woman on the other side said, "Oh, Joshie-baby. You are so cute."

Ruby's eyes bugged out. "Uh-oh. Sounds like you've got some competition."

I couldn't make out his reply, so I got up and stood with my ear to the fence. Ruby and Emily joined me.

"Oh, honey," said the woman. "Sometimes I forget what a funny boy you are!"

I tried to get a peek at her through the crack between the boards, but all I could see were the water meter, a hose bib, and some bushes.

"Baby, remember that time you…" The lady dropped her voice. "And then you…" Her sultry voice dropped again.

Josh laughed. "And you were completely soaked to the skin."

What? Soaked to the skin? As in wet T-shirt soaked to the skin? I needed to see her, so I started to drag a bench over to the fence. "Emily," I whispered. "Help me with this."

"Please tell me you don't plan to spy on your neighbor?" said my sister. "He might see you."

"I'll be very careful. I just need to see what she's got that I haven't."

"I knew it. You do have a thing for him." Emily lifted one end of the bench.

"I thought you were looking for a more feminine type," said Ruby. "Which Josh is so not."

"I am. It's just that—"

"You want Josh. Who wouldn't?"

"Me, for one," said Emily.

We set the bench down against the fence, making sure it wasn't wobbly.

"Let me look. That way you won't embarrass yourself." Emily set a foot on the bench. "If he sees me, he knows I'm gay, so he won't get any wrong ideas."

"Hold on," Ruby said. "Move the bench down to where the morning glories are growing and act like you're pruning them." She grabbed the clippers I'd left on the picnic table during my weeding on Wednesday.

We relocated the bench and Emily climbed up. She snipped a long runner and dropped it on the ground, then rooted around for another.

"Okay, I can see her sitting on the deck. Josh must be in the kitchen," she whispered, glancing down at us. "The woman's back is to me, but she looks good. Blond. Wearing a black print dress. Nice legs. Elegant. I bet she's hot."

"I need to see. Move over." I stepped up beside her. "She doesn't look that great. Her hair is definitely a dye job."

"Oh for God's sake, let me see," said Ruby. We scooted over and she climbed up, teetering in her four-inch heels. "If I fall, you two are nursing me, because I will not set foot in the hospital, you got that?"

"Yeah, I know," I said. "It's a deathtrap."

"Well, it is, so don't get sarcastic with me. Everyone I know is dying there." She peered over the thick vine straddling the fence top. "Yup. Definitely a dye job. No woman her age would naturally have hair like that. I should know."

"How do you know her age?" asked Emily.

"Elbows. A dead giveaway every time. You can lift your face, Botox it, fill it, and peel it, but nothing gives your age away like bony, wrinkly, old elbows. Like rings on a tree. And the upper arms, too. That's why I never go sleeveless."

"How old do you think she is?" I asked.

She bobbed her head back and forth, mentally calculating the unsuspecting woman's age. "It would help if I could see her face, obviously. But those elbows are telling me late fifties to midsixties. But well maintained, I'll give her that."

Emily and I were so engrossed in Ruby's calculations that we failed to see Josh step out on the deck. But he didn't fail to see us.

"Hey, neighbors," he called with a friendly wave.

"Duck," said Ruby.

It was a little late for ducking, so I grabbed the clippers out of Emily's hand and waved "hi" with them. "Doing a little clipping. Woo! This morning glory is out of control." I grabbed a hunk and whacked it off, revealing a snail family living on the fence railing. They immediately raced toward shade and Emily's hands.

"Oh, my God!" she shrieked. "Snails. Yuck. I hate snails. They're so slimy."

"You better get down then," I said, "or in a few minutes, they might get near you." I picked one up and waved it in her face. "Ooo. Emily, I'm going to slime you."

"How old are you two?" laughed Ruby, climbing down.

"When you guys are done playing," called Josh, "come over and meet my mother."

CHAPTER FORTY

Posted by Katy McKenna

The Jane Austen Book Club was scheduled to meet at Debra's, but one look at her when she opened the door to Justin, Chloe, and me made me think she should have canceled. Her normally vibrant golden-brown complexion looked dull, accented by dark hollows under her big red-rimmed eyes.

"You don't look so good," I said. "And I'm saying that with nothing but love."

Debra offered a weak smile. "Normally I would say I look worse than I feel, but today it would be a lie."

"You sure you want all of us here?" asked Chloe. "Maybe you should be in bed."

"I don't have anything you can catch, although most of you will come down with it sometime in the future. It's got a long incubation period." She chuckled and then broke into a coughing spasm.

Justin did a dramatic shudder. "Like a tropical disease?"

"More like menopause, or I should say perimenopause. Once I get to menopause, I'll be feeling a whole lot better than this. And the coughing is just really bad allergies. Blame it on the drought."

"TMI." Justin fluttered his hands. "But I feel for you in spirit, girl." He leaned in for a hug. "Good thing I brought chocolate."

"Is it dark?"

"Is there any other kind?" He uncovered a glass dish. "Home-made truffles." He put the plate in her hands. "Do not share with anyone."

I eyed the truffle-laden plate, then looked at Justin thinking, *He's perfect. I bet he vacuums too.*

———

We sat outside under a pergola, enjoying a gentle breeze from the overhead fan. After complimenting everyone on the delightful delicacies, Debra said, "I don't suppose anyone is actually reading a Jane Austen book?"

We all glanced at each other, looking guilty for not doing our homework.

"Shame on us," she snorted. "We are the worst book club, ever. Next question. Anyone got any good gossip?"

"Now we're talking. What's the latest on your charming ex, Katy?" said Justin. "I saw him at the hospital visiting Heather, so has he finally got his act together?"

"Oh, brother," Samantha snickered, fluffing her blond pixie cut. "Has he ever."

Justin shimmied forward in his seat. "Now you have to share."

"You're all over eighteen, so…" I turned my phone's screen toward the group and everyone leaned in. "Get ready to be scandalized."

"Oh, Lisa, baby. Unh-huh. Yeah. That's it, baby. God, I love your big hooters."

When my movie ended, Chris said, "I have to admit, Katy. Did not see that coming. I am impressed with you. You got balls, girl."

"Thank you." And thought, *I'm a bold, brassy broad with balls.*

Justin, overjoyed with the video, had done his happy-clappy-thingy throughout the movie. "This is priceless. Are you really going to post it on YouTube?"

"No. I can't do that to Heather, although I threatened to if he didn't shape up, and he swore he would. But he's already at it again. I shot this video over a week ago, and as of yesterday, he left on a trip to New York City with Lisa."

"You mean," Debra cracked a smile, "Big Hooters?"

I nodded, sipping my cabernet and thinking how good one of Justin's chocolate truffles would pair with it.

"Maybe he'll get hit by a subway train. Problem solved," said Chloe, dusting her palms.

"Wouldn't that be nice," said Sam. "Heather could grieve for him and never know what a complete—"

"Turd he is," finished Chris.

The rest of this post is private.

"There's one more person I'd like to add to the hit list," I said. "My great-Uncle Ted."

I shared Mom's story, finishing with the outrageous community service punishment.

"I don't even know what to say to that." Debra stifled a cough. "He's a child molester and he'll do it again. Somewhere out there are more innocent children he's going to hurt."

"Where's this perv live?" said Chris with eyes so cold it chilled me to the bone, making me wonder if she suffered from PTSD after all her tours in the Middle East. Would not want to get on her bad side.

CHAPTER FORTY-ONE

MONDAY · AUGUST 12
Posted by Katy McKenna

Heather's mother flew in this morning. Since Chad is still out of town, Heather asked if I would pick her up. I couldn't say no but sure wish she'd called someone else. When exactly did I become her bestie?

I knew Judy the moment she walked through the glass doors at the airport. Shoulder-length strawberry blond with freckles, late forties, with a bohemian vibe. Like a "Heather senior."

I stepped forward from the small crowd. "You must be Judy."

"And you are Katy. Isn't life strange?"

"You can say that again. Never saw myself becoming friends with Heather, but here I am."

Luggage bounced onto the carousel and she stepped close, ready to grab. I moved next to her. "Tell me which one is yours and let me grab it. You just had surgery and shouldn't be lifting."

"Shouldn't be traveling either, but I need to take care of my girl." We both let the reason hang in the air. "There's my suitcase. The one with the flowers on it."

. . .

While I stowed her luggage in the back of my car, Judy said, "I've only met Chad once. At the wedding in Vegas if you can call that a wedding. But so far, I am not impressed. You seem like a sweet girl, so how he could have cheated on you is beyond my comprehension. I'm just sorry it was with my daughter."

I was determined to take the high road and not say anything negative. "In her defense, she didn't know."

"But how could he go off on a trip at a time like this? Heather says it's business, but I don't get it. What can be more important than your wife and newborn baby? Especially after everything that's happened."

I bit my lips to keep my mouth shut and stay on that high road.

"And he hasn't been picking up her calls."

My lips cracked open a smidge. "He hasn't?"

"No. Heather thinks it's because the cell reception must be bad. In New York City? Right."

This high road thing was killing me, but I stayed the course. "Heather told me where the door key is hidden at the house. We'll go by there first so you can drop off your things. Then you can follow me over to the hospital in her car."

———

"How can they afford this?" Judy gaped at Heather's boxy contemporary concrete house when we pulled up in front. "Sure doesn't look like a house Heather would choose."

It looks like a house Chad would choose. Like the one we lived in, I thought, but didn't share. High road.

We found the key and let ourselves in.

"It's so cold and sterile." Judy glanced around the cavernous open-concept home. "All this glass and cement." She wrinkled her nose, shaking her head. "Listen to how my voice bounces off the hard surfaces. Just think what it'll be like with a baby crying at two a.m."

"Let's find the guest room so you can freshen up before we go."

Our footsteps echoed as we roamed around the house. We peeked in one bedroom and it was the nursery. "At least there are curtains and a rug." She went in and touched the top rail of one of the three white cribs. "Thank God one of my grandbabies survived."

We continued to the next room. "This must be the master," said Judy. "Look at the size of that bed. It's huge. It must have been custom made."

I glanced at the neatly made bed, flashing on the mess it was the last time I saw it.

Judy went into the master bathroom that was as big as my master bedroom, and I tagged along. "Sure is clean." She ran a finger across the bare concrete counter. "I always have stuff strewn all over the counter, and Heather has never been known for her tidiness, so it must be Chad."

"He didn't used to be."

She placed a hand on my shoulder. "I'm being inconsiderate. This has got to be terribly uncomfortable for you."

"Don't worry about me. I'm all right." *Not.*

She left the bathroom and crossed through the bedroom, out to the hall. "I'll hurry this up, so you can get out of here."

I hung back. Something felt wrong. I opened the closet door and snapped on the light. Chad was a clotheshorse and we always fought for closet space, but this colossal walk-in was three-quarters empty. Because Chad's clothes weren't in it.

Was he using another closet? I quietly searched the closets in the other rooms off the expansive hallway until I wound up in the guest room with Judy. Her bag was open on the bed and she was placing her clothes in a bureau. The wall-length open closet held nothing but empty hangers.

"You look disturbed, Katy. What's wrong, besides the obvious?"

"Chad's clothes aren't in the master closet, and I've checked the other rooms. I haven't looked in the drawers yet."

"Well, I will." She rushed to the master bath and slammed through the drawers, then the dresser in the bedroom. Everything male-oriented was gone.

"What kind of person does something like this?" She leaned against the dresser, looking at a framed Vegas wedding chapel photo of Chad and Heather. "Don't answer that. The kind who cheats on the good wife who nursed him through cancer." She set the photo facedown and collapsed on the gray love seat at the foot of the bed. "What am I going to tell Heather? She's been through so much already." She covered her face with her hands. "Oh, God. What if she has another stroke?"

I sat next to her. "Strokes aren't caused by stress. And she's on medication."

"Well, it's going to break her heart. There's no medication for that." Judy stood, smoothing her embroidered tunic top. "I need to get to the hospital."

"Are you going to tell her now?"

She shook her head. "No. Not until we have some answers."

The obvious answer was: Chad had not gone on a business trip. He'd moved in with his inamorata.

———

I had no idea where Lisa lived, so after I led Judy to the hospital, I drove to the country club. In the parking lot, I found Chad's Lexus SUV with its BADBOY vanity plates sitting under a tree. I parked Veronica out of sight, pulled on the wrinkled red baseball cap I keep in the car for dog-park visits, and feeling like a sleuth, settled in for my first-ever stakeout.

Halfway into the second hour I was getting drowsy and decided to sample the day-old leftover coffee in the flimsy, plastic cup holder hanging from the window channel. It wasn't bad. Not good but not bad.

Finally he sauntered through the parking lot like he didn't have a care in the world and tossed his clubs in the back of his SUV. I hunkered down, peeping over the windowsill, and saw Lisa rolling her pink bedazzled golf bag to the car.

And then they were off, with me in hot pursuit. In my orange 1976 Volvo wagon. Could I have been any more conspicuous? Realizing that, I hung back and let a few cars slip in between.

I must be a natural at this PI stuff because Chad never saw me, but I saw them turn into her plastic-flamingo-lined driveway. I jotted down the address, as if I was going to forget it, and then left the neighborhood because I didn't have a plan beyond locating Chad.

Samantha was on duty, so a few blocks away I pulled over and called to see if she could take a break. I needed her input and a text wouldn't suffice.

"I can break in about twenty minutes," she said. "I'll meet you in the cafeteria."

———

I found her sitting with Justin and Nora. Sam already had a cream-and-sugared coffee waiting for me.

"How much time do you two have?" I blew on my scalding beverage.

"We all just got here," said Sam. "So what's going on?"

I told them what was up with Chad and finished with, "What should I do?"

"I say it's time to pull out the big guns and go viral with that video," said Nora.

"I already threatened him with that, and it only kept him in line for a couple of days."

"He must have thought you wouldn't go through with it," said

Sam. "You know, because he figured you don't want to hurt Heather."

Justin fluttered his hands. "Before you do anything too drastic that you can't take back, I think you should talk to him one more time," he said, earning a round of groans.

I squirmed in my seat, whining like a five-year-old being ordered to eat her lima beans. "I don't wanna talk to him again."

Justin held up a hand, shushing me. "Trust me on this. You will feel better knowing you tried."

"Oh, all right."

"Promise?"

"Justin. Leave the poor girl alone," said my bestie.

"No, Sam. He's right. One more time won't kill me." *Although I might kill Chad.*

Nora's eyes lifted from our little group. "Debra! Over here. Come sit. You have to hear Katy's story."

"Let me get a water first," she answered. "Anyone need anything?"

"No, we're good." Nora lowered her voice, leaning in. "Debra looks dreadful, and I'm very worried. The constant cough, her weight loss. Look at the way her clothes are just hanging on her. If you ask me, this is a lot more than allergies and perimenopause." She looked past me and leaned back. "She's coming."

Debra joined us and immediately launched into a coughing fit. "Good grief," she sputtered. "You'd think I was a smoker, huh? My mother used to cough like this and she was a two-pack-a-dayer, and the main reason I never started. Damned allergies." She sipped her water. "Before you tell me your story, Katy, I have an announcement to make. I'm taking a leave of absence, effective as-of-now." She saw Nora's astonished face. "Don't look at me like that. I only just came to that decision this morning. I feel like crud and I need to get my act together."

"Is this a prelude to retirement?" asked Nora. "You're only fifty-three, you know."

"No. Not ready to throw in the towel yet. Maybe when I'm eighty-three, although some days I feel like I'm there already." She patted Nora's hand. "I just need to take a break and get well, that's all." Debra shifted to me. "That's enough about me. I'm guessing you have more revelations about your charming ex?"

CHAPTER FORTY-TWO

SATURDAY • AUGUST 17
Posted by Katy McKenna

I haven't posted for a few days. Time to catch up.

Tuesday, August 13
Part One

I should have stayed in bed. Should have bolted the doors, shuttered the windows and binge-watched *Bridgerton* on Netflix all day long. But no. I'd promised Justin I would talk to my was-band one more time. And I always keep my promises.

Around eleven thirty, I cruised past Lisa's house. Chad's spotless black SUV looked out of place next to the tacky pink flamingos lining the driveway.

I parked down the block and sat a while, building up my courage, thinking, *I really need to stay out of this. I have enough problems of my own without sticking my nose into everyone else's business.* Then I heard Justin nagging me, "Trust me on this. You will feel better knowing you tried."

Finally climbing out of the car, I muttered, "I sure hope Heather appreciates me." At the pink-and-purple front door, I tapped ever-so-gently and waited a few seconds. "Oh, darn. Guess no one's home."

"Woof! Woof! Woof!" A yippy little canine pawed frantically on the other side of the door.

Was this déjà vu? The last time a dog was barking in a house I shouldn't be visiting, it didn't turn out well.

I bent, whispering through the doorjamb. "Shhh. Quiet, doggie. Shhh."

The dog snuffled the bottom of the door, whimpering miserably. I started to leave, and then from somewhere deep inside the house, I heard Chad whimpering. "Help me. Please. Somebody help me."

Maybe he'd fallen and couldn't get up. Maybe I didn't care. Let Lisa deal with him.

"Help me, *pleeeaaase*."

"Oh for God's sake." I sighed, shaking my head. "So do not want to do this." I held my breath and tried the doorknob. It was locked.

"Okay, you tried the door. Now call the police and leave." Then my annoying good conscience said, *Go around back and try another door.*

I trudged through the front yard fairyland, sidestepping gnomes and creepy concrete forest creatures to the side of the house. And just my luck, the door next to the driveway was unlocked. Sometimes I really hate my good conscience.

I poked my head through the open door, keeping my feet planted outside. "Chad? You okay?"

I stepped inside and was immediately joined by a freaked-out white-and-brown spotted Chihuahua piddling on the tile floor. I stroked her while I read her rhinestone collar. "What's going on, Bambi?"

She rolled over for a tummy rub, then popped up and pranced

into the kitchen, checking over her shoulder to make sure I was following her lead.

I stopped a sec to marvel at the cookie jar collection covering every inch of counter space in the kitschy country kitchen, before skulking into a cramped dining room. To the right was a dark, narrow hallway. To the left, the living room, a tacky decorator's nightmare I would have loved to snap a photo of to show Sam, but before I could get my phone out of my red crossover purse, Chad moaned from the other end of the house. "Somebody. Help me."

I hurried down the hallway nearly tripping over the tiny dog. "Chad? Where are you?"

I found him in a bedroom sprawled on a bed that Lisa must have picked up at Liberace's estate sale. His wrists were tied with pink silk scarves to the gilt banisters. Probably an all-night orgy. How romantic. They were perfect for each other.

"Ahhh, you poor thing. Did your dominatrix leave you tied up? Well, you can just stay tied up until she comes back, 'cause I'm outta here."

"Nooo," he rasped. "Help me."

Now that my eyes had adjusted to the dim light, I noticed his sweaty, gray pallor. "I don't know what's been going on here, but you might want to rethink your lifestyle." I set my purse on the bed, then drew back the purple velvet drapes to let in some daylight.

He watched me through hollow, bloodshot eyes while I untied the knot on his right wrist. His arm flopped to the bed, then slid off the side, trembling spasmodically. Something clinked on the floor. A syringe. I kicked it away.

"Oh my God. What have you done?" I shook his limp shoulders as his pupils slid out of sight. "I'm calling an ambulance." I dug my phone out of my purse. "Hang on, Chad."

"Momma's home," Lisa warbled from the kitchen. "Where's my baby?"

Bambi bolted out of the room, running to her mommy, and a

few seconds later I heard, "There's my wittle baby girl. Momma's baby-waby. Have you been a good wittle-biddy-boo girl?"

I was trapped. Should I hide? Where? The closet? No, I'd have to come out eventually.

"Lover? Did you come home for a nooner?" Stilettos tapped down the tiled hallway. "I've got your favorite dress on. The red one you said makes my ass look sexy like J-Lo's." She stopped in the doorway, eyes bulging. "What the hell're you doing here?"

"Lisa, before you go ballistic, you need to hear me out." I stood by the bed, clutching my phone. Chad's spazzing arm brushed my leg, and Lisa went ballistic.

"Oh my God." She raged across the room, halting at the foot of the bed. "You're having an affair with my fiancé." Then she zeroed in on my phone. "Oh! And you're filming it? Figures, you sick perv. Get out or I'm calling the cops."

"Lisa. There's something seriously wrong with Chad. Look at him."

Instead she lunged at me, digging her gnarly purple acrylic claws into my puny biceps, screaming, "I'm gonna fucking kill you, you whore."

I shoved her away and toppled backward, falling hard on my back. She landed on top of me, pinning me with her massive thighs.

"Lisa!" Her big hooters blocked my view of her face. "Get off me!"

She slapped my face, and little Bambi jumped into the fray, licking my cheek like we were all playing a fun game.

"Bambi!" snapped her mother. "Go 'way so Mommy can kill this bitch!"

I struggled, screaming, "Lisa, you got it all wrong." Slap. Lick. Lick. "I'm not having an affair with Chad." I struggled for air. "I'm just trying to help Heather."

"Oh really? By screwing my fiancé?" Slap. She wrested the cell phone from my grip. "How about I make a little movie of you getting bitch-slapped?" She fumbled with the phone. "Dammit, what's your damned code?"

Lisa had to weigh at least one sixty and her thonged crotch was pressing hard into my chest. "I. Can't. Breathe."

"That's not a code." She flung my phone across the room. Slap.

I needed air or I was going to pass out, or worse. I looked for something to clobber her with and caught the glint of the syringe under the bed. I stretched my right arm toward it, my fingers almost touching it. All I needed was another two inches and I would have it, but I was fading fast. Lisa's screeching grew muffled as my vision blurred into shimmery white.

No! You have to hold on! This is not how you're going to die!

I stretched again for the syringe. Time slid into slow motion as I strained with all my might. One inch away. Half an inch.

Come on Katy, you can do it!

My fingertips grappled desperately on the dusty tile floor, then suddenly connected. I rolled the syringe into my grip, then with one final burst of adrenaline, I jammed it hard into her thigh.

"Oww!" She rolled off me. "You bitch! You stabbed me!"

Glorious oxygen flooded my lungs, and my head began to clear. I staggered to my feet, using the bed for support. Lisa yanked the syringe out of her leg, and blood bubbled from the wound. Clutching a bannister, I braced myself for her to attack. Then she finally got a good look at Chad's lifeless body.

She gawked at the syringe in her hand, putting two and two together, and getting the wrong answer. "Oh my God. You poisoned my fiancé."

"No! No! I just came here to warn him, that's all. For Heather. And then I heard him calling for help."

She flung herself on top of Chad, burrowing her head into his pillowy chest. "Oh, my sweet, sweet, darling love. Don't leave me."

I hung back, plastered against a purple-and-pink sponge-painted wall with freaked-out Bambi trying to wedge herself behind my legs and tinkling on my sandals. I should have run, but we needed to get help for Chad.

"Lisa," I whispered, afraid to provoke her. "We have to call 9-1-1."

She lifted her tear-streaked face, her blond bouffant flattened on one side, and glared at me. "Chad told me how unstable you are. And sweet little Heather took advantage of his innocent vulnerability and forced him to cheat on you. And then she fakes a pregnancy so he would have to marry her. Then she purposely gets herself pregnant with triplets so he would be trapped forever. And you," she said, wiping her nose on the sheet, "you've been stalking him, and when he spurned you…" She gasped an anguished sob. "…you murdered him. So, yeah. Call 9-1-1. I really want to see how you explain this to them."

She laid her head on his chest blubbering, and then she stopped, pressing her ear deeper into his ribs. "I think I hear a heartbeat."

"Let me check for a pulse." Like an idiot with a flat learning curve, I stepped toward her.

"Oh no you don't, bitch." She sat up, blocking me, and in a blink, slid open the nightstand drawer and whipped out a big black gun. "Don't you dare come near him, or I'll shoot. I mean it." No way could she miss me at that close range.

I stepped back, hands in the air. "I just want to check for a pulse, that's all."

"Oh, piss off, you douche bag. I know exactly what you want to do. You want to finish him off."

"Oh for God's sake, Lisa. You need to think. We have to call an ambulance."

"I am thinking." She stood, advancing on me, brandishing the gun inches from my face. "About how good you'll look lying dead on the floor."

I deflected her gun-toting hand with my forearm, and shoved her away. There was a deafening explosion. The sound of the gun going off ripped through my ears as if a bolt of lightning had blasted through the walls.

She teetered backward, thudding hard against the nightstand. The gun fired again.

Lisa collapsed onto Chad, her mouth gaping, then slid to the floor, her shirt and face smeared with blood. I reached over her and grabbed the landline and dialed 9-1-1. I couldn't hear a thing, so I yelled, "We need an ambulance. There's been a shooting."

———

The next thing I knew, an angelic curly redhead, backlit by the sun, was hovering over me. Her mouth was moving, but it was like my head was stuffed with cotton balls. I struggled to sit up, but she held my shoulder down, shaking her head.

My gurney was lifted into an ambulance. Inside, I scanned my surroundings, totally discombobulated. Another gurney with someone on it was next to me. And then the pieces shifted into place, as a searing blast of pain shot through me.

CHAPTER FORTY-THREE

SATURDAY · AUGUST 17

Guest posted by Samantha Drummond

Tuesday, August 13
Part Two

Katy asked me to write this post about what
happened when she was brought into the ER.

———

I was on duty attending a shrieking mother-to-be, who judging
from the decibel level of her shrieks, evidently had a very low pain
threshold. She was in early labor and only dilated to three centime-
ters with seven to go when Chris called from the ER and told me
Katy was on her way in with a gunshot wound. I got someone to
cover me and raced downstairs to the emergency entrance.

While I waited, every worst-case scenario ran through my
head. I was so scared I had to put my head between my legs to

keep from passing out. Finally the ambulance tore into the lot and screeched to a stop under the roofed entrance area.

The back door swung open and I stepped back so they could unload Katy. I was surprised when they hauled out Chad first. I knew he had to be the reason my best friend was in that ambulance. Had he tried to kill her?

Katy looked frightened and in pain, but alive. Her left pant leg was ripped to her crotch and a blood-soaked pressure bandage hid the thigh wound. The EMTs gave me the rundown as we wheeled her into a cubicle. Gunshot wound to the left biceps femoris muscle. Her blood pressure was low, and she'd lost a lot of blood. She was lucky though; the bullet hadn't torn through the femoral artery, or she would have bled out in minutes.

Chad was getting all the attention, so for the first several minutes I worked on my own. Katy already had an IV saline drip, but because her blood pressure was low, I feared possible hemorrhagic shock, which could flatten her veins, so I set up another IV, along with blood pressure and pulse monitors.

We would need an X-ray and possibly an MRI to evaluate the damage, but my first assessment was a clean exit with no serious damage.

I could tell her hearing was impaired so I shouted in her ear, "You're going to be okay, Katy. You've been shot in your left thigh. We have to stop the bleeding and then get an X-ray. How's your pain?"

She scowled, gasping, as she tried to shift on the bed.

"Don't move, you dope. I'll give you something for the pain."

I injected a potent painkiller into her IV and waited for the drug to work its magic. A few moments later her scowl softened, just as Dr. Prendergast (one of my favorite doctors) stepped in to take over. After a quick run-through of her vitals, he sent her up to X-ray. I went along to make sure she didn't get shunted into a side corridor. It happens.

———

After we had her back in the ER, the doctor scrutinized her X-rays. "This young lady is very lucky."

Katy was awake and smiling like a goofball. "What you say?"

"Your thigh bone. No damage," said the doctor.

"The thigh bone's connected to the knee bone," she sang like a drunken slob.

The doctor continued, "That's right. And no reason to think there's any nerve damage either. But we'll do an MRI to be on the safe side. If I don't, your buddy here will never give me any peace."

Katy took my hand and kissed it. "I love you, Sammy buddy."

I smoothed back her hair, my eyes tearing. "I love you too, Katy."

She grinned at the doctor. "I love you, Dr. Cutie-Pie."

"You gave her the good stuff, huh?" said Dr. Prendergast, with a wink.

"Are you married? 'Cause I'm not." Katy waggled her left ring finger in his face. "See. Totally available."

The doctor, old enough to be her father, shook his head. "Yes. Happily married for thirty-six years with three grown kids and a second grandchild on the way. But thanks for the offer."

"Oh, poopie."

"How's your pain level, Katy?" he asked, struggling to remain serious.

"Awesome." She dozed off, still grinning.

Dr. Prendergast chuckled. "Wish all our gunshot emergencies were as easygoing. Keep her comfortable and let's get the MRI. She lost a lot of blood, but she doesn't need a transfusion; nevertheless, I want to keep her overnight."

Katy's parents arrived while she was getting the MRI. I did my best to reassure them she would be okay, but I knew they wouldn't truly believe it until they saw her.

Once Katy was settled in her room, everyone gathered around her, and I could tell from the amused smirks on their faces that her decibel-defying snoring had reassured them.

CHAPTER FORTY-FOUR

SATURDAY · AUGUST 17
Posted by Katy McKenna

Still catching up.
Tuesday, August 13
Part Three

When I woke in my hospital room, my family was there to welcome me back to the real world. It wasn't long before I decided the real world sucks.

"I know you're hurting, Katy, but that's a good thing," said Samantha. "It means you're alive and there's no nerve damage. If the bullet had hit your femoral artery, you might have bled out before the EMTs got there."

The pain medication was wearing off, and I hunkered down in the bed wishing everyone would go away. "Why does this stuff always happen to me?"

"Because you have a bad habit of sticking your nose where it doesn't belong, young lady." Ruby crossed her arms, looking mad at me.

Ben put his arm around her rigid shoulders and pulled her close. "Go easy on her, girl."

"Mom, don't be hard on Katy," said Mom. "She's been through a lot."

"Well, so have we," grumped Ruby. "Scarin' the livin' daylights out of all of us."

Pop edged to the other side of my bed and hugged me. "Don't mind us, Katydid. We're all dealing with the aftershocks of Sam's phone call telling us you'd been shot."

"Jeez, Katy," said Emily. "I finally have a good relationship with my big sis and you go and get yourself shot? Seriously?"

"It's not like I meant to."

A petite nurse entered the room, cheerfully asking, "How's our pain?"

I glared at her, curling my lip.

"Then I think you'll like this." She injected a painkiller into my IV. "This should hold you awhile, then next go-round, we'll switch you to an oral dose of Vicodin."

"I hate that damn drug," said Ruby. "Always constipates me. Is there anything else she can take?"

"You'll have to take that up with the doctor," the nurse said.

At that point, constipation was the least of my worries. "Can I get rid of this damn IV? It hurts."

"I don't see why not, but I'll have to get your doctor's approval first."

"Well, you have my approval."

She peeked at my gauze-covered wound, seemed satisfied, and left with a warning that I needed my rest.

"I suppose we should get going." Mom looked like that was the last thing she wanted to do. "Tomorrow we'll pick you up and you'll spend a few nights at our house."

"No, don't go yet. Tell me what happened to Chad." For all I knew he was dead.

"His girlfriend managed to shoot him too," said Sam. "The

bullet just missed his heart and he's stable but comatose. Evidently he'd been injected with something before he was shot."

"He was in really bad shape when I got there. Barely conscious."

"Why the hell were you there?" snapped Ruby.

"*Ru-by*," warned Ben.

"Well after everything that man has put her through, I think it's a reasonable question to ask."

"It is, Mom. Just not now." Mom straightened and smoothed my sheet and blanket. "But be prepared to fill us in tomorrow, Katy. Because your father and I would also like to know the answer to that question."

"So would I." A blue-blazered, porcelain-skinned brunette stepped into the room followed by a tall, dark, and dangerously handsome man. She flashed her police badge. "I'm Detective Kailyn Murphy, Santa Lucia Police Department, and this is my partner, Mike Devlin."

She gazed coolly at me from the foot of the bed as Devlin flipped open a notebook and faded into the background. "You are Katy McKenna?"

"Yeth." The drug was making my tongue sluggish. "Am I in trouble?"

"I don't know." She titled her head. "Are you?"

"I dunno."

Her hypnotic gaze and tranquilizing voice were making my eyes blur. "I need to ask you a few questions about today's events."

"Can't this wait?" asked Pop. "My daughter's just had a painkiller. Now may not be the best time to be asking questions."

"I'm afraid this can't wait." Murphy gave him a watery smile. "We need to know what happened. I assure you it's in your daughter's best interest to cooperate with us."

Ben pulled away from Ruby and faced the detective. "I'm her attorney."

"Oh? Do you think Katy needs an attorney?"

He folded his arms over his chest, looking stern. "That depends on your line of questioning."

I'd never seen this side of Ben before, and I caught Ruby's impressed expression. Obviously it was new to her too, and she liked it.

The detective replied in her controlled, sedating tone, "Let's just try this, and if you don't like where it's going, I will stop, Mister…"

"Burnett. Ben Burnett."

Her eyes widened and her voice leaped an octave. "Not *the* Ben Burnett? L.A.'s illustrious criminal attorney? I was under the impression you'd retired a few years ago."

Ben edged into her personal space. "Katy is family and my license is up to date, detective."

Murphy stepped back and held out her hand to shake his. "Well, Mr. Burnett, it is a…" She paused with a rueful smile. "… mixed pleasure to meet you. I can't say I'm thrilled by all your courtroom successes considering who some of your clients were, but I am impressed." She glanced at me. "You're in excellent hands with your grandfather, Ms. McKenna. He's a rock star in the legal world.

My last thought as I drifted off to the Land of Nod was, *When did Ruby marry Ben?*

CHAPTER FORTY-FIVE

SUNDAY · AUGUST 18
Posted by Katy McKenna

Wednesday, August 14

I woke at dawn on Wednesday with no idea where I was until I shifted on the hard, narrow hospital bed, and my left leg clunked the metal rail. The resulting shock wave of agony jolted me into instant clarity. Clenching my teeth while tears dribbled down my face, I fumbled in the bed linens for the buzzer and pinned it down with my thumb, thinking that would make a nurse come faster. It didn't.

―――

After the miraculous meds had kicked in, a sense of soothing bliss engulfed me. I was floating back to dreamland when Detective Murphy's smug smile popped into my head and fizzled my bliss.

As I reviewed the bizarre events of the day before, I realized how it might look to the police. Me, the jilted ex, found in Chad's bedroom standing over his nearly dead body with a syringe. Okay, the syringe wasn't actually in my hand, but by the time the entire scene played out, it had my prints on it.

And who knew what Lisa may have already told Detective Murphy: *"She broke into my house, and when I came home I found her jamming the needle into him, cackling evilly, 'This is what you get for leaving me.' I tried to warn her off with the gun, but she grabbed my arm and forced me to shoot Chad. That's why I had to shoot her before she could get the gun away from me and kill me."*

The only one who could clear up this convoluted mess was Chad, and he was inconveniently comatose. *But that was last night. Maybe by now he's awake.*

I needed to check out this so-called coma for myself. From my bed I spied a wheelchair idling in the hallway and decided to take it for a spin up to Chad's room in the ICU.

"Ouch, ouch, ouch," I grunted, easing my legs over the side of the bed. Full disclosure: "Ouch" wasn't what I said.

Putting weight on the leg wasn't an option. But I wasn't giving up, so I hopped on my right foot to the wall, then worked my way to the open door. I peeked out, scanning the hall both ways, then crossed over to the wheelchair.

Voices from down the hall were heading my way, so I rolled in the other direction, searching for an elevator. This was my first wheelchair experience and along the way I crashed into a laundry cart, a recycling bin, and a wall.

Inside the elevator, I spent two minutes doing a three-point turn before I could press the button. At that point, I would've sold my darling Daisy for another Vicodin.

Ding. Third floor.

The doors opened and I rolled out, passing a sitting area and a long, U-shaped nurses' station, surrounded on every side by hospital rooms. No one paid me any attention when I wheeled by. I slowed at every room, peeking through the sliding glass doors until

I found Chad. His bed was on the far side of the room, next to the window.

He was hooked up to a respirator, a heart monitor, and an IV, but other than that he looked like he was napping. He was clean-shaven and not a hair out of place. It upset me to see him like that. It's not like it was scary or gory. Just surreal.

"Chad?" I whispered, rolling closer. "It's Katy. Can you hear me? If you can…" I took his pudgy, manicured hand. "…squeeze my hand."

I waited for a response, but all I got was the rhythmic whoosh of the respirator. "Chad, I know you're in there. It's time to stop screwing around and wake up."

They say it's important to talk to coma patients. That they can hear you even if they don't respond. I didn't have anything pleasant or inspirational to say to him so I turned the TV on to his favorite station. The Golf Channel.

"Oh look, Chad. A golf tournament is on. Woo-hoo!" I nudged his arm. "So who're you going for?" I'm not a golfer, so the only golfer names I could think of were Arnold Palmer, Jack Nicklaus, and Tiger Woods. I pointed at the man about to tee off. "I'm betting on that guy."

The respirator continued to pump, the monitor beeped, the IV dripped, but Chad just lay there like a big lump. Typical.

After staring at him for an hour or so, I caught the heavenly scent of eggs and bacon as the breakfast carts clattered through the halls, and my stomach growled its need for sustenance.

———

After a breakfast of oatmeal, a soft-boiled egg, and orange juice, I returned to Chad's room. The curtain was drawn across the glass wall facing the nurse's station, and Debra stood at his bedside checking his IV with her back to me.

"Hi," I said softly, trying not to startle her. "I don't want to disturb you. I'll come back later."

Debra jerked and spun around. "Katy." She gave me a motherly scowl. "Shouldn't you be in bed? You were next on my visit list." She looked sicker than the last time I'd seen her.

"You don't look well at all," I blurted, my mouth running ahead of my brain.

"I know." Her voice sounded wheezy and hoarse. "Even *he* looks better than me, huh?" She frowned, leaning into me, and tilted my chin. "What happened to your face?"

"His girlfriend smacked me around before she shot me."

She shook her head with a grim smile. "You need to pick a better class of people to hang out with, Katy."

"Is Chad a patient of yours?" I paused. "Oh, sorry. Doctor-patient privilege, right? But I thought you were on leave."

"I am, but I can't walk away from my patients entirely." Her gaze shifted back to Chad. "I've only seen him as a patient a few times, and that was a couple of years ago, long before I met you. But I thought I should check in. And I have to admit, after hearing all your stories about this guy, I was more than a little curious." She chuckled. "That doesn't sound very professional, does it?"

I laughed. "Who knew doctors are human?"

"Believe me, most of us are." Debra sat on the bedside chair. "How are you doing? The leg very painful?"

"I think I may have overdone it."

"You think? Mind if I take a peek at it?"

I rolled closer. "Be my guest. But it's all bandaged up, so I don't know what you'll see."

She gently lifted my hospital gown. The bandages were stained with blood, and it frightened me.

"Uh-oh. That can't be good," I said.

"It's dry, which means you're not bleeding now." She set the gown back down. "But you're overdoing it, and you need to keep it elevated."

"I will." I gazed at Chad's peaceful face. "Hard to believe how much misery that guy has caused. Lying there, he looks like he couldn't hurt a flea."

"Right now he can't," she said.

"This will probably sound crazy, but I thought maybe I could talk him out of his coma."

Debra patted my knee. "That's very noble of you, dear. But why, after everything he's done to you, would you care?"

"Believe me, I'm no Mother Teresa." I glanced toward the door to make sure no one was coming. "But I think I may be under suspicion of attempted murder."

"You're kidding! Why you?"

"Somebody injected him with some kind of drug. And I was the one who found him. Do you know what it was?"

"Potassium chloride. Really bad news if you get too much. Mimics a heart attack. Frankly, I'm amazed he survived," she snorted. "And then he gets shot and survives that too. Incredible. Clearly it's not his time. Hopefully, he'll make better use of the next chapter in his charmed life. But why would you be under suspicion?"

"Because my prints are on the syringe. Mine and his sleazy girl-friend's."

"You found the syringe? Where?"

"In the bedroom where I found him tied to the bed. It fell on the floor while I was untying him." I thunked my forehead. "Why did I think I could talk sense into him?"

"Did you go there because of what Justin said the other day about giving Chad one more chance to do the right thing?"

"Uh-huh. But I never had a chance to talk to him." I waved at the respirator. "And I'm not responsible for this."

"I can't believe the police will go after you."

"I certainly had motive. And desire. *Extreme* desire, although they don't know that. Even now I'd love to yank that pillow out from under his head and… But wanting to and actually doing it are two different things. We've all wanted to kill someone at one time or another, but most of us never do."

Debra laughed. "If we did, the morgues would be overflowing with corpses." Her expression changed to an empathetic, doctorly look. "Katy. Try not to worry. There's no way you're going to jail for this." She stood, leaning in for a quick squeeze. "I'm leaving now. You want me to push you back to your room?"

"I'm here, so I might as well keep trying for a while. I'll be checking out this afternoon, so this is my last chance."

CHAPTER FORTY-SIX

SUNDAY • AUGUST 18
Posted by Katy McKenna

There are many days when I don't feel like blogging, but when Samantha talked me into blogging several months ago, she said it would be cathartic.

At the time, I was not dealing well with Chad's betrayal, the divorce, his instant remarriage, and his pregnant wife. It was all just too much, and Sam was afraid I would slip into a deep depression. I was depressed, no doubt about that, but who wouldn't have been under the circumstances?

Before I post about last Thursday, I decided to look up the word "cathartic" to make sure I fully understand what she meant.

Cathartic: 1. A purification that brings about spiritual renewal or release from tension (the catharsis of tears). 2. Purgative, laxative.

I don't know about spiritual renewal, but it does seem to help me make sense of all the bizarre things that happen in my life.

And Ruby was right about Vicodin and constipation, but I don't think my cathartic blogging is gonna relieve that problem.

Now it's time to write about last Thursday, August 15

My go-to-sleep position is on my left side, curled up, face planted into my down pillow. That's not been happening with this damned gunshot wound. My leg has to be propped on top of the bedding with a big wooly sock on my foot and a light comforter draped over it.

The Vicodin I took at bedtime on Wednesday night knocked me out initially, but in the wee hours of Thursday morning, I tried to turn over without thinking. On a scale of one to ten, the pain was an easy eleven. I desperately needed another pill but didn't want to wake up the folks. So I lay there, being a martyr to my misery. I hate martyrs.

I must have finally dozed because the next thing I knew, Pop's voice was booming through the house. "Does Katy need an attorney present?"

"Why does he always have to shout when he's on his cell?" I grumbled, jerking the comforter over my head. And then thought, *Oh crap. Why is he asking if I need an attorney? Did Chad die?*

Now fully coherent, I seized the crutch propped against the wall by the daybed and hobbled to the living room at the other end of the house. "Pop! Did Chad die?"

"Hold on, Ben," he said. "No, honey. Samantha called from the hospital a little while ago, and there's been no change."

Mom hollered from the kitchen. "Is that my sleepyhead girl?

About time you got up. Do you need a pain pill, or is that a stupid question?"

"Yes to both." The throbbing pain in my leg had me trembling and nauseated.

Pop saw my distress. "Ben, I have to go. See you later." He climbed out of his power recliner and held my arm. "Let's get you into the recliner and elevate your leg before you fall on your face."

Getting me settled in the chair was brutal, but once he pushed the button to raise my legs, I felt some relief.

Mom brought me water and a pill. "Here ya go, sweetie." She finger-combed the hair out of my face. "Can you stomach a cup of coffee?"

I wiped a trickle of sweat from my brow. "Maybe I should go back to bed. I didn't sleep much last night."

"Not an option, Katydid." Pop gently draped a teal chenille throw over my lap. "The detectives are on the way to go over some things with you."

Mom was still hovering. "I'll get you a nice cup of tea. Easier on the tummy. Is Ben coming over, Kurt?"

"Yes. He thinks he should be here."

Not what I wanted to hear. "Am I in serious trouble, Pop?"

"I'm sure it's just a routine call." He smiled what he probably thought was a reassuring smile, but it sure looked forced to me.

Mom returned with a steaming mug. "Three teaspoons of sugar and milk. Just the way you like it. Be careful, it's hot."

I sipped the rejuvenating elixir and decided I might live.

The doorbell rang. "Omigod, Mom. I don't want to see anybody. I'm a total mess."

"This visitor won't mind how you look." She peeked through the sidelight. "Kurt, better grab her tea."

"Mom! Do not open the door."

"No can do." She turned the handle and was forced aside as Daisy barreled through, dragging Emily behind her. "Don't let her jump on Katy." Pop blocked Daisy from hurtling into my lap.

My girl quieted as she sensed my injury. She snuffled my thigh with little whimpers, while I gritted my teeth, then bathed my outstretched arm with sweet, sloppy kisses, and finally settled down beside my chair.

————

During my police "chat" (PC for "grilling"), I went through the scenario at Chad's house over and over. Why I went there. Why I went in the house. Why I thought he was dying. Even I thought my answers sounded bogus.

Ben's presence during the interview gave me a measure of reassurance. Who knows what trouble I might have talked my way into without him monitoring my answers.

Detective Murphy's parting shot was: "That's it for now, Katy. But as we sort through all of this, you may be asked down to the station for more questions."

I'm thinking that meant, "Don't leave town."

CHAPTER FORTY-SEVEN

TUESDAY · AUGUST 20
Posted by Katy McKenna

Yesterday

I was back in my cozy bungalow chilling on the couch, leg propped, and about to do a little online shopping when my phone buzzed on the tile counter in the kitchen.

"Want me to answer it?" yelled Emily.

"No." There was a reason the phone was on vibrate. I didn't want to talk to anyone.

"Too late." She entered the living room. "No, this isn't Katy. This is her sister, Emily. Hold on a sec and I'll get her." She was standing over me, holding out the phone. "It's Heather's mother."

"Hello, Judy." I glared at my sister. "Sorry I haven't called." Been busy recovering from a gunshot wound. Thanks a lot for not asking. "How's Heather doing?"

"Oh, not so good."

"Why? She didn't have another stroke, did she?"

"No, no. The thing is, she's not taking the news about Chad well. She's home now and wants to see you."

"Why?" I knew that sounded whiny, but I didn't want to see Heather. Or anyone for that matter.

"She wants to hear what happened. You know. When you found Chad. Can you blame her?"

"Hardly. But am I going to be brutally honest about everything? Like the part about him moving in with Lisa?"

"She knows about that. I had to tell her since it's on all the local news, including how you got shot. I'm so sorry, I should have asked how you're doing."

"Oh, I'm coming along."

"That's a relief," she said. "We've been so worried about you. I really don't want to bother you about this, but Heather needs to know if Chad was suffering when you found him. I hate to say it, but she still cares about him."

Mental sigh. "When do you want me over?"

"Oh no, you can't come here. Not with your injury. We'll come there if that's all right."

I thought it would be far harder on Heather coming to my house than me going there, so I fibbed a little. "You know, I was thinking I need to get out and get some fresh air, so this will give me the push I need. What time is good for you?"

———

"You poor thing," Heather said, patting the cushion. "Come sit by me."

I crutched my crocs to the love seat and eased myself down with her mother's help.

Heather pulled me in for a bear hug, not realizing how much it hurt my leg. "I'm so relieved you're all right."

"You should've let us come to your house," said Judy, setting my leg on an ottoman. "You look done in."

"I've been lying around for days. First at my folks' and now at home, and I needed a change."

"I just brewed a pot of coffee," said Judy. "Would you like a cup?"

"I would love it." My outing was already proving to be too much, too soon, and what I really needed was a double shot of espresso injected in my arm.

Judy called from the kitchen. "How do you take your coffee, Katy?"

"Half and half or milk, and three sugars."

"We don't have any sugar. Is agave okay?"

"Sure." *Meh.*

"And we don't have any dairy, so hemp milk okay?"

"Sure." *Next she'll say, "We don't have any real coffee, so is herbal coffee substitute okay?"*

Heather flashed me a sympathetic smile, as if she'd read my mind. "I talked to the doctor this morning. Chad's been taken off the respirator."

Of course, my first thought was: *Oh my God. They took him off to let him die.*

She interrupted my doomsday thoughts. "Evidently he is improving and breathing well on his own."

"But we are in agreement that he is not welcome back in your life. Right?" said Judy. She handed me a mug of coffee and set a plate of glazed almond-topped cookies on the coffee table. She must have caught my suspicious glance at them, because she said, "I hope you aren't gluten-intolerant."

"Nope. I love my gluten. In fact, if my doctor ever tells me to quit eating it, I'll change doctors." I grabbed one, hoping it would help me wash down the stuff in the mug.

"Don't worry, Mom, I'm done with Chad. I just meant it's good news for Katy since the police have been questioning her. They talked to me, too, did you know that?"

"You're kidding," I said. "They suspect you had something to do with what happened to him? That's absurd."

She twirled one of her long braids. "Yeah, but I had a pretty good alibi, so I think I'm off the list of suspects. But you know the spouse is always the first person they suspect."

"Or the ex-spouse, in this case."

Heather waited until I'd devoured another tasty cookie before saying, "Please tell me everything that happened. I know I said I'm done with Chad, and I mean it, but in spite of everything, I still love him and I need to know."

It was tough, but I told her everything while her big blue eyes shimmered with tears.

———

I left on an agave high, toting a bag of cookies that I had no intention of sharing with Emily. My ringer had been off while visiting Heather, so I took a quick peek to see if I'd missed anything. Sure wish I hadn't.

There were two recent calls from the Santa Lucia Police Department. I listened to the latest voice mail, certain I was going to toss my cookies all over Veronica's worn leather seats.

"This is Detective Kailyn Murphy with the Santa Lucia Police Department. I would like you to call me as soon as you hear this message."

———

Outside the police station entrance, I called the folks and gave them a heads-up in case I was truly in trouble, then did one of the hardest things I have ever done. I went inside.

At the counter, I identified myself and asked for the detective. The clerk told me to wait in the reception area. A few minutes later, Detective Murphy appeared. She shook my hand and thanked me for coming in so promptly. All very warm and friendly, like nothing was up.

I, on the other hand, was shaking like it was thirty below. "Am I in trouble?"

"No, no. We just want to ask you a few more questions. Is now a good time?"

No! Never is a good time. I wanna go home. I want my mommy. But I was supposed to say yes, so I said, "Yes."

She escorted into a room furnished with a long, battered table shoved flush against a blank puke-green wall. A one-way mirror covered most of the opposite wall, and there were two wall-mounted video cameras. Murphy motioned me to take a seat in a metal folding chair facing away from the back wall at the end of the table. The chair was set about a foot away from the wall behind me, making me feel cornered. I set my orange purse on the table and propped my bad leg on one of the other two chairs, shifting the weight off my sore thigh with a lot of dramatic groans.

Detective Murphy didn't looked impressed with my theatrics but had the decency to ask, "How's the leg doing?"

"I'll live." Wince. Groan.

"Would you like a water?"

I would like a big, tall glass of vodka, and I don't even like vodka. "Water would be good. Thank you."

Murphy left the room and I gazed at the mirror, wondering who was looking at me looking at them. After a few minutes passed, it dawned on me that they might be gauging my behavior. Did I look guilty? Heck, who wouldn't look guilty under the circumstance?

I rummaged in my purse and extracted my ibuprofen bottle and made a big show of dumping four in my hand. Maybe they would feel sorry for me and bring my water.

A minute later, Murphy, her sidekick, Mike Devlin, and Lieutenant Joann Yee entered. I know Joann from when I solved the Belinda Moore cold case back in April.

"Thank you for coming in." Joann tossed her sleek, black hair over her shoulders. "I'm sorry we had to call you in, Katy, but we have some problems with this case and need your help."

"I'll do whatever I can." *Oh thank goodness. They just want my help.*

Murphy handed me a bottle of water and just as I was about to swallow the pills, I remembered how they always get your DNA off the water bottle in the crime shows. It shouldn't have mattered since I was innocent of any wrongdoing, but I didn't trust any of them, so I set the bottle down.

"Not taking your pills?" asked Murphy.

"I just realized it's too soon since the last ones, so I better wait. Even though I'm in a lot of pain."

"I can't stay." Joann eased out the door. "Duty calls. But you're in good hands here. We'll do this as quick as possible so you can get home."

Detective Murphy tossed a thick red binder on the table, pulled out the remaining chair and sat facing me. Devlin did his usual fade into the background thing. Probably because I had my leg on his chair. Too bad.

It was all so different from the cop shows. Wasn't I supposed to be sitting on one side of the table and them on the other, instead of jammed against the wall? I would have preferred to have that barrier between us rather than having this cop practically breathing in my face.

Murphy opened the binder and flipped back and forth through pages I couldn't see, stopping to jot down a note here and there, while Devlin inspected his nails.

Finally she spoke. "We have a problem, Katy." She glanced back at the binder, tapping the page with her pen.

Those almond cookies crept up my throat and I needed a barf bag bad. "You two are really scaring me. Did Chad die?"

She leisurely shook her head, taking her sweet time to answer. "But he could have. The bullet just…," she glanced at the page again, "…missed his heart. Nonetheless it's going to take a while for that hole in his lung to heal."

"You do realize that was an accident. Lisa didn't mean to shoot him." I couldn't believe I was actually defending that vile woman. But it was true. She'd been pointing the gun at me.

"That's not our biggest problem right now," said Murphy, still smiling, her big brown doe eyes exuding reassuring compassion. The gun strapped to her waist, not so much.

Now they were both grinning at me like Cheshire cats. I felt myself shrinking as their eyes drilled into me, compelling me to ask, "Oh? What is?"

Devlin leaned against a wall, nonchalant, arms crossed. "The syringe."

The detective uncrossed her slim legs, edged her chair closer to me and leaned in. "Yeah. Your husband…"

"*Ex*-husband."

She sat back, shrugging a "whatever." "As you know, your *ex*-husband was injected with a lethal dose of potassium chloride."

I nodded slowly, wondering where this was leading. Then it hit me. Murphy had said lethal. "I thought you said he didn't die."

Murphy waved her hands in the air, blowing me off. "I stand corrected. Potentially lethal dose." She leaned forward again. "It's amazing he didn't die."

"So far," said Devlin. He pushed away from the wall and left the room.

"And then when your *ex*-husband didn't die, your friend Lisa…," said Murphy.

"She is not my friend." I shook my head so hard, it's amazing my neck didn't snap.

Another annoying "whatever" shrug. Detective Murphy reminded me of all those snotty, super popular girls back in high school that wouldn't give me the time of day.

"Shot him," she finished, crossing her arms over her perky cleavage.

Devlin returned bearing a large manila envelope and handed it to Murphy. She extracted a Ziploc bag containing a syringe and slid it down the table toward me. "Recognize this?"

What is going on here? I had been led to believe I was there to help with the investigation, but this was feeling more and more like I was being accused.

"Do I need an attorney?" I squeaked. "Should I call Ben?"

"Are you guilty?" asked Murphy.

There's a long list of laws I'm guilty of breaking: parking tickets, illegal U-turns, speeding, driving while under the influence of two glasses of wine, but not attempted murder. "No."

"Then no worries, huh?"

I glanced over at the one-way mirror, wondering if my friends Chief Yaeger and the lieutenant were watching on the other side. *Angela and Joann have to know I'm not capable of murder.*

Then Jeremy Baylor's body flashed in my head. I'd been the one who called the cops then, too. After letting myself in the house. Uninvited. Just like at Lisa's house. But Jeremy hadn't been murdered. He'd died of a toxic mix of alcohol, cocaine, and oxycodone. Then a shiver trickled down my spine. Or had he? A dribble of sweat rolled down my cheek. *Oh, crap. I am so screwed.*

"You all right?" Devlin loosened his tie and undid his shirt's top buttons, revealing a spray of curly, black chest hair and a gold cross. "Getting a little hot in here. Maybe you should drink your water."

He was right. It was getting hot in the windowless, claustrophobic room, but I wasn't touching the water. "Do I get a phone call?"

"Why? You haven't been arrested." Murphy advanced her chair toward me again. We were now so close that her stylish shoes were nibbling at my right foot's old green croc.

That was it. I've watched enough *Law and Order* to know how this was going down. "Either arrest me or I'm leaving."

Detective Devlin stepped forward, flashing a pair of cuffs. "Katy McKenna. You have the right to remain silent…"

———

It was too late in the day for my bail to be set, so guess where I slept last night? Yup. Jail. The hoosegow. The clink. The pokey. The big house. I'm innocent, but I suppose that's what all the jail-birds sing.

Like my cellmate, Ms. Dee Lite, a self-proclaimed victim of police entrapment. "Girl, I was profiled."

Right. Doesn't everyone wear thigh-high scarlet stiletto boots with skin-tight micro-minis and bustiers while waiting on a corner trying to catch a ride to their dear old granny's house?

Dee also swore he was a woman, but he wasn't fooling me. His makeup was too perfect, plus there's no hiding a five o'clock shadow against milky-white skin. On the plus side, his skin was flawless and he gave me some great beauty tips. I can't wait to try the mascara he told me about, because, "Girl, he had lashes to die for."

———

Today

Mom and Pop busted me out of the slammer shortly before noon and we went straight to a luncheon meet up with Ben. I hadn't eaten since the day before and was starving, so despite my jangled nerves, I wolfed down a veggie cheeseburger and a pile of sweet potato fries, while Ben attempted to make light of my impending doom.

"The cops are on a fishing expedition." He wiped his wire rims with a napkin. "If they had something solid on you, we wouldn't be sitting here now. And the judge released you on your own recognizance, because she knows the police don't have a solid case." He put on his glasses and looked at me in earnest. "So who would want Chad dead?"

"That's easy," I garbled through a mouth full of fries. "Me for one."

"And me." Pop patted my hand. "He hurt both our girls."

"Add me to the list," said Mom. "And he continues to harass Katy."

"Actually he had stopped before all this happened," I said. "I think he really cares about Lisa. Go figure."

"Maybe so," said Mom. "But you can still add me to the list of suspects. And Ruby, too."

Pop gave me a rueful look. "I know you don't want me to say this, but if anyone had a motive, it would be his wife."

I dropped my burger in the basket, shaking my head. "No way. Besides, she's not strong enough. She just had a baby and a stroke."

"What about her mother?" asked Mom. "With everything he's done to her daughter, what mother wouldn't want to protect her child?"

I had already briefly considered Judy as a suspect. "I don't think so. She just had surgery, so I doubt she could have done it."

I popped a couple ibuprofens in my mouth and drained my iced tea. "The big problem is that the only fingerprints on the syringe are mine and Lisa's. I know I didn't do it, and I'm pretty sure it wasn't Lisa. The only people who know what happened in that bedroom are Chad and the person, or persons, who did it. And Chad's not talking."

CHAPTER FORTY-EIGHT

WEDNESDAY · AUGUST 21
Posted by Katy McKenna

Late this morning, I had an appointment at the medical center next door to the hospital. My doctor said the wound is healing nicely and traded out my crutch for a cane. On the way to my car a tantalizing aroma caught my nose, leading me to Chad's favorite food truck parked around the corner.

I've read how a person's long forgotten memories can be triggered by an aroma. It's true because every time I catch a whiff of Old Spice, I remember my grandpa and it always gives me the warm and fuzzies. So I thought maybe the smell of Chad's favorite food could weave its way into the deep, dark crevices of his comatose little pea-brain and wake him up. It was worth a try.

I ordered his favorite, a green chile chicken empanada, and a spinach, mushroom, and goat cheese empanada for me. Since Chad wouldn't know the difference whether his food was hot or not, I plunked down on a bench under an olive tree and devoured mine.

———

"I have a big surprise for you," I merrily singsonged, setting the greasy white bag on Chad's hospital tray table. "Yummmm. Green chile chicken empanada from the Ensenada Empanada food truck. Your favorite."

I unwrapped the pastry, resisting the urge to take a chomp, and swished it under his nose. "Remember that smell, Chad? Mmmm. Doesn't it make you want to wake up and eat it?"

I wondered what would happen if I slipped a teeny-tiny little morsel into his mouth. Not enough that it could choke him, but just enough to tease his taste buds. Then we'd be working on two of the five senses.

I washed up, then broke the empanada in half, and dug my finger inside to get a dollop of the green chile goo. I peeped around the curtain to make sure the coast was clear before proceeding. "Okay, Chad. Open up."

Fighting back the chili-willies, I parted his slack lips and slithered my finger inside, depositing the green glob on his tongue. "If anyone comes in here now, this will be a little hard to explain."

After scrubbing the Chad-saliva off my finger in the sink, I again waved the food under his nose, cooing, "Mmmm. Yummy to your tummy. Chad wants to wake up now and eat his empanada, doesn't he?"

Chad did not, and then I had another brilliant idea. "Perhaps you'd like a little dinner music, huh?" I scrolled through iTunes on my phone and downloaded his favorite song. "Taste, smell, hearing. Three out of five senses ought to do something."

The song loaded. "Okay, Chad. Here's my last ditch effort. Your all-time most favorite song. "Who Let the Dogs Out?" Remember how you sang it every morning in the shower?"

I turned up the volume and prayed I wouldn't get kicked out. As the song played, I continued the aromatherapy until the final "woof."

"Dammit, Chad. If you don't wake up, I could wind up in prison for attempting to murder you. And we both know it wasn't me, but you're the only one who can set the record straight." I watched his face for a few more minutes, then shoved the phone into my purse. "I give up. You win. I'm outta here."

Halfway to the door, he whispered, "Woof."

CHAPTER FORTY-NINE

THURSDAY · AUGUST 22
Posted by Katy McKenna

Private Post

Mom asked me to join her for lunch at Suzy Q's today. From the tone in her voice, I knew she was upset, and I figured it had to be about Uncle Ted.

I found her sitting outside on the patio in the shade of an arbor cloaked in crimson bougainvillea and grapevines. I set my cane against the table, and she helped me get settled in a rattan chair opposite her.

I noted her forlorn expression, so I decided to lead off with a hair compliment. "I love the new golden highlights in your hair, Mom. Really flattering."

Her posture straightened a tad as she ran her fingers through her chin-length brown bob. "Thank you, honey. I think Jeri did an excellent job." She tasted her iced tea, then added two packets of raw sugar. "I know I shouldn't burden you with this, not with everything else going on in your life, but you're the only one I can really talk to about this. Your father gets too upset."

"Is it about Uncle Ted?"

Mom nodded, pulling an envelope from her handbag. "He sent me a letter." She handed it to me. "Here. You read it."

My Dear Marybeth,

I know I am probably the last person you want to hear from. What I did to you was truly unforgivable, I know, but in my defense, I am a sick man. I suffer from a cerebral dysfunction.

This frontotemporal disorder creates an obsessive-compulsive behavior that I wasn't able to control. Much like pathological gambling or kleptomania. So you see, I was as much a victim as those I preyed upon.

I know I cannot undo what is done, but I hope to put this painful chapter in my life to rest. Therapy and finding God has given me purity of heart. I'm a harmless old man now who just wants to live out his days in peace, worshipping the Lord, surrounded by family.

Presently I am on house arrest, but in a few months I will be allowed to travel. At that time I would like to come and reconnect with my sister and to ask for your absolution for the distress I caused you so long ago.

Marybeth, forgiveness is divine. God has forgiven me. Now will you?

Fondly,
Uncle Ted

I read the letter twice, feeling Mom's eyes burning a hole through the back of it. "Mom. I don't know what to say. Tell me how you feel about this?"

"He's acting like it's not his fault. Like being a pedophile is no worse than having a gambling addiction. Like he's a born-again Christian in AA, for God's sake." She snatched the letter. "*I'm a harmless old man now.*' Harmless? Ha! He's a serial pedophile in his early seventies. My God! How could he still have his freedom?" She slapped her forehead. "Oh, that's right. I forgot. God has forgiven him and I guess the system has, too. Well, I haven't. And I never will." She crammed the letter into her purse and gulped her tea down. "If I didn't have to do a hair weave this afternoon, this would be wine."

Mom dragged the letter out again and smoothed it on the table. "'*Forgiveness is divine. God has forgiven me.*' I know for a fact he was not a religious man, Katy, but evidently now he's found religion and he's all holier than thou. How convenient. Defile little girls and then when you finally get caught, claim you've found God and all is forgiven. Makes me want to kill him."

There was a chorus of throat clearings around us and several sharp glances pointed our way.

Mom met their disapproving looks with a harsh glare. "Well, excuse me for not being a fan of child molesters." She returned her attention to me, dropping her voice to a whisper. "You know what, Katy? I will have a glass of wine." She picked up her phone. "I'm texting Jeri. She had a cancellation, so she can take my appointment."

I caught the waiter's eye and beckoned him over. "You ready to order?" He smiled anxiously. Apparently he'd heard Mom's rant.

I hadn't even glanced at the menu, and I doubted Mom was hungry. "How about two glasses of the chardonnay, and when you get back, we'll order."

He departed and Mom said, "I'll behave now. But, Katy. What am I going to do?"

"You are going to give me the letter and let me deal with it."

"Sweetheart, I can't expose you to that monster."

"Mom, I'm pushing thirty-two, so not really his type. It's better I do this than you or Pop. Pop would probably kill him. We already have enough legal problems in the family without Ben having to defend both Pop and me."

"What do you plan to do?" She reached across the table, clutching my hand. "I do not want you talking to him. Please."

"No worries there. I will simply write to him and make it very clear he is never to contact you again."

"What about Mom?"

"Her, too. And Aunt Edith and Emily. He is to leave all of us alone or…" I paused, thinking of what "or" could be. "Or we'll tell his parole officer that he's harassing you and you're one of his victims."

Mom looked sick at that idea. "Then Mom would find out."

"No matter what, you have to quit putting it off and tell her." I sipped my water, wishing the waiter would hurry up with the wine. "Ruby has to hear this from you." I tapped the letter. "Not him. Besides, I don't know how much longer I can stall her from searching for Uncle Ted online."

———

After lunch, I went home to compose my letter. I was feeling protective and enraged that this scum would have the audacity to contact my mother.

Several drafts later, I finished the letter and then set it aside to simmer. I've learned never to send the first draft of an angry missive, whether by e-mail, snail mail, or text. If I wait a day or two, often whatever it was I was all worked up about usually turns out to be no big deal. I speak from bitter, humiliating experience.

Of course, this was different. I would be just as furious no matter how long I waited to send it, but I wanted to make sure my letter was worded just right.

Out of curiosity, I googled his house and virtually stood on his sidewalk, staring at the glossy red front door of his midcentury tan rancher, willing him to magically step out on the porch so I could blow him away with a flick of my mouse.

I reread my letter, made a few changes, and set it back on simmer.

CHAPTER FIFTY

FRIDAY • AUGUST 23
Posted by Katy McKenna

Sam called this afternoon with a Chad update. "He's asking for you, Katy."

My first thoughts were, *Yippee! He's alert and talking. He'll clear my name.*

Sam interrupted my cerebral happy dance. "There's just one tiny little hiccup."

I stopped dancing. "What?"

———

Not knowing what kind of minefield I was about to step into, I paused in the hospital room doorway to assess the situation. Sam stood at the end of Chad's bed while his attending nurse did his routine duties. Blood pressure, pulse, temp.

I leaned into the room. "Psst. Sam."

She stepped over to me. "Before you see him, Dr. Russo wants a word. Wait at the nurse's desk and I'll have him paged."

A few minutes later, I instantly aged ten years as the doctor shook my hand. He must have been old enough to be a doctor, but he looked like he was still in middle school.

"Right now, Mr. Bridges's mental state is very delicate," he said.

I forced myself to pay attention while I inspected his shiny cheeks for a hint of stubble.

"He cannot be aroused or provoked in any manner."

I certainly have no plans to arouse him, so no worries.

"In other words," Dr. Russo continued, "agree with whatever he says. He's confused at the moment, that's to be expected. I'm sure that in a few days, he'll be back on track."

———

"Chad?" I apprehensively approached his bed. "How're you doing?"

His face lit with the goofy grin I once adored. "There's my darling wife. Where've you been?" He held out his hand, and I limped around to his side and reluctantly took it. "Why are you using a cane?"

"It's nothing. Just had a little accident. I'll be fine."

Sam stood up from the bedside chair. "Katy, you should sit down and rest your leg."

"Sam, please don't leave."

"Relax. Not going anywhere."

Chad held his arms outstretched. "Before you sit, my love, can you give your hubby a hug?"

Sam took the cane and I leaned in for the embrace.

"And a kiss?"

I flicked a "help-me" glance at Sam and she bobbed her head, meaning "do it."

I brushed his chapped lips. "Baby, you can do better than that." He hauled me in, smooshing my face against his, and slithered his tongue into my mouth.

I should win an Academy Award for that performance. Not only did I kiss him, but I didn't throw up in his mouth. "Chad, your injury. You need to be careful." More stellar acting. "There will be plenty of time for that later when you're completely healed."

He smiled, shaking his head. "I must be the luckiest man on earth. I've survived a bullet, a coma, and I have you."

What about being poisoned? I assumed no one had told him, so I kept my mouth shut and plastered a sunny grin on my face. "Right back at ya, Chad."

"Sweetie?" He shifted in bed, wincing. "Could you fluff my pillows?"

Sam stepped in. "Let me do that for you."

"No, I want Katy to do it. She knows how I like it."

Oh, good grief. I leaned over his head, adjusting the pillows, and felt his hand cup my boob.

"Woof," he whispered in my ear.

That was it. Time to tell him what's what. "Chad, there's some things I think you should know."

Samantha tapped my shoulder. "We'll be right back, Chad." She grabbed my arm and wrestled me out to the hall. "You cannot tell him. It's too soon. Right now he's very fragile, so we can't have him getting upset. Chances are by tomorrow his memory will've returned."

"But Sam. What if it doesn't? Are you going to tell me we have to live together as man and wife so I don't upset him? Because that is not happening."

Samantha managed to keep a straight face, but her pressed lips were quivering.

"This isn't funny, Sam."

"Oh, come on. You have to admit, it kind of is."

We returned to the room, and Samantha made a big fuss about Chad needing his rest. "Time to scoot, Katy."

"Wait," he said. "What were you going to tell me, Katy?"

"That. You." Sam cleared her throat. "Need to rest. That's all."
I pecked his cheek and Sam handed me the cane. "Doctor's
orders."

"Will I see you later?"

"Chad, it's getting late," said Sam. "The dinner cart will be
coming around soon." Her tone was akin to the one she uses with
little Casey. "Hey, are you up for a little gelatin?"

He hates gelatin. He always called it "flu food."

"Ooo," said Chad, rubbing his hands together. "That's sounds
good. I hope it's cherry."

I was actually considering staying a while longer to watch him
eat his gelatin, when Lisa shrieked from the doorway, "What the
hell're you doing here?"

"Lisa!" I held up my hands to halt her charge into the room.
"We need to talk. But not here. There's something you need to
know.

She advanced on me, purple acrylic claws flashing. "Out of my
way, bitch."

Sam blocked her, pushing into Lisa's personal space. "Oh no,
you don't. This is a hospital, and if you can't behave, you're
leaving."

Lisa jutted her chin, virtually spitting in Sam's face. "This is a
public facility and you can't make me."

"This is not a public facility, and yeah, I can."

"Katy," whimpered Chad, clutching his blanket. "Who is that
mean lady?"

I moved to the head of his bed and murmured, "It's okay. She's
leaving."

"Like hell I am." Lisa elbowed Sam in the stomach, crashing
her into the wardrobe cupboard. "Baby, it's me. Your fiancée."

Chad gawked at her like she'd just landed from Mars. "You're
crazy. I don't even know you and besides, I'm already married." He
pointed at me, now hiding behind his IV drip pole. "To her. She's
my wife."

That shut Lisa up as she rubbernecked us, trying to grasp the situation. She didn't notice Sam dash out of the room.

"Lisa," I said from my hiding spot. "If you will go out in the hall with me, I can explain everything."

My voice reanimated her and just as she stepped toward me, a Marine Corps-wannabe security guard entered the fray. "You'll need to come with me, miss." He patted the baton hanging from his belt like it was a loaded Glock and reached for Lisa's arm.

She stepped away from his grasp and pointed at me. "I'm not going unless she goes too."

Chad burst into tears. "Please don't make Katy leave." His bristly lower lip quivered. "I'm scared."

Feeling like I was protecting a little boy, I stepped away from the pole and patted his head. "It's okay. I won't leave you."

He gazed at me, his teary eyes as big as one of those little waifs in the Keane paintings. "Promise?"

Lisa looked like she was choking on a mouthful of nails, and I couldn't help but feel a tiny bit sorry for her. But only a teeny-tiny bit.

"Chad. What's wrong with you?" she asked, smearing a mascaraed tear across her cheek. "Why are you acting this way? I'm your fiancée. The love of your life. Your soulmate."

I should have restrained my scornful snort, but it just popped out of me. Kind of like a burp or a fart you don't know is coming until it erupts.

Lisa's gaze swung to me, hands clenched and glassy-eyed like a cat about to pounce on its prey.

"Let's go, lady," said the guard.

"All right. I'm going. But just one thing first." Her balled fist shot out, lightning fast, and sucker-punched me in the eye, sending me sprawling across Chad's body.

"That's it, lady!" The guard whipped out handcuffs and dragged Lisa away from me.

Sam hauled me off Chad (now blubbering inconsolably) to a

sitting position and inspected my eye. "You're going to have a nasty shiner. I'll get you an ice pack."

From the doorway, the security officer said, "Do you want to press charges?"

With one hand clapped over my broken eye, I peeked at Lisa, now cuffed, her body tensed like she'd tear me apart given the chance. "I don't know. Just get her out of here."

As he escorted Lisa down the hall, she screamed, "You stay away from my fiancé, or I will fucking kill you."

"So that's Lisa," said Sam. "Nice girl."

The dinner cart clattered into the room, pushed by a perky senior volunteer. "Who wants gelatin?"

CHAPTER FIFTY-ONE

SATURDAY · AUGUST 24
Posted by Katy McKenna

Private Post

Today should have been my turn to host the book club, but with my injuries I was relieved from duty, so we gathered at Samantha's. The minute I entered the house, I was the center of attention.

"OMG. You poor, poor thing," said Justin, rushing to me all dithery. "First you get shot and now a black eye?"

"Aunt *Kaaaateee!*" Casey tore into the room making a beeline for me.

I braced myself for the attack, but Sam intercepted him before he lunged. "Auntie Katy has some owies and can't pick you up, Casey."

The little guy looked at me and his big blue eyes got bigger. "Wow. What happened to your eye? Did a bad guy punch you out?"

"You could say that." I laughed and found out that laughing hurt my sore eye.

"Can I touch it?"

"Sure, if you're very gentle, but I can't bend down, so Mama will have to pick you up."

Sam hoisted him to her hip, and he cautiously touched my eye. "Wow. That's so cool. I bet you beat the bad guy up, right?"

Before I could answer, I caught Sam's *we don't condone violence* look. "No, sweetie. I called the police and the bad guy went to jail."

"Okay, mister. Time to go watch your movie and let the grown-ups have their meeting." Sam set Casey down and swatted his tush. "Scoot!"

As soon as he was out of earshot, Justin said, "Now dish, girl. What happened?"

I smiled mysteriously. "All will be revealed after I get a plate of food."

———

Settling in the recliner in Sam's spacious kid-cluttered living room with a plate piled with scrumptious eats on my lap, I brought every-one, minus absentees Heather and Debra, up to date on my latest bizarre misadventures.

"Wow," said Melanie. "Your life is like one big never-ending soap opera. Only worse. You can't make this stuff up."

"Are the police still after you about Chad being injected with potassium chloride?" asked Nora, delicately nibbling a salmon-and-cucumber canapé.

"I don't know. But my grandma's boyfriend is a big time defense lawyer, and he told me not to worry. And since I don't have access to a drug like that, their case against me is pretty flimsy." I glanced around the group, giving them the evil black eye. "But all of you do."

"Hello. I'm a nurse anesthetist," said Justin, waving his hand. "Easy-peasy."

"It's true," said Melanie. "I'm a hospice nurse, so while I do have access to potassium chloride, it's certainly not a drug I would ever use. It causes severe heart arrhythmias and often leads to sudden cardiac death."

Chloe crossed her tanned arms. "Well, I for one, as a patient rep, do not have access to any drugs."

"So what you're saying, Melanie," I said, "is that all of you…"

Chloe cleared her throat.

"Except Chloe, could be guilty. The only other members with no access to potassium chloride, or any other drugs other than over-the-counter, are Heather and me, and yet I seem to be the number one suspect."

"Don't forget Debra," said Sam. "She could have done it too. She certainly has the means."

I thought a moment. "Trouble is, none of you have a motive. So that narrows it down to me, Heather, her mother, and his girl-friend, Lisa, although she really has nothing to gain by his death. And now that I think about it, she was really surprised to see him tied to the bed. She actually thought we were having a kinky affair." I shook my head, hating the fact that I was once again, standing up for that nasty woman. "So now we're down to Heather, her mother, and me."

"The guy's a big phony loser," Sam said. "So we really don't know how many people he's screwed, you know."

"That's true. In fact, now that I think about it, there was a man at the country club who made it very clear to me that Chad is not a popular guy there. Even asked me if the jackass owes me money." I paused for a quick sip of Merlot. "And you should see Chad's house. No way could he afford a house like that on what the book-store makes. Plus, he drives a new Lexus SUV."

"Maybe he owes money to a loan shark," said Chris. "They don't like it when they don't get their money. A few years ago, my cousin's house was burned down when he couldn't make his payments. And then his dog was poisoned. A cute little beagle. Who does that?"

"This is starting to sound like an Agatha Christie novel," Chloe said. "Maybe we should be a murder-mystery club."

"Ooo. Good idea, honey bunny." Justin sat up straight, clearly excited by the idea. "We could be amateur sleuths and solve crimes and—"

Chloe rolled her eyes. "I was just kidding, you big knucklehead."

"I knew that." He slumped back in his chair.

I actually liked the idea, thinking it would be way more fun than talking about Jane Austen, but kept my mouth shut. And yes I know, we never talk about her, or her books.

"Anybody know how Debra is doing?" asked Sam.

"I saw her at the hospital a couple of days ago, and she looked absolutely awful," I said.

Nora leaned in, dropping her voice. "You all know she's my closest friend and in the past we've always shared everything, but I think she's keeping a big secret. I'm terribly worried about her."

"Does she have any family?" asked Melanie.

"She has an elderly aunt in Florida, but she has Alzheimer's now and has no clue who Debra is. Bloody awful disease."

"I agree with you, Nora, about Debra," said Sam. "Whatever is going on with her has got to be a lot more serious than just peri-menopause and allergies. The weight loss, the constant cough. It could be any number of things. But she's a doctor, so I have to assume she knows what she's doing."

"This is off the subject," I said, "but since you all know about my uncle, I want to read a letter he sent to my mother. And then I want your opinion on the response letter I wrote." I held out my wineglass and Chris refilled it. I swallowed a swig, then read my uncle's letter.

When I finished, Chris said, "What a bunch of bullshit."

"Your poor mother." Justin reached for Chloe's hand. "I do not want to get into this, but I had a funny uncle too."

We all made conciliatory groans of commiseration.

"It's okay, guys. Years of therapy helped, but the one thing that truly gave me peace was when one of his other victims murdered him. It was like the weight of the world had been lifted from my shoulders. Am I awful?"

Chloe hugged him. "No, honey bun. You're human."

He fanned away his threatening tears. "Enough about me. Let's hear your letter, Katy."

I cleared my throat, feeling timid. "First off, what I want from you guys is your honest opinion. I want my letter to drive home in no uncertain terms that there is no hope of forgiveness, reconciliation, nothing." I took a breath. "Okay, here goes."

To Ted Peckham:

I am Marybeth Melby's daughter, and I am writing to you on her behalf. This will be the only communication you will receive.

Leave my mother alone. She doesn't want to see you or hear from you. You do not deserve her forgiveness, and you will never have it. You are not to contact her. You are also never to contact your sisters or my sister. If you do we will report you to your probation officer. We will inform him that my mother was one of your victims, and you are harassing her.

Katy McKenna

"I like that it's to the point." Nora donned her specs and took the letter. "You kept your feelings out of it and said what you had to say. He should get the message."

"You didn't see the first draft. That was three pages long. When I read it later, I realized it was a crazy rant. You know, like, *'You better watch your back, you big pile of steaming shit, because I'm coming for you and you are a dead man.'* Then I realized that probably wasn't a good idea. You know, in case I ever do decide to finish him off. Don't want my written confession sitting in his house."

"If it were my mom, he'd be on ice already," said Chris. "I got a long-range rifle with night vision, and the bastard would never know what hit him. Just sayin'."

CHAPTER FIFTY-TWO

SUNDAY • AUGUST 25
Posted by Katy McKenna

My weirdo was-band called at the crack of dawn this morning, wanting to know when I'd be coming over.

"I'm not sure if I can get there today." I yawned, rubbing my crusty eyes as I leaned over to check the time.

"Why not?" he whined. "I miss you."

"Because." I couldn't tell him the truth, so what could I say? "Because I need to look for a job, that's why."

"What are you talking about? We have the bookstore. Why would you need to look for a job?"

Oops. "Uh, well. You know. Um. I thought it would be good if I brought in some extra income to help cover your medical expenses."

"That's why I love you so much. Always thinking ahead. Now get your sweet ass out of bed and come snuggle your lonely hubby."

We said good-bye, and I rolled over and snuggled Daisy instead, who groaned with sweet, uncomplicated doggy love.

"One more day, Daisy. That's all I'm giving him and then the hell with how upset he gets. He never worried about how much he upset me."

Daisy sealed my promise with a big lick on my cheek.

———

I found Lisa sitting on Chad's bed when I dragged myself into his room a little after ten a.m. My first thought was: *Yay! He's got his memory back*. Then I saw his mottled face and red-rimmed eyes.

"Is it true, Katy? What this woman is telling me?"

I leaned on my cane at the end of his bed, avoiding Lisa's haughty glower. "What exactly did she tell you?"

"I told him the truth," she sneered. "Somebody had to."

Chad raised the head of his bed to a sitting position. "She said that she's my fiancée and you and I are—"

"Divorced." Lisa's eyes challenged me to argue the truth.

Chad looked at me with pleading eyes. "Tell me I didn't leave you for this," he said, waving his hand at her, "th-this—"

"Bunny boiler?" I figured there was no point pussyfooting, so I gave it to Chad with both barrels. "Actually, you didn't leave me for her."

"Oh thank God." Relief flooded his pathetic face.

"You left me for a twenty-two-year-old named Heather. Your personal trainer at the time."

"What are you talking about?"

I held up my hand. "Not done yet. You had cancer."

"I had cancer?"

I moved to the side of his bed, opposite Lisa. "Yup. Testicular."

His hand dove under the covers, presumably to do a self-inspection. I guessed that with the catheter still in place, he hadn't noticed his loss.

His face turned a lighter shade of pale at his discovery. I was afraid he might vomit, so I took the plastic kidney-shaped dish from his bedside table and set it on his lap.

"I nursed you through the cancer, and then you got a trainer to get back in shape, and that's when you dumped me."

"I couldn't have. I love you."

"You don't love her, you love me!" Lisa yanked his hand from under the covers and clasped it to one of her big knockers. "And I don't care if your sack is half full."

Chad looked horror-struck, jerking his hand away. "I never could love—"

"Still not done," I continued, like a train wreck in slow motion. "You got Heather, the trainer, pregnant, then divorced me and married her."

"That's not true!" said Lisa. "She was faking it so Chad would have to marry her."

I laughed at her. "Yeah, right. That's what he told you. Now I'm telling you the truth." I returned my gaze to Chad. "Anyway, Heather lost that baby and then got pregnant again. With triplets. Then you started harassing me with texts, phone calls, thinking you could win me back. As if. Somewhere in there, you started screwing around with…" I tipped my head toward Lisa. "…*her*. Then Heather went into labor, lost two babies, and had a stroke. And then you moved in"—I pointed at his fiancée—"with *her*. By the way, you have a baby boy. Noah."

Chad looked stunned. "I can't be that awful."

"Heather is a sweet girl who really loved you." I paused. "I guess you could say that about me too." I glanced at Lisa. "Her? Not so much. And she's the one who shot you. She may also have been the one who shot you full of potassium chloride." I was pretty sure she hadn't, but I knew it would really piss her off. "It's amazing you survived."

Lisa stood, fists clenched, looking like she wanted to give me a matching shiner. "For all we know, it could have been you."

Chad's eyes darted between us. "What're you talking about?"

Lisa moved to the bedside chair, hugging her big rhinestone bedazzled purse to her chest. "Don't listen to her, Chad. She's lying."

I set my cane on the tray table and sat on the bed, my hands in my lap, out of Chad's reach. "I know that's a lot to take in all at once, Chad. And to be honest, she shot you by accident. The gun was actually aimed at me."

"You got shot, too? Is that why you're limping?"

"Yup."

Lisa picked at a plastic ruby on her purse. "It was an accident, and you know it."

I pinned her with a righteous glare. "You shoved the gun in my face. I thought you were going to kill me."

Lisa dropped her handbag on the floor and reached out to Chad. "I was only trying to protect you. You have to believe me."

"Well, I got a big hole in my leg and could have bled to death, thanks to you. And you never even said you're sorry. And then you punched me in the eye. I could still press charges, you know."

"Sorry." She practically spat the word at me.

"Yeah, well, I guess we'll see how sorry you feel when I file a lawsuit." I turned back to Chad. "About the potassium chloride. Someone tied you to your bed and injected you with it. Not a good thing when you get too much. The police questioned both of us. But I didn't do it and though it *kills* me to say it, I really don't think she did either."

Lisa shook her head vehemently. "I didn't. I swear, Chad. I didn't. You are the love of my life."

Chad grappled for my hand like a scared six-year-old reaching for his mommy, but coldhearted me wouldn't give it up. "I don't know about this Heather person or a baby," he said, "but I believe you, Katy. I know you wouldn't lie to me."

"Chad, you have to try very, very hard to remember what happened. Even though the police seem to have let us off the hook, you're the only one who can clear our names."

What I didn't say was: *Someone tried to kill you and I'm afraid they may try again.*

What I wondered was: *Why aren't the police protecting him? And come to think of it, why are Lisa and I even allowed to set foot in the hospital? I guess we really are off the hook.*

"Will you help me?" he asked.

I sighed, knowing I had no choice. "Yes."

———

Once back in the warm, comforting confines of good old Veronica, I had a good cry. That surprised me, because I thought I'd wrung out every last tear I had left for Chad, long ago.

CHAPTER FIFTY-THREE

MONDAY · AUGUST 26
Posted by Katy McKenna

Last night Emily made me watch the first episode of *The Walking Dead* and in return, she watched *Downton Abbey's* first episode. Neither of us won the other one over. We wound up staying up way too late drinking wine, snacking and arguing the merits of our polar-opposite shows. Good times.

I woke with a pounding head, stuffy nose, and cotton-mouth this morning. I need to remember to take an antihistamine before drinking wine. Or maybe quit drinking wine.

I pondered that idea for a short while. It would save money, that's for sure. Decent wine isn't cheap, and neither are antihistamines and ibuprofen. Think of all the money I'd save.

I glanced at my fully stocked wine rack on the kitchen counter. I can't let all that good wine go bad, can I? That would be wasteful. But I will cut back. That'll save money and calories.

After gulping down a couple of ibuprofens, I posted a reminder note on the wine rack to take an antihistamine before drinking, then poured a big mug of coffee and curled up in a comforter on the couch to recover and check my messages.

Sam had texted: *Chad was moved out of ICU this morning. He's starting physical therapy today and asking for you.*

The phone chirped and a text came in from Mom: *Need you here. Telling Mom everything.*

———

Mom and Ruby were holding hands on the living room sofa when I arrived. My grandmother looked shell-shocked and every one of her seventy-four years, and then some.

I perched on the edge of an easy chair opposite them. "How are you doing?"

"I feel like the worst mother in the world. My baby…" Ruby broke down, teardrops staining her beige linen skirt.

"Mom, it's okay. *I'm* okay." My mother stroked her hand.

"Why didn't you tell us? We always tried to be supportive parents."

"I was just a little girl. I didn't know what to do. I didn't want everyone to be mad at me."

"Oh, honey," said Ruby. "How could we have ever been mad at you? You did nothing wrong."

"I know that as an adult, but I didn't know it as a six-year-old. And then you had your big fight with him after Grandma died, and he was finally out of our lives. So I just tried to forget about it." She paused, expelling a hard sigh. "Until I found out about his arrest and his outrageous sentence. And when you got your reunion idea, I knew I had to tell you." Mom shook her head, pressing her lips tight to hold back tears. "But I have dreaded hurting you with this."

"Grandma." I moved to her side. Feeling protective, I draped an arm around her slim, trembling shoulders.

"Marybeth told me you knew about this."

"Yes, but it wasn't my story to tell."

"Sweetheart, I understand that, so don't feel bad." She groaned with exasperation. "I'm sorry that I asked you to find him for me. How hard that must have been for you."

"You didn't know."

"Katy?" said Mom. "Did you bring the letter? I want Mom to read it."

"It's in my purse." I moved back to the chair opposite them and took the folded, crinkled letter out of my bag.

———

"My God, what a demented pervert," Ruby said when done reading. "Marybeth said you've already responded."

"Yes, I mailed it Saturday. I made it very clear he's not to contact any of us."

She sat up straighter, her mouth set grim with determination. "I'd really like to get my hands on him and finish off the son of a bitch."

My mother shook her head. "He's not worth the jail time, Mom."

"Bullshit," said Ruby. "Nothing would give me greater satisfaction than to stand over his cold, dead body."

CHAPTER FIFTY-FOUR

TUESDAY · AUGUST 27
Posted by Katy McKenna

My amnesiac lothario keeps texting me 24/7.
  When are you going to be here :-(
  I really love you xoxoxox
  Miss you…

———

After a leg checkup this morning, I coerced myself into visiting
Chad. The doctor's office is next door to the hospital, and I was
feeling kind of bad for the poor guy… Wow. Never thought I'd call
Chad-the-Cad a "poor guy."

———

I found him in rehab, slowly walking between parallel bars with the
encouragement of his physical therapist. I observed from across the
room for a while, debating whether to say hello or not. Or not was

winning when he saw me and his face lit up like a kid on Christmas morning.

"Katy! Look at me. Walking. Pretty soon I can come home. Right, Holly?"

The slender brunette PT nodded. "That's right, Chad."

Whoa. Was he thinking about coming home to our house?

He cleared up that question immediately. "I can't wait to be back in our bed again."

I couldn't let that slide and crossed the room. "Chad? Remember what I told you? We are not married anymore. You left me. Remember?"

His face dimmed like a kid who just found out there's no Santa. "What are you talking about? Of course we're married. We've been married over five years. Don't kid around like that."

Holly gestured me to meet her in the far corner. "He's having some short-term memory issues."

"Along with amnesia?"

She nodded, keeping tabs on Chad's progress over my shoulder.

"This is too much," I said. "I can't do this."

"You'll need to talk to his neurologist about how to handle it."

"No." I shook my head, feeling my lower back muscles seizing up. "Not doing that. We are divorced. He walked out on me for another woman and married her. Therefore, he is not my problem."

I turned to watch him and Chad flashed us a silly grin. He'd already forgotten what I said.

Holly smiled back and waved. "Keep going, Chad. You're doing great." Then to me, "So where's his wife?"

"It's a long story. Suffice it to say, he dumped her, too, though they're still legally married."

Chad was gripping the parallel bars for dear life, perspiration dribbling down his face, dragging his reluctant feet across the floor. He gave us a thumbs-up and nearly fell on his face.

"Really hard to believe." Holly slowly shook her head. "He seems so sweet."

I was tempted to share my porn video with her, but I restrained myself. "You don't know the half of it. While she's been recovering from the loss of two babies and a stroke, he dumped her for another woman." While I jabbered on saying way too much, her benevolent smile dissolved into a contemptuous scowl.

"Oh my God. What a pig." She glanced at me with a rueful smile. "This is why I gave up on men and married a woman."

Chad was nearing the end of the bars. "Holly, I need help turning around."

"You're a big boy. Figure it out."

————

On my way out of the hospital, I swung by the pharmacy to say hi to Nora.

"Hello, Katy," she called from behind the glass window. "I'm absolutely knackered and was about to take a break. Have you time for a coffee?"

We sat outside on the brick-walled patio, watching a little brown sparrow hop from table to table scavenging for crumbs.

"I hear your ex is up and doing physical therapy."

"Yes, he is." I added two packets of sugar to my coffee. "I was just—hold on. My phone's vibrating." I plucked it out of the side pocket of my purse. "I don't recognize this number. Area code 559. I'll let it go to voice mail."

"Five-five-nine is in the Central Valley, I think," said Nora. "Didn't you say your uncle lives in Clover?"

"Yes, but how would he have found my number?" I waited a minute and then listened to the voice mail. *"Hello, Katy. This is Uncle Ted calling."* His voice was a smooth baritone, reminding me of a slick radio announcer.

I shuddered, feeling like he was standing next to me. "I can't believe it. It's him. My uncle. I'll put it on speaker."

"Hello, Katy. This is Uncle Ted calling. Your letter arrived yesterday afternoon. I'm afraid I cannot do as you say. As soon as I'm free to travel, I'll be coming to see my sister and niece. I look forward to meeting you. I've seen your photo online, and you are a very pretty young woman. You have your mother's eyes.

Katy, I am an old man who needs some peace. I'm not a threat to anyone. I'll let you know when I am coming."

"This can't be happening." My hand shook as I attempted a swallow of coffee. "I really thought my threat to tell his probation officer would stop him."

"What do you think you'll do, love?" Nora's faint British accent calmed me a little.

"I have no idea. I really don't want to contact the probation officer because that means dragging my mother and grandmother through all of that. But the part about being a harmless old man now? What a crock. It was just in this past year that he was groping his granddaughter. As long as he is alive, he will never be harmless."

Nora reached across the table and took my hand. "If there is anything I can do."

"I know." I patted her hand then pulled away, shoving my chair back. "I'm sorry, Nora, but I need to go home and think. I can't let this happen."

CHAPTER FIFTY-FIVE

FRIDAY · AUGUST 30
Posted by Katy McKenna

Private Post
Wednesday, August 28
Part One

I am an old man who needs some peace. I'm not a threat to anyone. His words spun like an endless loop in my brain. Over and over.

———

Wednesday morning, after a long toss-and-turn night, I concluded that the only way to shut this down was to drive to Clover and finish this insane business face-to-face. I would make him understand that he would be spending his golden years behind bars if he bothered my mother or grandmother again.

It's only about a two-and-a-half-hour drive, but I threw a few things into a duffel bag if I was too emotionally drained to drive home. Daisy saw the bag and danced around, barking, "Road trip! Road trip!"

"No, baby. Mommy has to do this all by herself. I do not want you exposed to that terrible man."

She may not have understood everything I said, but the word "no" definitely deflated her high. She collapsed on the floor with a huff and gave me her mopey look.

"Daisy. The expected high today in Clover is ninety-eight." I hugged her and got coated in dog hair. "I'd love to have your company, but you'd be miserable. You're much better off staying home with Tabitha and Auntie Emily."

————

About ten miles out of Clover, I switched on the GPS app on my phone to guide me to his house. My GPS buddy was taking me on the long route, which was fine with me. I was in no hurry for my meetup with the devil.

I cruised through downtown toward the rolling hills beyond into an upper-middle-class neighborhood. A high canopy of sycamores and elms lined the peaceful, shady streets. Expansive green lawns fronted circa 40s–50s single-level sprawling ranchers, Tudors, and Craftsmans.

Too soon, my GPS announced, "You have arrived at your destination." I cruised past his house, then parked several houses down. Now moments away from meeting this contemptible person, my initial righteous resolve had fizzled out, replaced with ramping trepidation.

I would have gladly stood on a stage in front of ten thousand people singing "The Star-Spangled Banner" in my birthday suit rather than knock on his door. I was about to turn tail and run when my cell phone chirped with a text from Mom.

I'm worried about Mom. Haven't seen her this down since Dad died.

Anger reignited; I left my cane in the car, jammed the keys into my pants pocket, and hobbled to his front door. I stood on the wide slate porch facing the ominous red door, staring at the wrought-iron knocker. I stabbed the doorbell three times, waited about ten seconds, and punched it again. I knew he had to be there since he was under house arrest, so I hammered the knocker for good measure.

I waited a minute more, then tried the door handle, thinking, *I seem to be making a career out of entering houses uninvited*. It wasn't locked. I pushed the door open, poked my head inside, screwed up my courage, and whispered his name. At least there wasn't a dog this time.

I had two choices. After my recent trespassing experiences, you'd think this was a no-brainer. Obviously, the smart choice was to leave. Not known for making smart choices, I stepped inside, shut the door, and stood in the expansive foyer, pondering my next move as I looked around.

The decor was an eclectic mix of contemporary and antiques. It worked. So much nicer than the last house I'd broken into. And then I caught the murmur of voices. Whoever was in the house must have heard me beating on the door but probably thought the crazy person gave up and left. *Nope. Still here.*

My inner alarm was clanging, *Get out. Get out.* Then I thought, *Oh God, what if he's molesting a neighborhood child?*

I looked around for some kind of weapon, wishing I had my cane. There was a heavy, red ceramic vase sitting on a console table. I grabbed it and crept down the hallway toward the voices. If he were hurting anyone, he was a dead man.

Then I heard, "You're really going through with this?"

I know that voice. No, it can't be. I inched toward the open doorway.

"We can still leave, you know."

My heart clawed its way up my throat, and my shaking hands were so slick with sweat I had to set the vase on the floor and wipe

them on my pants. *This makes no sense. Oh God, why didn't I stay home?*
````

"No. I have to do this. And we can't leave. He can identify us."

"We should have covered our faces. What were we thinking?"

"Go wait in the other room and leave me to this. If we leave now, he'll wake up and call the police. It has to be done."

*Do what? What could they do that would get them in trouble with the police?*

"You're right. But I'm not leaving you. Please, just do it before I change my mind again."

I decided to leave before they discovered me and then heard, "There. It's done. Now he can never hurt anyone again."

"Oh my God. Oh my God. What have we done?"

"You haven't done anything. I did it."

"But I drove you here. I let you do it. I wanted you to do it."

"Because we agreed it was the right thing to do. He is a despicable, evil man who hurts innocent children, and he would have continued to do that. Somebody had to do something. The judicial system failed all of his victims. Someone had to set things right."

I stepped into the room.
````

CHAPTER FIFTY-SIX

FRIDAY · AUGUST 30
Posted by Katy McKenna

Private Post
Wednesday, August 28
Part Two

"Katy!" Nora screamed.

Debra crumpled onto the bench at the foot of the king bed, clutching her heart, gulping for air.

"What are you doing here?" Nora stepped toward me trying to block my view of the person on the bed.

I moved closer, edging her aside, looking at the pale, unconscious silver-haired man. Well dressed. Respectable looking. Not the scuzzy, meth-addicted pimp I'd imagined. "Is that my uncle?"

"Please, Katy. Let's go to another room where we can talk." Nora helped Debra to her feet.

I felt completely off-kilter, like I'd just stepped through the looking glass into an alternate dream world. "I don't understand what's going on. What'd you do to him? Did you drug him with something?"

"We can explain." Debra wiped her mouth with a tissue. "But not here."

"Let's find the living room," said Nora. "We'll talk there."

I took another glance at the stranger sleeping on the bed and left the room with the ladies following. In the hall Nora picked up the vase. My spine suddenly prickled with fear, thinking she might slam it over my head. I spun around just as she set it back on the entry table.

"I think the living room is that way." She pointed beyond me.

The spacious room was accented with vivid, splashy art—my uncle's name in bold black letters slashed across the lower right corners. Painted by anyone else, I would have loved them but instead they creeped me out.

Nora shut the plantation shutters lining the windows facing the street, then sat next to Debra on a leather sofa. "Please sit, Katy."

"I don't want to sit," I said, hugging myself, feeling chilled to the bone. "I want to know what the hell is going on here."

"This was my idea, so it's mine to explain." Debra glanced at Nora. "I could use some water." She turned the leather-strapped watch on her bony wrist to check the time.

Nora left the room. While we waited, I paced, panicky and completely baffled. All I wanted to do was get out of there, but first I had to know what was going on. I stopped pacing and studied Debra's sickly countenance. She averted her eyes under my stare but said nothing. It had been only a few days, maybe a week since I'd last seen her, but she was wasting away. Her complexion was blotchy and withered, and blood stained the crumpled tissue she clutched

Nora returned and set a tall glass on a coaster. Debra took a pillbox from her sweater pocket and struggled to open it.

"How's the pain level?" Nora opened the box and dumped a pill in Debra's hand.

"Bad." She gagged down the pill, then checked her watch again. "Katy. I know I look bad, and I'm sure you're wondering, so I'm going to be blunt. I'm dying."

"What do you mean?" I sank into a leather sling chair facing her.

"Just what I said. I am dying. Soon. I have stage-four metastatic lung cancer."

"But you don't smoke, do you?"

"No. But I grew up with two smokers. So maybe this is the result of that. Who knows?"

"Are you doing chemo?" I asked.

"I chose not to. I have no family and…"

"That's not true," said Nora. "You have me. If you'd told me sooner, I could have helped you."

Debra smiled sadly, shaking her head. "Maybe if my daughter had lived." She stopped talking, lost somewhere in time for a moment. "Some people, when given a terminal prognosis, choose to spend their final days working their way through a bucket list. But I have no desire to jump out of a plane or climb mountains. I chose to work as long as possible, doing what I love most. Caring for my patients. Chemo would have halted my life immediately."

"I'm so sorry about all that, really, but it doesn't explain why you're here in my uncle's house. And why you've done whatever it is you've done to him."

"Hear me out, Katy." She stifled another coughing spasm. "I couldn't let that man in there…" She glanced down the hallway. "…be free to hurt other children. And I couldn't let him hurt your mother again. I just couldn't." She glanced at her watch again, then nodded to Nora.

Nora stood, brushing away the stray hairs clinging to her face and tucking in her wrinkled white blouse. "We should go now."

"Not just yet. I have to explain this so Katy truly understands, because now she has to make a decision too."

I sucked in a slow, shaky breath, pretty sure of the answer to my question now, but still I asked again. "What did you do to him?"

"We sedated him and then—"

"Oh, thank God. I thought maybe you'd—"

"Nora, I'm going to check him now." Debra used the sofa arm to push her spindly body erect.

"I'll go," said Nora.

"No. You're not a doctor. You stay and talk to Katy."

I watched her lurch out of the room, using furniture and walls for support, then said to Nora, "I still don't understand."

"Katy." Her warm brown eyes were filled with compassion. "Yes, you do."

Debra returned and Nora helped her sit. She sipped her water, then said, "It's done. We should leave soon."

I rushed to my uncle's bedside. His crotch was damp and the odor of feces drove me back. I kept a hand clamped over my nose and mouth while I watched his chest for movement. I studied his slack, unfamiliar face, a thick wad of terror clogging my throat. How could I be related to this man? And then I realized he had Ruby's nose.

"He's gone," said Debra from the doorway. She advanced toward me holding out her hand, revealing a syringe.

I recoiled, remembering another recent run-in with a syringe. "What are you doing?"

"Showing you what I used. I injected him with a lethal dose of a neuromuscular blocking agent."

"An overdose causes respiratory failure," said Nora.

I said nothing, watching the syringe in Debra's hand. Was I next on their extermination list?

Debra swayed on her feet and grasped the bureau for support. "How many times have you wished him dead, Katy?"

"Too many times to count. But I didn't really mean it."

"I don't believe that. And neither do you."

Debra was right. From the moment I first heard what he had done to my mother and his granddaughter, I wanted the son of a bitch dead. I'd had wild daydreams of killing him myself. He was a perverted human being who finally got exactly what he deserved. Now my mother and grandmother would no longer live in dread, wondering when he would come knocking on the door. Or when he'd hurt another child.

I gazed at him, my feelings a mix of disbelief, fear, gratitude, horror, relief. "She's right. I'm glad you're dead."

"So now what do we do?" Nora moved to stand beside Debra.

"That all depends on Katy," said Debra. "Can you live with this, or are you going to turn me in?"

"Us in," said Nora. "You couldn't have done this alone. Not in your condition. And we agreed it was the right thing to do."

I contemplated the situation as best I could, considering my current state of total discombobulation. If I turned in Debra, Nora would be an accessory. These courageous women had done society a great service at a tremendous risk to themselves. And they'd done it for my mother and grandmother. And for every other child he'd hurt in the past or would hurt in the future. And I was glad they had done it. How could I possibly turn them in?

"One thing you should think about, Katy." Debra drew in a wheezy breath. "If you don't go to the police now. Today. You could be held responsible too."

That hadn't occurred to me, but she was right. If I chose to turn a blind eye to this, I'd be an accessory to murder. This was a life-altering decision I had to make in a matter of seconds, and once made, there would be no take-backs.

I turned away from them, gazing out the window at a tin bird feeder hung in a sycamore maybe fifteen feet from the house. Two finches were quarreling over its one perch. One gave up and flew off. Was this decision as easy as that? Yes, because there was no decision to make. I had to do the right thing.

"I'm sure. I owe you both a huge debt of gratitude." I pointed at the corpse. "In a way, so does he. You released him from his terrible demons."

"Thank you, Katy." Debra stood, appearing energized by my decision. "We have to make sure we leave nothing behind that will lead back to us, in case there's any suspicion of foul play."

"What if they do an autopsy?" Just asking made me want to throw up.

"The drug only remains in the liver for a very short time after death," said Nora. "And it could be days before anyone discovers his body, so you don't have to worry about that."

"A man his age dying of an apparent heart attack shouldn't raise any suspicions." Debra handed the syringe to Nora. "Put this in your purse, and we'll get rid of it on the way home."

She removed her turquoise neckerchief and wrapped the syringe in it. "Are we going to leave him like that? Just lying there on the bed, fully clothed? Won't that look a trifle odd?"

"You're right," said Debra. "If he'd had a natural heart attack, he'd be on the floor or sitting in front of the TV. Something like that." She thought for a moment. "We can't move him. He's big and trying to drag him through the house would most likely be detected by homicide detectives."

"We could make it look like he was taking a nap," I said, suddenly no longer an innocent bystander.

"Good idea." Debra started to untie a shoe, then wavered. "I can't do it. I'm afraid I'm spent." She dropped into an easy chair by the window.

"I'll do it." I untied his brown oxfords. While struggling to pry them off, the leathery odor of his warm, damp socks, mixed with the foul smell of his excrement made my stomach lurch convulsively. I held my breath, fighting the urge to spew the bag of Twizzlers I'd consumed on the drive over. That would've given those homicide detectives a field day.

I dumped the shoes by the bed and Nora picked them up and

laid them straight. "Look around you, Katy. This man is, was, an OCD neat freak, and these look like very pricey shoes."

I backed away and watched her mess his hair just enough, then set his tortoise frames on the nightstand, all the while intoning an eerie mewling hum. She took a hardback book from the dresser and placed it on the bed near his hand, marking a random page with the cover jacket. *The Wasteland* by T.S. Eliot. I don't read poetry, but I found the title fitting for this man's wasted life.

"Put this over him, Katy." Debra held out a moss-green throw that had been draped on the chair.

I spread it over his body, wanting to cover his face.

"Did we really just do all that?" Nora stepped back to survey the tableau we'd created.

"He really looks like he's taking a nap," I said.

"It does to me, too," said Debra. "Time to go."

"Let's leave through the kitchen door, in case there's any neighbors walking by out front." Nora helped Debra to her feet and retrieved a bloody tissue that fell from her lap. "There's an alley that runs behind the houses."

At the bedroom door, Debra stopped. "Katy, Nora. You better check yourselves. Did you lose an earring? Hair clip. Anything?"

My silver hoops were in place. No clips in my hair, and my purse was in the car. I patted my keys in my jeans pocket. I took one last look at the dead man, then followed the women through the house to the sterile Euro-modern kitchen.

On the table, a laptop was open. Curious, I tapped the touchpad with my knuckle and the computer sprang to life. He'd been trolling child pornography sites. Any lingering doubts about my uncle's death and my role in it vanished.

Debra and Nora stood beside me and I embraced them. "Thank you so much."

The doorbell rang.

"What should we do?" whispered Nora.

"Nothing. They'll go away," said Debra.

"Yeah, just like *I* went away."

"Most people don't walk in when no one answers, Katy," said Debra. "And we should have locked the door when he let us in. Did you lock it?"

"No."

"Oh God." Nora grasped my arm. "What if he was expecting someone?"

A truck roared to life out front. "That sounds familiar." I went to the living room and peeked through the shutters. "It's okay. UPS. He must've left a package on the porch."

As soon as the truck was out of sight, I inched the door open, stuck my arm through and grabbed the small Amazon package on the doorsill. I left it on the foyer table and locked the door.

Back in the kitchen, I said, "I didn't think it was a good idea to leave it sitting out there. A neighbor might notice it and wonder why he hasn't brought it in."

"Good thinking," said Debra. "We ready to go now?"

"The water!" I retrieved the glass from the living room, dried it and set it in the kitchen cabinet with the dish towel. Then I went around wiping off any surfaces we may have touched—the vase, doorknob, his shoes, the Amazon box—before returning to the kitchen.

"Okay. Ready," I said, out of breath.

At the kitchen door, I used the dish towel to open and close it. Once out of the house, I wanted to run, but I kept pace through the yard with Debra and Nora, thankful for the mature canopy of trees and tall shrubbery hiding us from any curious neighbors.

As we neared the back gate, I said, "What I don't get is why he let you in, or how you controlled him so you could do this? He must have put up a fight."

"Oh my God. Thank you, Katy," said Debra, as Nora snatched the towel from me and rushed back to the kitchen door.

"What'd I say?"

"We left something very damning in there. How could we have forgotten it?" said Debra, wringing her hands. "Nora's waving. Oh God, I think the door's locked."

CHAPTER FIFTY-SEVEN

Posted by Katy McKenna

Private Post
Wednesday, August 28
Part Three

Nora was doubled over, clutching her stomach moaning. "What're we going to do? We'll be arrested for murder. What will my daughter do? Oh God, what was I thinking?"

I placed my hands on her shoulders, forcing her to straighten up and look me in the eye. "Nora. Get a grip and for the love of God, pipe down. Do you want the neighbors calling the police?"

She hung her head, shaking it. "No. I just want to go home and forget this bloody-awful day ever happened."

I pulled her close and patted her back. "I am so thankful for what you've done for my family. You cannot begin to know. And think of all his future victims you have saved. Nora, you're a hero. You're *my* hero." I felt her tense muscles release, and I stepped back looking her square in the face. I spoke in a composed voice when I really wanted to shriek like a banshee. "Tell me what you left in the house."

"A gun."

My stomach plunged as the banshee reared its ugly head, ready to cut loose. "You used a gun?"

"I feel like I'm going to pass out." She put her head between her knees, and I placed a hand on her back, ready to catch her if she keeled over. "It's just an old air pistol. But it looks like the real thing. That's how we got him to let us in the house. I must've left it in the bedroom. I can't believe we forgot it."

"Where in the bedroom?"

"The dresser, I think." She slammed her fingers into her hair, crying. "I don't know."

How could we have not noticed a gun sitting on the dresser? This can't be happening. This whole day can't be happening.

Across the yard, I saw Debra leaning against the fence in the blistering sun, looking ready to drop. "You need to pull yourself together and search for a key while I get Debra situated. Then I'll start checking the windows. Maybe something's open."

I rushed back to Debra and settled her on a bench in the shade of a sprawling sycamore. "I think you should go to the police," she said. "Right now. Say you walked in on us and when you saw what we'd done, you ran out. This is your chance, Katy. Your finger-prints aren't on the gun, so there's nothing to tie you to this. I can't have you going to prison because of us. "

"I could never live with myself if I did that. And what about Nora?"

She clenched her gnarled, veiny hands, shaking her head. "I'll say she had no idea what I was doing."

"But she did. The gun proves that. Even if it isn't a real gun." I squatted, looking into her dear face. "I promise I will get us safely out of here." *What if I can't?*

Nora was hunting for a key under pots near the back door, so I checked the windows, working my way along the back and sides of the house. Every window was locked. Obviously, I couldn't check the windows facing the street. And if I broke one to get in, that could raise questions, leading to an autopsy. But we couldn't leave that damned gun in the house.

I returned to Nora and found her prying the screen off the window over the kitchen sink. "The window looks slightly ajar. I need to get this off without bending it out of shape like I've done to the ones on my house. I hate these damned things."

Together we got it off without mangling it and then pried the window open. I'm at least ten years younger and several inches taller than Nora, so I knew I was the one going in.

We set a wrought iron chair under the window, and I wriggled in headfirst. I grabbed at the counter edge beyond the sink and worked myself in with Nora's help. Once there was more of me inside than out, I lost my grip on the counter and slid through, out of control. The faucet slammed into my pelvic bone, and the windowsill dug into my thigh wound before I landed chin first on the floor. On the way through, I heard something rip.

"You okay?" Nora poked her head in the window.

"I think so." I lay there a few seconds accessing my physical damage. Adrenaline had been masking my leg pain, but now it had awakened with a ferocious roar, overshadowing all the other new injuries that would announce themselves later.

I stood, keeping as much weight off my left leg as possible, and limped toward the bedroom. The last thing I wanted to do was see his body again.

In the foyer I stopped, recalling Debra's words, *I think you should go to the police. Right now. This is your chance, Katy.* Oh, how I wanted to open the front door and run to my freedom. I stepped to it, placing my hand on the lever. Breathing hard, I turned the handle and pulled. The door seal whispered a soft whoosh as a waft of sizzling summer air filtered through the crack.

"Katy?" called Nora from the kitchen window. "Are you all right? Do you want me to come in?"

"No. I'm fine. You say you left the gun on the dresser?"

"I remember now. I left it on the bathroom counter when I got tissue for Debra."

I closed the door. Then wiped off my prints with my T-shirt. Like a criminal.

———

About twenty miles out of Clover, I pulled into a convenience store parking lot. I needed a Sprite and a bathroom. A couple tequila shots to dull the aftershocks would have been nice, too.

I opened the car door; barely registering the blasting heat, then froze with one foot on the scorching asphalt. A video camera hung from the top of the grimy, stucco building.

What am I doing? My face will be on the video camera. Proof I was in the Central Valley on the day of the murder.

I pulled in my foot and slammed the door, then looked at the camera through the rearview mirror. It was aimed right at Veronica's rear end, but after a brief panic attack, I observed the broken lens and wires hanging out of it.

I needed to get myself home before I did anything else reckless. My gas tank was over half full, and my bladder would have to hold until I was back on home turf. If I wet my pants along the way, so be it.

———

I arrived home around eight fifteen. Emily's Subaru sat in the driveway, blocking the garage door. It pissed me off, but in the big scheme of things, it's not like she'd just covered up a homicide.

Before going in, I rested my aching body on the front steps, inhaling the cool, refreshing honeysuckle-scented evening air, trying to gain control of my emotions. Across the street, Lynyrd

Skynyrd was rocking the house. Instead of getting annoyed, I pulled comfort from the now-familiar neighborhood sound.

I became aware of voices filtering through the living-room window behind me. Great. Emily had company. Just what I needed. I strained to hear the conversation and realized her company was Josh. Really great.

Haven't seen the guy since meeting his mother, and he has to pick tonight of all nights to pay a social call. I peeked in the window. He was lounging on the couch with Emily, swilling wine and having a good old time.

Daisy was scratching and whining at the front door, and I knew she wouldn't give up until I went inside. I opened the door, and she nearly knocked me off my feet.

"Daisy! Off." I shoved her away with my good leg. "At least let me get through the damned door first."

She gave me a crushed look and I patted her head. "Sorry, baby. Mom's had a rough day."

"Whoa. I'll say you've had a rough day. You look terrible." Emily gave me the once-over and headed for the kitchen.

"You been in a fight?" asked Josh as I eased my bones onto the sofa.

"No. Why do you ask?" I was being pissy but really didn't care.

"Well, your chin for one thing and…"

I followed his eyes to my leg and saw the right-side pocket was torn away, giving Josh a nice shot of my bruised, snow-white thigh.

I vaguely recalled hearing something rip when I plummeted through the window. "It got caught on something, and I took a tumble. Clumsy me."

Emily returned with a tall glass of sauvignon blanc for me. "How's your leg feeling?"

After a long pull of the chilled wine, I said, "Killing me. Actually, everything hurts. Could you get me some ibuprofen?"

"Will do. And I'll get a bag of peas for your chin, too."

Josh reached for my hand and gave it a friendly squeeze, along with a sympathetic smile that ignited his aquamarine eyes that on any other day would have left me panting.

"Emily told me what happened. You know, about your gunshot wound. So sorry I wasn't around to help out." He released my hand as Daisy snuggled between us, resting her head on my lap after giving her boyfriend a lovesick look.

"Where've you been?" I asked, not really caring and no doubt sounding grumpy.

His hand massaged Daisy's neck, scratching under her collar, causing her mouth to distort in doggie pleasure. "Remember I told you about the big family reunion my family was having on the East coast, and then my plan to drive through the Catskills with my cousin?" He paused, waiting for a response. "You know. I told you about it when you met my mother."

"Oh, yeah. Totally forgot about that. Hope you had fun."

"Jeez, Katy. What's up with you?" Emily handed me a pack of frozen peas and two ibuprofens. "Why're you so cranky?" Her eyes widened. "Oh, it's that time, huh? Boy, there are a few days a month that I absolutely want to kill everyone in my line of sight. Katy will vouch for that. Huh, Katy?"

I gave her an icy glare, then realized she'd given me the perfect excuse to be unfriendly. "I guess that partly explains my horrible day. That and taking that tumble."

"Have you eaten anything?" asked Josh. "I know how I get when my blood sugar's low."

"No, but I'm not hungry." I tapped my glass. "The wine will do me nicely."

"Come on. You gotta eat. I've got some leftover mac and cheese from Suzy Q's in my refrigerator, and I know how much you love it." He stood, much to Daisy's disappointment. "I'll be right back."

After he left, Emily said, "You know, Katy. I really think he likes you. He kept asking about you. And I know for a fact you like him. When are you two going to hook up?" She sniffed, wrinkling her nose at me. "You kinda reek. You might want to freshen up a little before he gets back."

"If I stand up now, the only place I'll be going is bed." I shifted to accommodate my dog's weight, now crammed against me, and we both groaned.

A few minutes later, Josh tapped on the front door and Emily answered.

"I'm not coming in," he said. "Katy's had a rough day and doesn't need to entertain visitors. Here's the mac and cheese and a couple of pieces of carrot cake."

"You sure you won't come in and at least finish your wine?" said Emily. "I feel bad about this."

"Don't. We all have rotten days. Just make sure she eats."

I listened to this conversation wishing I could be friendly. Wishing I cared. But my ongoing crush on Josh no longer mattered. My life had taken an abrupt, ugly turn, and there was no room left in it for romance.

CHAPTER FIFTY-EIGHT

SUNDAY · SEPTEMBER 1
Posted by Katy McKenna

Private Post

It's been four days now. Every time the phone rings, my heart races zero to ninety in a nanosecond. I check the caller ID, but whether I know the caller or not, I don't answer.

The only people I want to talk to are the ones I absolutely must not. I'm afraid if I do, they'll sense the insanity in my voice, then ask what's going on, and then I'll come unhinged and dump my pile of guilt on them. I cannot let that happen. Mom, Ruby, Pop, Emily, Samantha… If any of them knew what I have done, they would then be ensnared in the culpable noose that is strangling me.

Until now I have always shared everything with Samantha, down to the dirtiest detail, ever since we became friends in elementary school. But if I tell her, it would always be there, hanging over our heads like a dark, ominous cloud, and over time would drive our friendship into extinction. I couldn't bear that.

To keep everyone at bay, I texted that I'm down with that awful flu bug that's been going around. Of course, that also means I have to fake it for Emily, but she's been so busy writing her book that she barely comes up for air.

That'll work for a while until I can pull myself together. However, the only way I'm going to be able to do that is when I know I'm safe from prosecution. As for dealing with the guilt, I'm so conflicted that I don't know what to feel. But I'm not sorry he's dead. And I am not sorry about what I did.

CHAPTER FIFTY-NINE

MONDAY • SEPTEMBER 2
Posted by Katy McKenna

Private Post

Over the past few months, I've gained about ten pounds—okay, more like fifteen, but I don't recommend my new diet plan. The "I'm-so-freaked-out-that-I-will-vomit-if-I-eat diet."

I've been drinking wine, however—lots of it. I had meant to cut back, but instead, I'm drinking more. I am taking antihistamines, though.

Emily cornered me this morning and did an annoying mini intervention. "Katy, I'm really worried about you. Ever since the other night when Josh was here, you've been acting really weird. You're drinking way too much. Plus, you're living in your pajamas," she ticked off my infractions on her fingers, "not showering, not putting on any makeup. And you always put on makeup. Even just to walk out to the mailbox."

"In my defense I've had the flu, you know." I coughed a few times to sell my excuse.

"Oh, come on. This is more than just the flu, and you know it. If you don't get your act together, I'm telling Mom and Pop."

"Give me a break. This is one of those bugs that really drags you down. I'm just glad you haven't caught it. And it doesn't help that Chad keeps texting and calling. That whole thing has really bummed me out."

She bought that since she's seen how many times a day that lunatic texts and calls. He continues to forget we're not married. I actually feel kind of rotten that I haven't visited him in days. With his short-term memory issues, hopefully he doesn't remember that.

We ended my intervention with me promising to get my act together, and she's not buying me any more wine. If I want it, I have to go to the store and get it myself. I really don't want to shower, dress, and put makeup on.

I guess that means that is exactly what I need to do. Get my act together.

CHAPTER SIXTY

TUESDAY · SEPTEMBER 3
Posted by Katy McKenna

Private Post

I promised Emily I would pull myself together, so this morning I forced myself out of bed, showered, dressed, and put on a little makeup. I have to admit, it made me feel better. Or at least fresher. Then I prepared a Swiss cheese, spinach, and mushroom three-egg omelet, split it in half, and surprised my sister with breakfast in bed.

I tapped on her door. "Who wants breakfast?"

Her response was a groan followed by, "Go 'way."

"That's not happening." I opened the door and set the bamboo tray on the bureau, swishing a mug of steaming coffee near her nose. "Wake up, little sleepyhead."

The tantalizing aroma did the trick, and Emily sat up, reaching for the cup. After a few swallows, she said, "This is nice. Thank you."

I placed the breakfast feast on the bed and sat cross-legged facing her.

"That looks delicious." Emily tossed back her long black hair. "Why the special attention?"

"Your little talk yesterday got to me." *Not really, but I can fake it until I feel it.*

Waving a forkful of omelet at me, she looked pretty pleased with herself. "You just got scared when I said I'd tell on you."

"Well, you got my attention. Sitting around moping isn't solving anything."

"Yeah. Chad. What a mess. Hopefully, time will resolve that issue."

"Yeah. Hopefully." *Nothing can resolve what I'm moping about.* "Anyway, I'm over the flu, and I'm getting out of the house today. Poor Daisy needs some attention, so we're hitting the dog park, and then we'll see what the rest of the day brings." I washed down a nibble of blackberry-jammed rye toast with a swig of orange juice. "Maybe I'll call Ruby and bug her about finding me a job."

"Did you ever get paid for the Clunker Carnival job? Last I heard, you hadn't."

"Nope. And I need to come up with an idea to make them pay me. Especially after my run-in with the bookkeeper. She flat-out told me they weren't paying me, and I said to her that nobody pushes Katy McKenna around, and, yes, they were going to pay me."

"Whoa. You go, girl."

"Yeah, well that was weeks ago, before I got shot. She probably thinks I caved. I don't know how I'm going to collect, but I'll think of something."

———

Daisy was over the moon when she realized we were headed for Lago Park. By the time I had the car parked and the back door open, she was in full tilt doggy boogie while I battled to untether her from the backseat.

"Daisy! Calm down so Mommy can untie you."

She looked at me like I was nuts and continued to bounce around, slapping me with her tail and smacking me with kisses.

A crowd of doggie playmates barked encouragement to Daisy as she towed me to the park gate. Once I'd wrestled her through the motley crew and set her free, I collapsed on a bench to soak up some much-needed vitamin D.

Watching my girl frolic with her pals put a smile on my face. Also much needed.

———

On the way home, I stopped at a drugstore and bought melatonin. My perimenopausal insomniac mother says it helps her sleep. It's worth a try. There's a Starbucks next door, so I treated myself to a grande cappuccino. Yes, I am aware of the paradox.

At home, I toted my coffee and laptop out to the patio to do some Central Valley recon. Daisy followed me out and flopped in a sunny spot in the grass to catch some Z's. What bliss it must be to have a guilt-free mind.

I typed in "Clover HubBub" in the search bar. HubBub is great for finding out what's going on in just about any town. Obviously, what I was looking for wouldn't be in *USA Today*. The top stories for Clover were:

- *Dairy farmers struggle to survive prolonged historic drought.*
- *Clover man who killed boyfriend sentenced to fifteen years.*
- *Clover teenager suffers head injuries during a game of mailbox baseball.*

And down at the bottom of the front page: *Convicted sex offender found dead in bed.* I clicked the headline.

A 72-year-old man was found dead in his home on Monday after he failed to report to his probation officer last week. Theodore Peckham, a convicted sex offender charged with child molestation, was under house arrest at the time of his death. He appears to have died in his sleep. The coroner's office is listing it as a cardiac arrest.

The story continued with his sex offender conviction, but I didn't have the stomach for it. Instead, I sat there, absorbing the fact that it had gone down like I had hoped it would. His body wasn't discovered until five days after his death, so no trace of the stuff that Debra had injected in him was left in his system.

At the bottom of the story, there were hater comments posted already. The one comment that stood out was:

The only good pedophile is a dead pedophile.

"Could not agree with you more, buddy," I muttered, tempted to click the thumbs-up button but instead clicked out.

I leaned back in my chair. *Is this really the end of it? No, but it is the end of the worst of it. Now I have to learn to live with what I did. And I can do that.*

I joined Daisy in the grass, nuzzling my head on her warm, plush tummy. Gazing at the clouds scuttling high in the infinite deep blue, I gave thanks to anyone out there listening.

CHAPTER SIXTY-ONE

WEDNESDAY · SEPTEMBER 4
Posted by Katy McKenna

Private Post

Last night I climbed into bed early thinking I'd read for a while, then pop a melatonin and go night-night. Next thing I know, sunlight is glaring in my eyes through a gap in the drapes.

I started the coffee, put the dirty dishes in the dishwasher, and wiped down the counters—reveling in my freedom to do everyday mundane chores.

My paper girl scratched at the front door, ready to do her job. From the porch, I watched Daisy pounce on the paper at the end of the walk. Paper in mouth, she proudly pranced it up the stairs and dropped it at my feet.

Across the street, my beefy neighbor was climbing into his yellow muscle car. I waved as he rumbled away, thinking, *Howdy, neighbor. Great day, huh? Guess what? I'm not going to prison!*

After Daisy and Tabitha had finished their morning repast,

they joined me in our chair by the living room french doors to catch up on current events:

Federal agents raid gun shop, find weapons. Second arrest for gun shop owner.

"Hello. It's a gun shop."

County to spend $425,000 to advertise lack of funds in the hopes that voters in November will approve higher taxes for public-safety services.

"Key word—lack of funds. Gee, I wonder why?"

A Highway Patrol officer arrested a deputy U.S. marshal for stealing 37 pounds of marijuana from drug traffickers with the intent to sell the pot. Drug traffickers file a civil suit.

"How about they take the money from the pot sale and use it to pay for the county's advertising campaign? Oh, here's something that may interest you, Daisy. The humane society is having a fashion show fundraiser."

My pound puppy set her paw on my thigh and gave me one of her deep, soulful sighs and then my phone rang.

"Hey, Ruby. What's up?"

"You certainly sound chipper," she said. "You finally getting over the damned flu?"

"I am, thank you."

"Well…" Long sigh. "I have some news you need to hear."

I sighed back. "Good or bad?"

"I know it's bad, but frankly I am at a loss for how I feel. My brother died."

I considered what tone my response should take.

"Katy? You there?"

"Yeah, I'm here. I'm stunned by what you just said." I was thankful we were doing this over the phone, so I didn't have to control my facial expressions. Texting would have been better, though. "So, uh, how did he die?"

"Heart attack according to the coroner's office. I was notified early yesterday morning, but wasn't feeling ready to share." She snorted a laugh. "They offered their sympathies." Another snort followed with a labored groan. "Here's the kicker. They want to know if I'm going to claim his body."

"What'd you say?"

"I didn't say anything. I was shocked by the news of his death, to say the least. I sure wasn't ready to make any snap decisions."

"Please don't tell me we're going to have a funeral for that man."

"Not unless we can build a funeral pyre, toss a match, and do a happy dance."

I felt relieved that she hadn't lost her sense of humor. Still, this was her brother, so it had to feel weird.

"Anyhoo," she sighed. "I'll tell Marybeth today. And then I need to call my sister. That's going to be a very difficult phone call. I haven't told her about any of this yet."

"You know, you don't have to call Aunt Edith today. Another day or two isn't going to change a thing. In fact, wait until the weekend."

"Good idea. Your mother will be enough. I guess I'll need to come up with an answer for the coroner's office."

"And your answer will be?"

"Bury him in a pauper's grave for all I care."

I knew she cared. "How do you really feel?"

"I keep thinking of that cute little scamp who was my baby brother. That's what I'm going to hang on to because the person he grew into was someone I didn't like, even before learning about all this." She paused. "He hurt my baby. I hope he rots in Hell."

———

Late this afternoon, I called Samantha. "Hey. It's me."

"Well, it's about time you called. What is going on, Katy? We haven't talked in days and you don't return my calls. I know you've had the flu, but did I do something to upset you?"

"You didn't do anything. I've just been really dragging. The flu,

Chad, worrying about my mother's uncle coming here. But I'm feeling better now. And I have some news." I told her about my uncle's death.

"Heart attack? Well, amen and pass the biscuits, as my grandmother always says. Sometimes there is divine intervention, huh?"

"Sometimes." *And sometimes it gets a little earthly nudge.*

"Please tell me you don't feel bad about this." She waited for a response, then said, "You don't, do you?"

"No. It's just the whole thing. I've been so worried about Mom and Ruby and …" I stopped before I said too much.

"Yeah, it's got to feel strange. One minute you're fretting about him showing up on your doorstep and the next thing you know— he drops dead. When I think about it, there have been a few perfectly timed deaths lately. And all well deserved. Hold on. Casey's calling me." She held the phone away and hollered, "Yes, baby. We're going in a few minutes."

"Where are you going?"

"Soccer practice. Hey, did you hear Chad was transferred to a memory-loss care facility? Now he's living with a bunch of elderly Alzheimer patients."

"Are you kidding? When?"

"Day before yesterday."

"Does this mean he's not going to recover?"

"Hard to say at this point. He was well enough to leave the hospital, but he can't function on his own at this point, so I guess that was the best option for now. I hear he's very popular with the old ladies. It also means he won't be harassing you anymore because they took his phone away."

"Wow. I'm completely gobsmacked. I wonder what Heather will do."

"Who knows? My heart certainly goes out to her, but my advice to you is stay out of it. You already have enough on your plate."

She was right about that. But what will Heather do about the store? Her marriage? Will she have to pay for the memory care facility? And Chad's the father of her baby. Talk about having a lot on your plate.

"You still there?" asked Sam. "You're awfully quiet. You okay?"

"Yeah, just thinking."

"I'm so glad you called. I feel much better after hearing your voice. Just don't do that to me again. You know you can talk to me about anything. An-y-thing. Whatever is bugging you. Big and small. Day or night. Doesn't matter. That's what best friends are for. We don't judge." She snickered. "Well, we try not to judge. But no matter what, we listen. That's our job."

There are some things even best friends can't share.

"Gotta get going now," she said. "Oh, by the way. Did you get the group message that Saturday's book club meeting has been canceled?"

"No. Why?"

"Debra's too sick, Nora can't come, and of course Heather can't."

My book club days are over.

"Anyway, we couldn't have gone either because Casey has a soccer game Saturday and he said he wants his Aunt Katy there. One o'clock."

"I'll bring the Ding Dongs."

"Make it orange slices. The Ding-Dong days are over."

"I meant for you and me."

———

All evening I've been thinking about Chad. Call me crazy, but I feel bad for him. He can't contact me (yay!) and he's not going to understand why I don't visit him. That's really sad.

Something's been niggling at me too. Like something I'm supposed to do or remember. I don't know what it is, and it's driving me bonkers.

Ruby always says if you can't remember something, take ten

slow deep breaths. Get that oxygen flowing in your brain, and usually it will come to you. That may work for when you walk into a room and have no idea why you did, but I've been deep breathing to the point of hyperventilating and it's not working.

Who have I talked to today?

Mom. She sounds more like her old self. Sometimes one person's death is another person's rebirth.

Ruby and Samantha.

And then I remembered. Sam had said, "When I think about it, there have been a few perfectly timed deaths lately. All well deserved."

What are the odds of every rotten person I've recently encountered, been told about, or been related to turning up dead? Or nearly in Chad's case.

CHAPTER SIXTY-TWO

THURSDAY • SEPTEMBER 5
Posted by Katy McKenna

Private Post

I called Debra this morning and finagled an invite via a series of thinly veiled hints. Although I'm sure she would've rather ignored them, she asked me to come over at three thirty.

Arriving on the dot, bearing lattes and cheese danishes, a note on the front door told me to come around to the backyard. I found her on a chaise lounge, wrapped in a wooly blue blanket in spite of the warm summery day.

"Hey, Debra." She looked wretched, so I didn't follow up with *how're you doing?* I sat beside her on a matching rattan chair, setting my offerings on a glass-topped table next to a tissue box and a water bottle. A portable electric oxygen concentrator sat on the concrete beside her, softly ticking with every breath she inhaled through a nasal cannula.

"Hi, Katy."

"You cut off all your beautiful curls."

"Too much trouble." Debra ran a hand through her cropped, gray hair. "Seems I cut off all the color too. Oh well." She inhaled and the machine ticked its response. "I was surprised you called. I figured you'd keep your distance. You doing okay?" She erupted into a string of deep, phlegmy coughs that made *my* chest hurt.

"I'm okay. Pretty much. You know he was found?"

"Yes. Nora told me. What a relief it is to know everything went as planned. How's your mother doing?"

"Good. Really good, in fact. Thanks to you and Nora. I wish I could tell her what you did for her."

"No!" A fragile hand snaked out from under the blanket, seeking mine. "You can never tell her."

I held her hand, surprised her grip was so strong. "I won't. I just wish I could. But I need to ask you something."

"About that day?"

"No." I paused, trying to find the least offensive way to ask my question. If I was wrong, what would she think of me?

"Please, Katy. Just ask."

I gazed at our hands, clasped together in her lap. "Have there been others?" I peeked up to catch her reaction.

She bowed her head and I took that for a "yes."

"How many?" I expected the answer to be four, including Chad-the-Undead.

"I'm not sure." She thought a moment, pulling her hand away. "Eighteen. Maybe twenty."

To say I was astounded would have been an understatement, and I'm sure it showed on my face.

"Katy. Only a few were amoral, evil people like your uncle. The rest were terminally ill and suffering needlessly. They begged me for release and I merely eased them along. It's done all the time. It's the merciful thing to do. I wish somebody would do it for me."

I kept my gaze focused on a shiny black beetle trudging across the patio. "Who were they?"

"Most you wouldn't know. Just know they were in their final days and in utter misery."

"What about Jeremy Baylor?"

I asked because Angela had told me he'd died from a toxic mixture of cocaine, alcohol, and oxycodone. It had been assumed that he'd gotten the oxycodone on the streets. But now I was wondering if Debra had anything to do with it.

She nodded yes. And yes to Melanie's brother-in-law, Travis, and yes to Chad. That hit me hard. Chad was a selfish bum, but he didn't deserve what he got. Of course, maybe my reaction was based on the Chad he had become at the hands of Debra.

I remembered Ruby talking about the numerous recent passings at Shady Acres. I asked her about the two I actually knew. Ronald, the retired mortician. And Beverly, who had tripped over her diaper. Yes to Ronald, and no to Beverly.

"She asked, but I thought she would recover, and go on to enjoy life again," she said.

"Was Nora an accomplice to these..." I stopped, unwilling to say the word.

"Mercy *coups de grâce*? No."

I was going to say murders, but her words put a nicer spin on it.

A tear threaded through the grooves of her withered cheek. "Please don't tell Nora. It's bad enough I've left her with the memory of your uncle's death weighing on her dear, innocent soul."

"I promise." I forced myself to look her square in the face. "When Sam and I got to Jeremy's house, I think he was already dead. But we must have come right after you left."

"Yes. You did. In fact I passed you on the street." Her latte shook in her palsied hands as she swallowed. "After knocking on the front door and getting no answer, I went 'round back and saw him through the window, sleeping on the sofa. I tapped on the glass, but he didn't wake up. The slider was unlocked and I went in. There was a dog, a Puggle, I think, barking at me." She stopped for a few breaths. "But Jeremy slept right through the racket. There were empty beer cans strewn about, so I assumed he'd passed out. I felt bad putting the dog in the bathroom, but I was afraid I'd have trouble doing what I came to do with it jumping around me." Debra winced, groaning as she hunched into the pain, clutching her chest.

I half-stood. "Do you want me to get you something?"

"In a minute," she gasped, holding out her coffee. "I need to finish."

I set her coffee on the table and waited while she worked through the pain, finally breathing easier.

"After I put the dog in the bathroom, I looked in Jeremy's room and saw he'd been snorting lines of cocaine. My original plan had been to use potassium chloride, but when I saw the cocaine I decided to inject him with oxycodone instead. There's been several teen deaths in the past year from that lethal mixture, so I figured it wouldn't raise any eyebrows."

I couldn't believe we were talking so matter-of-factly about premeditated murder. "Did he suffer?"

"No. Unlike his victim, Brittany." Her chest whistled each time she inhaled oxygen. "Killing that boy was probably the hardest thing I've ever done since burying my little girl. I knew how awful it would be for his parents. But at the time I thought he was infecting innocent girls with HIV. When I learned it was all a hideous joke…" She paused to compose herself. "And then Brittany killed herself because of him."

She hung her head, picking at a frayed edge of the blanket. "I know now I shouldn't have gone after Chad. I deeply regret that."

"What I don't get is how you tied Chad up all by yourself? He had to have put up a fight."

"Not really. When he saw the air pistol, he let me in. Once I had him on the bed, I had him inhale an anesthetic. He was hyper-ventilating at that point, so it only took a whiff to knock him out. Tying him up had not been in the plan, but the scarves were already hanging from the bedposts, so…" She shrugged. "He was only out for a minute or two, so it was a good thing that I did."

"In the hospital you told me you'd seen him as a patient a few times. Was that really true?"

She shook her head. "You caught me unawares, and I made that up to cover for why I was really there. Truth is you saved his life twice, because I was there to finish what I'd bungled the first time." She was wheezing hard and gasping to catch her breath.. After a long pause, she continued. "The whole thing was a horrendous mistake. You and Heather are both strong, resilient women. Survivors. All I did was botch things for you. I'm so sorry. Please know, I never would've let you go to prison for it."

We sipped our lattes, lost in our own musings. I listened to her shallow, rattily breathing as I thought about all the miserable terminally ill people she'd helped gently pass and realized I had no problem with that. We always say we would never let our beloved pets suffer, but yet we let our beloved humans suffer long, horrendous, undignified deaths.

I know Ruby keeps a stash of leftover painkillers, tranquilizers, and sleeping pills in her freezer. Some are years out of date. She said that even though they may weaken over time, they don't go bad. The day I found it while scavenging for ice cream, I confronted her with the plastic bag.

"Honeybunch," she said, unfazed. "Nowadays too many people live way past their expiration date. Rotting away in lonely misery, propped up by modern medicine administered by young doctors who don't see us as human beings who had careers, passions, lives, loves. They see us as machines that must be kept running, no matter what. God forbid we should actually be allowed to die with a little dignity."

"But I don't want you to die, Grammy," I cried, hugging her tight.

"As long as I'm enjoying life, neither do I." She gave me a jab in the ribs. "I want to play with my future great-grandkids."

Finally I spoke to Debra. "Is there anything else I should know?"

"No. I think we covered everything." She smiled, looking wistful, and I caught a glimpse of the healthy, pretty Debra. "It certainly is a lovely day, isn't it? The breeze is a little chilly though."

"Would you like me to help you inside before I go?"

"No. I'm enjoying the sunshine. But could you bring me a sweater? There's one sitting on a kitchen chair. Oh, and my purse. It's on the counter. My cell's in it. I should check in with Nora. She worries."

I set the purse in her lap and draped the sweater over her shoulders. She held out her hand and I took it. "I don't think we'll see each other again, Katy."

"I know." I gently squeezed her icy hand.

"Your mother raised a lovely woman. Tell her I said so."

CHAPTER SIXTY-THREE

FRIDAY · SEPTEMBER 6
Posted by Katy McKenna

I received a group e-mail from Justin Fargate today:

> *I have really sad news. Debra passed away yesterday. Nora found her and said she died peacefully in her sleep. I don't know what the funeral plans are, if any, but I'll keep everyone posted. We will all miss our dear Debra.*
>
> *Hugs*

CHAPTER SIXTY-FOUR

SATURDAY · SEPTEMBER 7
Posted by Katy McKenna

Today was Casey's first soccer game. I wasn't in the mood to go, but I'd promised the little guy I'd be there. I packed goodies for Sam and me and loaded a lawn chair and an exuberant canine soccer fan into the car.

From the parking area, I saw Sam trying to tie a fidgety kid's cleats. When he spied Daisy and me approaching, he ripped away from her, laces flopping, and ran to throw his arms around Daisy.

"Aunt Katy. This is my first real game. Are you gonna watch?"

"You bet I am. I'm really, super excited. So is Daisy."

He eyed my cloth sack. "Is that snacks for me?"

"No. You'll get team snacks. Way better."

He raced off to join his team, shouting, "Yay! Team snacks."

I unfolded my chair and set it next to Sam's and before I got my tush deposited, Daisy hopped in. "No, sweetie. That's Mommy's chair. Next time I'll bring one for you."

With a great deal of attitude, she slowly hauled her carcass off the chair and lay on the grass with a "harrumph." It's probably a good thing she can't talk.

Sam plopped next to me, stretching out her spray-tanned legs. "This has been a very long morning. Casey was up at the crack of dawn putting on his uniform. Not fun making a kid wait for seven hours."

"No Spencer?"

"No, and he's heartbroken about missing this game. We had a long talk on FaceTime last night about the future. He loves flying, but he wants to quit."

"Is he serious?"

She swatted a fly off her leg. "He said you only get to raise a kid once, and he's right. I may be exhausted most of the time, but at least I'm not missing out on every milestone. And Chelsea definitely needs her dad around too, especially with her flakey, absentee mother."

"And if he weren't on the road all the time, you'd have more free time to play with me, 'cause you know, it really is all about me."

"Duh. I know." She pulled me into an embrace. "I have missed you, girl."

"Me too." It felt good to be back in the game of life. Then I thought of Debra. "So sad about Debra, huh?"

"Yes. Nora told me she had lung cancer and it had metastasized to her brain. I figured it was something like that. Anyway, poor Nora is devastated. They were best friends, and then for her to find her like that. I can't even think about it. It kills me that Debra kept it to herself. Only Nora knew and even she wasn't told until close to the end." She brushed a tear away. "You better never die on me, okay?"

"I'm not going anywhere." I glanced out to the soccer field. Chelsea stood between the teams, trying to get them to pay attention. "The assistant coach has her hands full. How'd you get her to volunteer to do this?"

"I'd love to say it was her idea, but the reality is, this is how she's paying for her cell phone privileges."

"You finally got her a phone? She was like the last teenager on the planet without one."

"I know—because I hate how her friends have all turned into cell phone zombies. Personally, I'd rather she didn't have a phone until she's twenty-one—but since the school has adopted a no-phone policy this year, and she has to turn it in to me every night at 8:30, I'm not too worried about her getting addicted."

"I gotta say, I'm impressed. Uh oh, the game's about to start."

Sam scrambled to get her phone out of her purse. "I promised to send some video to Spencer."

Chelsea tossed a coin in the air, and Casey's team, The Hawks, got the first kickoff.

"Oh God." Sam covered her eyes. "Casey's doing the first kick. I can't watch."

"You have to watch. You're filming it. He'll be fine. He's good at kicking things."

Chelsea yanked Casey's finger out of his nose and pointed at the ball. He wiped his snotty finger on his shorts while the other kids hovered, waiting to pounce. Swinging his leg with gusto, he tipped the ball and landed on his rear end. The ball rolled a few inches and the children went into a free-for-all, kicking at the ball and each other while Casey lay on the ground howling in humiliation.

Daisy was suddenly faced with a dilemma. One: a ball. And two: her buddy was screaming. She bolted across the field and the ball won. Who knew she could dribble?

CHAPTER SIXTY-FIVE

MONDAY • SEPTEMBER 9
Posted by Katy McKenna

"I'm sorry, Ms. McKenna," said Nina, the snotty Clunker Carnival bookkeeper. "As I've told you numerous times already, we're not paying you. Just write it off on your taxes."

"What taxes? You have to earn money to pay taxes. You have to get paid the money you earned so you can pay the stupid taxes."

"Sorry." Click.

"Oh yeah? Well, you can just shove it," I screamed at the dead phone.

I poured another cup of coffee and cozied up with Daisy in our chair to ponder my dilemma. Tabitha leaped to the top of the chair and gently massaged my head while I deliberated. "I can't afford to hire a collection agency, so I need to come up with a creative idea to get my money."

I thought about my redneck neighbors across the street. "Maybe they could go with me to the dealership and intimidate Nina."

I eased Daisy's head off my lap and went to the front door to see if their cars were in the driveway. Randy was on his knees, planting pretty begonias along the porch. Yeah, real intimidating. As I watched him, a frazzled mother trudged by, dragging a little boy in the throes of a mega hissy fit, and it got me thinking.

"Hmm." I tapped my chin. "It's wacky-crazy, but it just might work. And even if it doesn't, at least I'll have had some fun revenge. Now all I have to do is get Sam on board and muster up the courage to go through with my diabolical scheme."

———

I parked near the service area at Clunker Carnival. Before climbing out of the car, I turned to my compadres-in-crime in the backseat for a last-minute pep talk.

"Okay, guys. Casey, please quit picking your nose and listen up."

He smeared his slimy findings on his pants and gave me his full attention. His little buddy, Jonathan, said, "When're we gettin' ice cream?"

"Soon. But first we have an important job to do. Then we go for ice cream. Remember?"

"You have'ta get your money, right, Auntie Katy? And we're helping you because we're big boys. Right?"

"That's right, Casey. And do you remember what you're going to do while we wait for my money?"

"We gonna play a game where we act really, really bad. Right?" He growled and they both burst into a giggle fit.

I waggled a finger at them. "But only if I tell you to. We might not get to play the game. We'll just see how it goes."

"Will we still get ice cream even if we're not bad?" asked Jonathan.

I kept a poker face to match the little red head's serious mug. "Yes. I promise."

I had the mothers' permission to do this collection sting with their kids, but I think they would have agreed to anything to get a free babysitter for a couple of hours.

Holding the sticky little hands of my A-Team, we boldly marched into the building. Inside, several people sat waiting on the worn leather sofas in the quiet lobby. I tousled Jonathan's curly hair, then tapped on the accounting window and waved at Nina—my nemesis.

The stringy-haired bleached blond slid the glass aside. "May I help you?" Then her eyes narrowed with recognition. "Oh. It's *you*."

I smiled, all super sweet. "Yup. It's me. Here to pick up my check."

She leaned out, gagging me with her tobacco breath. "I told you, we're not paying you. When're you going to give it up?"

"I think you might change your mind, so I'll just wait until you have my check ready."

"Not happening, sister."

My darling Casey loudly announced, "That lady smells yucky."

"You might want to teach your brat some manners." She slammed the window.

Oh, this is going down, you stinky bee-yatch. I pulled my team away from the window, squatting in a huddle with them. "Okay, guys. You stay here and after I sit down over there on the couch, I'll give the signal like we practiced."

"Like this?" Casey nodded vigorously, flopping his shaggy blond hair into his eyes.

"Maybe not that hard, but you'll know. And when I nod, what does it mean?"

"It's go-time." Jonathan puffed out his chest, snarling like the Hulk.

"And you both remember what I told you to do?"

Casey said, "Be really, really bad and…" He furrowed his brow, scratching his head. "What am I 'posed to do?"

"Yell, scream, throw magazines." Was I really telling four-year-olds to do this? "Jump on the chairs."

"Can we jump off too?" asked Jonathan, all serious.

"Yes. You may jump on and off the chairs. But there's something else, really important, that I told you. Do you remember what it is?"

Jonathan looked stumped, but Casey came through. "This is the only time we get to be bad boys. Right?"

"You got it, buddy." I left my crew and sat on the end of a sofa, steeling myself for the impending explosion.

A rosy-cheeked, elderly woman perched on the seat of her red walker leaned to me. "What darling boys. You must be so proud."

"I should warn you. This company has refused to pay me for a job I did for them, so those darling kids over there? That's my collection crew."

The dear lady shared a larcenous grin with me, patting my knee. "Oh, this is going to be fun."

"Well, it's definitely going to be something." I gave the boys the nod, mouthing, "Go."

The little guys hung back, timid. Each waiting for the other to start the game. Understandable, considering their proper upbringing. I nodded again, harder this time, looking directly at Casey. That got the ball rolling. I had released the beasts.

The little Tasmanian devils charged at the seating area, whooping and hollering. Neatly stacked magazines on the big round coffee table were ripped and tossed. A dusty plastic fern flew into a paunchy middle-aged man's lap.

"Can't you control your children?" snarled a skinny purple-head, ducking to avoid a flying *Sports Illustrated*.

"Sorry. Hyperactive." I gave her a what-can-you-do look.

"Rooooaaarrr!" Casey pranced around the sofas and chairs. "I'm a lion! I'm a lion!"

My silver-haired pal murmured, "Oh, they're good."

Meanwhile, Jonathan attempted to shinny up a massive ficus tree near the showroom windows. "Look at me, Katy."

The tree rocked precariously, and I was about to run to his rescue when a salesman beat me to him, shouting, "Get down from there."

Too late. Jonathan and the tree crashed to the floor, cracking the heavy terra-cotta planter and spilling dirt on the tile floor.

The salesman yelled at me, "You're paying for this."

Jonathan was splayed on the floor, looking stunned but unhurt so I whipped out my cell and snapped a photo before running to him, crying, "Baby, are you okay?"

I knelt beside him, and he whispered, "I'm okay, Katy. That was really fun. Can I do it again?"

"No, sweetie. But I want you to yell really loud, 'My back hurts,' and then pretend to cry."

He took a deep breath and bellowed, "My back hurts! My back hurts. Waaaa!"

I shouted at the beleaguered salesman, "Why do you have such dangerous things in your lobby for children to get hurt on?" Then I snapped a few more photos. "These are for my father. He's a personal injury attorney."

In the meantime, Casey had morphed into a kitty and crawled around the seating area, meowing and rubbing his head on people's legs. The disgruntled patrons shot me killer glares as they scrambled to get away from the creepy cat attempting to climb into a burly biker's lap.

"Dude, not cool. Chill," he said, setting the kid-cat on the couch next to him. "Act normal."

"He *is* acting normal," I snapped at the biker, then got weepy. "And I am doing everything the child psychologist has told me to do."

The poor guy looked miserable. "I'm sorry. That was un-PC of me."

I sat next to my friend and retrieved a *People* magazine off the floor. I flipped through the pages, the picture of calm as the kids screamed bad kid words.

"Stupid, stupid. You are stupid," sang Jonathan. "Everyone is ugly and stupid."

"Dumb dodo," Casey trilled. "You are a stupid dumb dodo head."

Out of the corner of my vision, I saw several people tapping on the accounts window and gesturing wildly at my children.

I was getting worried. *What if they don't break down and give me a check? How much longer can my gang maintain this level of bedlam? I wonder where the security guard is? They wouldn't call the cops would they? Omigod, what am I doing?*

Mr. Chuckles entered the lobby and the kids ratcheted up the manic another notch. "A clown! A clown! Aunt Katy? Can we see the clown? *Pleeease?*"

I glanced up from my magazine and smiled coolly at Matthew. "Of course you can. Mr. Chuckles loves to give piggy-back rides."

The kids charged him. Jonathan grappled his legs while Casey tried to climb up his back, but wound up pulling Mr. Chuckles's rainbow pants down.

"Get these damn little monsters offa me," yelled Mr. Chuckles, yanking up his big pants.

"Ummm." Casey's eyes bugged out. "You said a really, really bad word."

My lady friend wheeled her walker over and got in Matthew's face. "You, young man, are a disgrace to your race." She winked at me as he stomped away in his enormous clown shoes.

The kids threw their arms around my legs, and Casey rubbed his snotty nose on my jeans. "Please, Aunt Katy. Can we go get ice cream now?"

I squatted and hugged my A-Team, ready to accept defeat. "Yes. You kids did great. I'm so proud of you."

"You have got to be kidding," Nina said from behind me.

"You're taking these little shits for ice cream after what they did here?"

Jonathan pointed at Nina. "Shit's a bad word and you stink."

I released the children and faced her. "Sorry, boys. Looks like we can't go just yet. Go play some more."

"Hold it right there, brats." She held out a check. "Here. You win."

I accepted the money with a gracious smirk. "Pleasure doing business with you, Nina."

CHAPTER SIXTY-SIX

TUESDAY · SEPTEMBER 10
Posted by Katy McKenna

Private Post

Got a text from Nora last night. *Can you come for tea tomorrow at 3?*
   Really didn't want to. But how could I say no?

———

Nora, always the perfect hostess, had set up a tea tray in her living room on the fringed ottoman that doubles as a coffee table. I made myself busy doctoring my Earl Grey, then leaned back into the brocade sofa cushions, sipping my tea and waiting for her to initiate the conversation.

   "This is certainly a bit uncomfortable, isn't it?" she said, stirring her tea.

   "A lot has happened." I tried to sound light but wasn't feeling it. "But I need to thank you again for what you did. I don't know how I can ever repay you."

"There's nothing to repay, Katy. I don't plan to ever do anything like that again, but I'm not sorry we did it. Especially after we discovered the child pornography on his laptop. Such a contemptible man."

She picked up a plate of warm snickerdoodles. "I know what a sweet tooth you have."

I wasn't the least bit hungry, but I nibbled one to be polite while she topped my teacup.

"I have something for you. A letter from Debra. I found it..." She blinked rapidly, clearing her throat. "When I found her." She pulled an envelope from under a floral napkin on the silver tray. It had my name on it and looked like it had been sealed, then torn open. "I know it looks like I snooped, but I didn't. It was already like this."

I started to open it and she gestured me to stop. "No. Not here. It's meant to be private, so please, wait until you get home."

I tucked it in my purse. "Are you up to telling me about when you found her?"

"Debra knew I'd be the one who found her. I'd been checking in on her several times a day, either by phone or I'd drop by, bring groceries, sit for a bit, do chores. You know." She shrugged with a trace of a smile. "The day I found her..." She paused, pressing her lips tight, and smoothing the napkin in her lap. "She'd texted, asking me to come over at six. I found her on the patio. She spent a lot of time out there. She joked that she'd be in the dark soon enough." Nora stopped, dabbing her tears with the napkin. "She was bundled in her blanket with a sweater over her shoulders, in spite of the warm weather. Her purse was in her lap. I hoped she was just napping and not..." Nora shuddered, struggling. "I checked her pulse."

I moved to Nora's side and embraced her. "I can't imagine losing your best friend."

"It's really hard even when you know it's coming. I thought I was prepared. I really did. I knew there would be a day when I would find her…" She lifted her chin, swallowing. "Gone."

Nora stopped, unable to speak for a few moments. I refrained from the usual lame platitude: It'll be okay.

"I found that letter for you, and one for me, when I moved her purse." She paused, fighting her tears. "Katy, she killed herself. She injected herself with the same medication we injected into your uncle."

"It was better this way, Nora. She was so miserable."

"I know. I just wish she would have let me help her," she sobbed, pressing her face into my shoulder. "She shouldn't have died alone."

"Honey, she couldn't risk you getting charged with murder."

"It's so stupid. It's what she wanted." She pulled away, her eyes imploring mine. "And there was no hope, so why? Why couldn't I help her, Katy?"

Nora stood and crossed the room to close a window, then returned, sitting opposite me. Trying so hard to be stoic.

"Her letter to me was labeled, 'Read me now, dear friend.' In it she asked me to get rid of the syringe. She didn't want anyone to know she'd committed suicide. Evidently she had been keeping that filled syringe until the time was right." She swallowed. "I had to pry it from her hand. I hid it in my purse before calling anyone." She drained her teacup and then refilled our cups. "Katy, please do me a favor."

"Anything." I spooned sugar into my tea, afraid to hear her request.

"Please tell everyone that Debra didn't want a funeral."

After I had left Nora, I was driving home, thinking about Debra and my final visit with her, when it hit me. Nora had found Debra with her purse in her lap. I had put the purse in her lap. The syringe must have been in the purse. I had assisted Debra's passing. I pulled over under a shady tree and sat, trying to take that in.

"It's okay," I whispered. "I didn't know and it's what she wanted. Needed." I thought a moment. "And I would have done it even if I had known."

———

After a healthy dose of doggy smooches and a cold Eskimo kiss from Tabitha, I took Debra's letter to the backyard and sat under the pepper tree. Anxious to read it, terrified to read it, my hands trembled as I removed the two-page letter from the envelope, treating it like an ancient document. Taped to the second page was a small key with a tag attached.

The pages were dated two days before her death. I read the first page.

Dearest Katy,

 The key is to a safety deposit box containing a letter of confession. I had my lawyer help me draft it. He knows nothing about you and Nora. The box is only to be opened if you or Nora ever need to clear your names.

 But I do not think that will happen. Your uncle's death was a heart attack. That is true and there is nothing to suggest otherwise, so why would the police pursue it?

 I'm sure you will never need to use it, but it is your insurance. Your "get out of jail" card, so to speak.

 Burn this first letter now, then place the other letter and key in a fireproof safe.

Your friend,
Debra

Beneath the typed portion of the first page, Debra had continued in shaky, barely legible handwriting. Clearly she had added this right after our meeting on the patio.

I'm so sorry, Katy. You asked me about the others and I couldn't lie to you. Please know they didn't suffer. But now I'm worried that by you knowing everything I have done, you could be considered culpable. Not just for your uncle's death, but for all of them.

I dropped the letter on my lap, dumbfounded. *Oh my God. How could I have not thought of that? She's right. In the eyes of the law, by withholding information, I am now involved in—how many did she say? Eighteen, maybe twenty murders. Twenty-one, if you count Debra's suicide.*

My heart was pumping so hard I thought I'd keel over dead, right there in the grass, and be found holding the damning evidence. This wasn't good. I picked up the letter and tried to focus on the words.

So now that confession letter is even more important to you.

I read the first page several more times, then took it in the kitchen and burned it in the sink, flushing the remains down the garbage disposal, then read the second page.

To Whom It May Concern:

I have asked Katy McKenna to safeguard my safety deposit key, to be used at her sole discretion. She does not know the contents of my box. If there is ever a time that she deems it necessary to open the box, she must have a witness present and she is not to open the sealed document inside. It is to be given to the District Attorney.

Debra Ann Williams

Box #701

Santa Lucia Central Coast Bank

Santa Lucia, CA

I placed the letter and key in my underwear drawer, hidden beneath a pile of panties. Then grabbed my purse and dashed to Office Max and lugged home the biggest fire safe they had. After locking the letter and key inside, I stashed the safe in the back of my closet.

———

Was it just yesterday that I thought this was all behind me? It will never be all behind me. I will always be involved in a murder. No, make that murders, although I prefer the term that Debra used. *Mercy coups de grâce.*

No matter how you frost it, I am now a criminal in the eyes of the law. If the truth ever comes to light, I could be facing serious prison time. That's not something you can just blow off. But I have to learn to live with it and get on with my life. And I will.

EPILOGUE

Posted by Katy McKenna

Ruby and I were sharing tapas and a bottle of Sauvignon Blanc at a new Vietnamese-French fusion restaurant in town. The Red Door. Very swanky. Thank goodness she was picking up the tab.

"So. What's the latest on Josh? Every time I run into him at the office, he asks about you. When are you two going out?"

"Well, Granny. He's never asked me."

"What's that go to do with the price of tea in China? It's the twenty-first century. You can ask him out."

"I'm not comfortable doing that. Besides, he's not my type."

"Oh puh-leeze! He's everyone's type."

"I have reassessed my idea of the ideal man."

"Can't wait to hear this."

"I am looking for a sexy-sissy man. A BFF with—"

"I know. Benefits. And I have just the man. Duke."

I groaned like a drama queen. "Duke, the Dial-a-Ride guy?"

"You promised you'd go out with him." She reached across the table and squeezed my hand. "Sweetie. He is perfect for you."

313

"Is he in touch with his feminine side? Because I am so done with hunky, macho men."

"Honey, I thought he was gay for the longest time."

I topped off our wineglasses and then chugged a glass of water.

"How old is he?"

"He's legal." She smirked. "I don't know. Maybe mid to late thirties."

"Is he in good shape?" Just because I'm done with hunky, doesn't mean I'm into chunky.

"Mmmm. He could lose a few pounds. All that sitting on the job. Not to mention the goodies the gals ply him with."

I could stand to lose a few pounds, too. But regardless of my current shape, I prefer to date a guy with a six-pack not a keg. Does that make me shallow?

"Is he handsome?"

"Mmm. More like nerdy-cute."

"Techie or Star Trekkie?"

She shrugged. "I'd say Techie."

"Hair?"

"Most of it."

"Tall?"

"You'll need to wear flats."

"So here's the Duke rundown according to you, Ruby. He's pudgy, nerdy, balding, and height challenged."

"Did I mention he's English?" said Ruby.

Oooo. I do like an English accent.

Dear Reader,

Like most writers, much of what I write is drawn from my life. The good, the bad, the sad, the weird, and the funny. It's also why I'll never write a Cold War spy thriller or a Zombie Epic. I've met a few zombies along the way, but I don't know enough about their lifestyle to write a book about them.

Like Katy's mother, I, too, was molested by my uncle. I was six years old, and until that fateful day, he'd been my favorite uncle. It was the late 1950s, and like all kids, I'd been instructed not to talk to strangers or get in their car. But I knew nothing about pedophiles. I never told anyone until years later, but the horrific memory remains fresh and painful.

The bill-collection episode really happened, even though to this day, so many years later, I can't believe I had the nerve to do it. Or that my friends allowed me to employ their kids.

It was the late eighties, and I lived in Anchorage, Alaska, with my husband and two young boys. Spencer was in preschool, and Casey was a third grader. The economy had slipped into a recession, and businesses and banks were shutting down right and left.

I was a freelance graphic artist working out of my home. A car dealership owed me $1500, and they flat out told me I would not be paid.

It went down pretty much as it did with Katy's A-Team. I recruited my four-year-old son, Spencer, and a couple of his fun-loving friends. I cannot tell you how mortifying it was to sit in the lobby and watch Jonathan and Sara run wild—screaming, flinging magazines, and jumping on the furniture. Spencer, however, sat quietly next to me. He was used to attending business meetings with me, and could not bring himself to be part of the ruckus.

Within twenty minutes, I had my check, and we had the best ice cream party ever! Sure wish I had a video of the event!

Respectfully yours,
Pamela

P.S. Writers live for your kind comments.
Plus, it boosts our writing energy
and helps our sales.
So if you enjoyed *Better Dead Than Wed*,
please leave one on Amazon:
<u>Better Dead Than Wed</u>

Thank you.

I live on the California Central Coast with my husband, Mike, and our furry canine writing muses. We have owned two restaurants for over three decades now. In my spare time, I enjoy gardening, reading, yoga, riding my electric bike (I peddle, just not up steep hills), playing guitar, binge-watching TV shows, and playing with our four awesome grandkids.

You will find recipes from the books on my website.
Pamelafrostdennis.com

Try the
Pasta Mama
Really good!

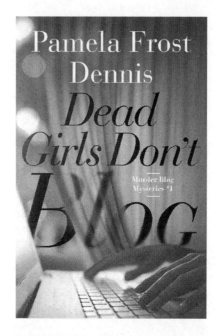

DEAD GIRLS DON'T BLOG #1

Katy McKenna's life takes a dramatic turn when she stumbles upon a newspaper story about the upcoming parole hearing for one of the men who raped and murdered her high school friend, sixteen years ago. Fearing he could soon be set free to prey on other innocent young girls, Katy sets out to make sure this doesn't happen, not realizing she might not survive to blog about it.

Awarded the B.R.A.G. Medallion
for excellence in independent publishing

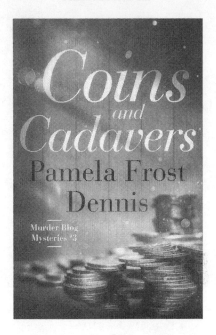

COINS AND CADAVERS #3

While battling a furry vermin invasion in the spooky attic of her old house, Katy discovers a vintage wooden chest hidden behind a wall. Although everyone assures her the box is legally hers, its incredible contents compel Katy to search for the rightful owner.

Meanwhile, she takes a temp job assisting her hunky P.I. neighbor, Josh Draper. The assignment: Trap a sleazy wife-cheater. During a cozy stakeout in Draper's two-seater, things get awkward as the sizzling tension builds. Who will make the first move?

Since she's already been searching online for past owners of her home, Grandma Ruby asks Katy to use her sleuthing skills to discover what happened to her bigamist great-great grandfather. Katy's quest leads her to find an extended family she never knew existed.

Family secrets are revealed ... *for better or worse.*
Romance blossoms ... *for better or worse.*
And Katy's good intentions lead her into a
terrifying dilemma she may not survive.

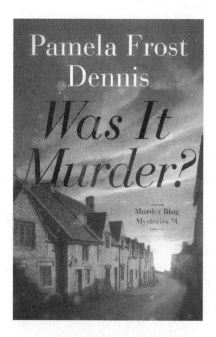

WAS IT MURDER? #4

Katy finds herself at loose ends. She's jobless, but not penny-less thanks to a recently discovered box of rare coins in her attic. But she's clueless as to what her next career will be. Plus, her sizzling romance with Josh, is doing a fast fizzle since he left town to continue nursing his ex-wife through her cancer battle.

Just as Katy is settling in for an extended pity-party of weepy old movies and tubs of mint-chip ice cream, her mother calls with tragic news. A dear family member has met an untimely end. Now

Katy and her grandma must travel to the scenic Cotswolds of England to sort out legal matters. When they arrive, they're overwhelmed by the friendly villagers who offer help and moral support.

However, when Katy and Ruby become the target of vandals, they realize that not everyone in town is pleased about their presence.

Is murder next on the list?

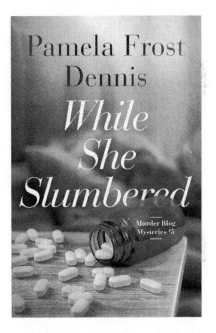

WHILE SHE SLUMBERED #5

Can Katy McKenna outwit a cranky, cozy mystery writer?

With her boyfriend nursing his dying ex in Los Angeles, heartbroken Katy finds comfort blogging her woes and visiting her elderly neighbor, Nina.

One day, Nina tells Katy that her mystery-writing niece, Donna, is coming for a few days. "I'm looking forward to her visit. I haven't seen her in years and have always thought of her as a daughter."

However, two days into the stay, Nina has already had enough of her overbearing niece. She confides to Katy, "This visit can't end soon enough for me."

A couple of days later, Katy drops by for a visit. The surly sixty-something author forbids her from seeing Nina with the excuse that her aunt has a cold and is napping.

After many failed attempts to see her neighbor, Katy fears her friend may be in mortal danger, so she doubles down on her efforts to get beyond Nina's front door.

Is Katy's imagination running wild, or is Donna slowly killing her aunt?

———

I hope you enjoy the first two chapters of
Coins and Cadavers
on the following pages.

COINS AND CADAVERS - CHAPTER ONE

WEDNESDAY • JANUARY 14
Posted by Katy McKenna

For over a week now, my upstairs, furry "tenants" have been throwing all night ragers—jumping, thumping, and no doubt humping. I'm running on empty and have the dark circles to prove it.

———

My folks have complained for years about pesky squirrels getting into their attic, and I've always wondered what the big deal was. It's not like they're rats. But after several sleepless nights, I googled "squirrels in the attic" and learned that they're rodents, and like rats, could do severe damage to your home.

For example:

- A dear old granny in England died after squirrels gnawed through gas piping, causing her ancient stone cottage to explode.

- In Ireland, a family of four was crushed when their home collapsed after squirrels chewed through the attic timbers.

There's even a website dedicated to documenting the number of attacks on our power grid each year. In the site's first year of collecting data, there were nearly two thousand "cyber squirrel" attacks impacting millions of people across the nation.

"The number one threat experienced to date by the US electrical grid is squirrels." — John C. Inglis, Former Deputy Director, National Security Agency

I'm not making this stuff up.

Yesterday
Rodent Elimination: Phase One

I hadn't visited the gloomy, spooky space since the first time I looked at the house. But I couldn't risk having my home cave in just because I was too chicken to go in the attic.

After a trip to the hardware store to purchase ultrasonic pest repeller beepers guaranteed to drive away mice, cockroaches, rodents, spiders, ants, rats, and squirrels, I was ready to face the enemy.

In the hallway, I stood on a stepstool and unlatched the door in the ceiling to release the antique retractable stairs. After they had clunked into place on the wood floor, I gazed up at the exposed rafters.

"Really do not want to go up there." I pulled in a deep breath. "I mean, what's the rush? I can wait until my sister gets home, and we can do it together."

Mission aborted, I stooped to close the stairway when my cat zoomed in and tore up the stairs like her tail was on fire.

"Tabitha! Stop! Get back down here!" Her catnip mouse lay nearby on the floor. I clambered halfway up the wobbly steps and swung the fuzzy toy over my head. "Look what Mommy's got. Mmmm. Catnip. You know you want it, so come and get it."

Nothing.

"Dammit."

I stepped back down, grabbed the bag of sonic beepers, and climbed into the attic. Weak sunlight filtered through the grimy octagonal windows revealing a large and even creepier space than I remembered.

"Here kitty-kitty-kitty."

Something thumped in a dark corner, and Tabitha moaned mean and low.

Oh God, she's got a squirrel. Thoroughly pissed off now, I shouted, "Dammit, Tabitha. Leave the poor little animal alone."

Suddenly, she bolted past me and careened down the stairs, scaring the bejeebers out of me. I wasn't feeling brave enough to hunt around the spooky attic for the squirrel, so I switched on the beepers and placed them around the floor, then scrambled down the steps and slammed the stairway into the ceiling.

After getting my heebie-jeebies under control, I laughed at my silly behavior. I mean, come on, I'm a five-foot-nine, thirty-two-year-old woman, weighing in at one-hundred-thirty-six-ish pounds, and how big is a squirrel? A pound, maybe?

———

Around midnight, my half-sister, Emily, opened my bedroom door. "You awake?"

"No."

"There's a weird sound coming from the attic."

I switched on the bedside lamp. "It's the ultrasonic pest controllers I put up there to shoo the squirrels out. It's supposed to be too high-pitched for human ears."

"And you're saying you can't hear it?"

"Yeah, I can hear it. But if it works, it's worth it."

Emily sat on the end of my bed. "Well, from the sounds of it, whatever is up there—and I seriously doubt that it's squirrels—is enjoying it."

She was right. It sounded like they were having a gay old time, groovin' to the beat of the beep.

"Tomorrow I'm pulling out the big guns. Humane catch and release traps."

"So you're going to catch rats and—"

"Squirrels."

"Whatever." She shook her head. "And release them where?"

"In the woods, where they can frolic and live happy squirrel lives."

Today
Rodent Elimination: Phase Two

This morning, I went online and learned that most animals don't fare well when released in a new area. The humane society says that 97% won't survive. The frightened critters suddenly find themselves dumped in unfamiliar terrain, and it's too traumatic. Makes sense.

So I researched other ideas to humanely evacuate my pests and came up with peppermint oil. Supposedly, rodents hate it, but it won't hurt them, and my house will smell minty fresh.

Feeling bolder than yesterday, I climbed into the attic with a bag of peppermint soaked cotton balls and glanced around, thinking, *If this was finished it would make a nice office or guest room.*

A past owner must have had the same thought. The wall facing the back yard had three plywood planks, roughly four by six, nailed to the studs, the last one ending halfway between studs. I wondered why they hadn't finished the entire wall.

I tucked a few cotton balls behind the wall and something sharp gashed the palm of my hand. Curious about what cut me, I peeked in. Lodged behind the plywood was a rectangular wood chest about the size of a knee-high boot box. Its rusty handle faced me, and I tried to pull it towards me, but the box was wedged in tight. I gave it a hard jerk, and the handle snapped off, propelling me backward onto my rump. The heavy padlocked chest tumbled after, landing on my bony shins.

You know the agony of ramming your bare toes into a table leg? Well, this hurt like that times ten. The room turned bright white, and I knew I'd better lie down before I passed out.

Finally, I was able to sit up and tip the box to the floor. That move took me back to Ground Zero pain, and back down I went to wait out the accompanying nausea. When my head cleared, I rolled to a fetal position and considered lying there until my sister, Emily, got home from her shift at the Burger Hut.

Why didn't I bring my damned cellphone with me?

My yellow lab yelped frantically at the foot of the steps. Then the stairs thudded against the downstairs floor.

"No, no. Stay off the stairs, Daisy. Mommy's all right." *No, I'm not. My legs might be broken.*

I struggled to a sitting position again, biting my lip to squelch the shrieks of agony that would have distressed Daisy. The wooden chest was within reach, so I jiggled the corroded padlock, hoping it would pop open, but it didn't.

Standing was not an option, so I slithered my butt a couple feet across the rough wood floor, then reached back to drag the heavy box with me. One mighty tug and I wrenched my lower back.

I left the mystery box behind and worked my way to the steps wondering how I was going to get down without breaking my neck. I wound up jostling down on my rear end, one creaky rung at a time. By the time I hit bottom, I was in tears, and Daisy liberally applied first-aid kisses to my face.

Too bad she couldn't carry me to the couch, get some frozen peas for my shins, a heating pad for my back, several ibuprofens, and a glass of wine.

COINS AND CADAVERS - CHAPTER 2

THURSDAY • JANUARY 15

Posted by Katy McKenna

Before my baby sister moved back to Santa Lucia, she'd been living in San Diego and working two jobs to pay the rent. Emily told our folks she wanted to come home and work a part-time job while she wrote a paranormal mystery series (she really is). She failed to mention that the main reason she wanted to come home was because she'd just broken up with her girlfriend. She also neglected to tell her family she's gay.

Mom was going through a trying time, so I offered up my guest room. Reluctantly. Very reluctantly. After the initial period of adjustment, it's been fun getting to know my sister. The nine-year age difference had always been a barrier between us, but now that we're all grown-up, more or less, the years no longer matter so much.

Last night, when Emily got home from her part-time job at the Burger Hut, she found me sprawled on the couch, shins smothered under thawed-out bags of veggies. Doctor Daisy sat on the floor by me, keeping a watchful eye on my vital signs.

"Good grief, Katy. What happened?"

"A heavy wooden treasure chest fell on me and almost broke my legs."

She shook her head with a hint of a smirk. "Sounds reasonable. For you, that is."

"I'm not kidding. Anyway, I took some leftover Vicodin from when I got shot in the leg, but it barely touched the pain."

She removed the dripping bags of peas and corn from my shins and took a good look. "Wow. That's gotta hurt."

"You could say that."

"I'll stash these bags back in the freezer for your next crazy escapade."

"You sound like Mom."

"That's because living with you is rapidly aging me." Emily laughed. "Oh, my God. I *do* sound like Mom." She scooped up Tabitha, who'd been weaving between her legs. "These guys must be starving. I'll feed them, then you can tell me all about your treasure chest."

"With the agony I'm in, it damned well better be a treasure chest."

After Emily fed the pets, she set a fresh batch of frozen veggies on my shins and then flopped in the armchair across from the couch. "So...a treasure chest. Really?" She pulled the elastic band out of her long goth-black hair and scratched her scalp.

"Yup." I sat up, pointing at the ceiling. "In the attic."

———

When I concluded my story, she still looked skeptical. "Get the flashlight and go see for yourself if you don't believe me."

"I believe you, but I will anyway." She went to the hallway and hollered, "How do you get up there? Do you have a ladder?"

"Use the stepstool to unlatch the door in the ceiling. Be careful not to let the stairs bang your head because I can't save you."

The stairway creaked down and struck the floor.

"Wow. This is so cool," Emily shouted as she climbed.

I wanted to watch, but when I tried to swing my legs to the floor, I thought better of it. "Emily! I need more Vicodin."

"In a sec. Okay, I'm at the top, and I see the box. Let me see if I can lift it."

"No! It's too heavy. We'll figure something out tomorrow." Emily is a petite little thing, and I was worried she'd hurt her back.

"Whoa. You're right. Darn it. I wanna find out what's inside." Then she shrieked. "There's a rat!" Another spine-chilling scream. "Three rats! I'm outta here!"

Emily squealed her way down the steps, then slammed the stairway into the ceiling so hard the house rattled a 4.0 on the Richter scale. Wish I'd gotten a video of her hopping around and shaking her head like she had rats in her hair. It would have gone viral on YouTube, for sure.

————

Emily woke me at eight this morning. "Wake up, sleepyhead." She handed me a steamy cup of French roast, perfectly doctored with sugar and a healthy dollop of half and half.

I sipped the tasty brew, giving thanks to the gods for inventing coffee. "What're you doing up so early?"

Usually Em sleeps past nine, then grabs a coffee and holes up in her bedroom to work on her book until it's time to go to her job. Her mystery takes place in a medieval fairy forest full of evil trolls and goblins. I'm proud of her for sticking to it. It can't be easy writing a book.

"Aren't you dying to see what's in the box?" she said. "I know I am."

"Oh my God! The treasure chest!" I flipped back the blankets, disturbing Miss Daisy. She rolled onto her back stretching her long legs with a big yawn, then smacked her lips and collapsed back to sleep.

"Eeew." Emily eyeballed my legs with a grimace.

Eeew was right. The blossoming bruises and lumps could win a spot in the Guinness book of world records.

"Maybe you need to see a doctor," she said. "Those bruises are the worst I've ever seen. You might have cracked something, you know."

"I was able to walk to the bathroom last night—"

"Yeah. Barely. Remember I had to help you."

"Anyway, I'm probably fine." I chugged my coffee, then stood, testing my limbs. Yes, it hurt big time, but I was pretty sure nothing was broken.

"I definitely could use three or four ibuprofens, though. I can't take any more Vicodin. It was making me nauseated. Then we need to figure out how to get that box down."

———

After debating several treasure chest extraction schemes, we settled on one of my ideas: a rope tied several times around the box with another long rope attached. Then slide the box down the stairs with Emily controlling its descent from the attic. Trouble is, I didn't have any rope, so we used extension cords.

"Okay, ease it down nice and slow," I said.

"I'm trying." She grunted with the exertion. "This thing weighs a friggin' ton. Probably full of gold bars, don't ya think?"

"Probably more like lead bricks." I reached for the box. "I got it, but don't let go yet." I guided the box to a comforter protecting the floor. "Okay, you can let go now."

Emily clambered down the rickety stairs, and then we stood contemplating the mysterious wooden chest.

"This is so Nancy Drew," she said.

"You're right. Did you read Mom's books?"

"The whole collection. Some more than once."

"I had a huge crush on Ned Nickerson," I said. "Did you know that most of the books were Grandma Ruby's from her childhood?"

"I did. It made them even more special. Did you have a favorite?"

"I liked them all," I said. "But a few of my absolute favorites were *The Secret at Shadow Ranch*—probably because I wanted a horse. *The Bungalow Mystery*, and *The Secret in the Old Attic*. Wow, I'm amazed I can remember the titles after all these years. What was yours?"

Emily glanced up the attic steps. "My favorite was *The Hidden Staircase*. Kind of ironic, considering I had no idea about your hidden staircase." She patted the mystery box. "You know, this could be a new Nancy Drew mystery."

"You're right. The Secret of the Old Box."

She crouched and rattled the rusty padlock. "We need to pick it."

And I needed to get off my feet. Emily dragged the blanket and box into the kitchen, and together we hoisted it onto the table. Then I collapsed on a chair, feeling lightheaded.

"It shouldn't be too hard to spring the lock, since it's so corroded," said Emily. "Got any ideas, Nancy?"

"Give me a minute. I feel like I'm going to be sick." I rested my forehead on my folded arms on the table.

"You want a glass of water?" she asked.

"Yes, and bring me a wet, cold face towel."

She did, and after I wiped my face and sipped the cool water, I felt revived. "Can you get my laptop? I think it's in the living room. I'm sure we can find a video on how to pick a lock."

First, we watched the one for how to pick a padlock with a paperclip. We followed the geeky prepubescent boy's methodical directions, but no luck. Then we tried how to pick a padlock with a screwdriver, and finally, "how to pick a padlock with a steak knife."

I tapped the lock. "Clearly, we'll never make it as burglars. So now what?"

"You got a hacksaw?" she asked.

"No. But I'm sure Pop does. He's probably at his shop now, but I have a key to the house. He won't mind if we borrow it."

A few years ago, Pop took early retirement from the police force after getting shot in the knee. Now he owns a quaint old-school fix-it shop near the downtown area of Santa Lucia. It's next door to Mom's hair salon, Cut 'n Caboodles.

"Or I can go to the hardware store and buy one," said Emily. "Then you'd have one of your very own. And the hardware store's closer."

After she left, I watched one more video, "How to pick a padlock with a paper clip for beginners" and voila! It popped open.

Now for the big reveal. I unhitched the lock and set it on the table.

Would it be riches?
Or was I opening Pandora's box?

———

Coins and Cadavers
is Available on Amazon

Made in the USA
Columbia, SC
13 February 2023

12028420R00205